ROLLING THUNDER

A NeWest
MYSTERY

Praise for *Rolling Thunder*

"Professional wrestler-turned-PI 'Hammerhead' Jed is back, and not a moment too soon—trouble is brewing in the Greater Vancouver area on the roller derby circuit. *Rolling Thunder* is sheer fun. The dialogue is snappy, the action fast-paced. A.J. Devlin is the Canadian Carl Hiaasen. In fact, America will trade you Carl Hiaasen for him. I feel that strongly about this kid's future."
— *New York Times* bestselling author and humorist Andrew Shaffer

"A.J. Devlin's latest crime novel packs a punch with nonstop action! His witty, entertaining style hooked me quicker than a figure-4 leglock and pinned me to the pages.

"'Hammerhead' Jed's colourful stable of heels and babyfaces create a suspenseful, romantic, comedic vice. Very entertaining! His rock-star persona makes him the ultimate chick magnet. His story takes me back to my four seasons at The Riviera hotel in Las Vegas with the Gorgeous Ladies Of Wrestling and the words of my trainer, the legendary pro wrestler Mondo Guerrero, come to mind—'No guts, no glory.'

"*Rolling Thunder* is a must read for everyone who is a fan of sports, wrestling, suspense … or all three!"
— Jeanne "Hollywood" Basone, the first G.L.O.W. girl hired by creator David McLane

"*Rolling Thunder* has everything! Action, humour, mystery, and most importantly pro wrestling. I'm totally invested. Can't wait for the next one!"
— Cat Power, pro wrestler and former ECCW Women's Champion

Praise for *Cobra Clutch*

"…masterfully blends humour, mystery, thrills, action, romance, and heart into a hell of a story featuring a lively wrestler-turned-PI hero. The action scenes are intense, the quiet times heartwarming and engaging, and the humour expertly interjected to accentuate characters and breathe realism into the story."
— John M. Murray, *Foreword Reviews*

"Set in Vancouver, BC, this intriguing debut offers a fast-paced, graphically violent mystery…. Fans of pro wrestling will appreciate 'Hammerhead' Jed."
— *Library Journal*

"…a very authentic-feeling world full of colourful characters, twists and turns and plenty of banana milkshakes."
— J.P Cupertino, *Gremlins Online*

"*Cobra Clutch* uses humour and gritty realism and includes a former tag-team partner, a kidnapped snake, sleazy promoters, and violence inside and outside the ring."
— *BC BookWorld*

Library and Archives Canada Cataloguing in Publication

Title: Rolling thunder / A.J. Devlin.

Names: Devlin, A. J., author.
Description: Series statement: A Hammerhead Jed mystery

Identifiers: Canadiana (print) 20190167599 | Canadiana (ebook) 20190167602
| ISBN 9781988732862 (softcover) | ISBN 9781988732879 (EPUB) | ISBN
9781988732886 (Kindle)

Classification: LCC PS8607.E94555 R65 2020 | DDC C813/.6—dc23

Board Editor: Merrill Distad
Cover and interior design: Michel Vrana
Cover images: Photo by Chris Bojanower (https://www.flickr.com/photos/
bojphoto/7595237790) is licensed under CC BY 2.0 (https://creativecommons.
org/licenses/by/2.0/) cropped and converted to halftone. Illustrations by
Jay Stephens.
Author photo: Gina Spanos

NeWest Press acknowledges the Canada Council for the Arts, the Alberta
Foundation for the Arts, and the Edmonton Arts Council for support of our
publishing program. We acknowledge the financial support of the Government
of Canada. NeWest Press acknowledges that the land on which we operate
is Treaty 6 territory and a traditional meeting ground and home for many
Indigenous Peoples, including Cree, Saulteaux, Niitsitapi (Blackfoot), Métis,
and Nakota Sioux.

NeWest Press
#201, 8540-109 Street
Edmonton, Alberta T6G 1E6
www.newestpress.com

No bison were harmed in the making of this book.

Printed and bound in Canada

1 2 3 4   22 21 20

For my grandfather Bill Gillis

ROLLING THUNDER

A "HAMMERHEAD" JED MYSTERY

A.J. DEVLIN

NeWest Press

Rolling Thunder:

[**roh**-ling] [**thuhn**-der]

noun; verb (used with object)

1. The action of a forward roll towards an opponent using the complete rotation to spring up onto their feet and into the air and perform an attack. The most popular version of this ends with a jumping somersault senton.

ONE

Two thoughts popped into my head when the three-hundred- pound woman on roller skates slapped me on the ass.

First, that she must have been skating very fast before delivering the spank as the force with which she pummelled my posterior sent shock waves throughout my body and caused me to stumble forward, no small feat when you consider that I'm six-foot-three and weigh close to two-forty, give or take a few pounds, depending upon whether there's been a spike in my milkshake intake.

The second thought was that the sheer size of this heavy-set hellion on wheels' hand was astounding, for when she delivered her vigorous blow to my buttocks, her giant meathook nearly engulfed the entire circumference of my behind.

I regained my balance and was rubbing my stinging rump when I realized what had just transpired turned a simple bum assault from a playful incident into a full-blown calamity—upon impact the large, delicious, Dairy Queen banana milkshake I had been nursing flew out of my hand and splattered onto the concrete floor.

I was no longer annoyed. Now I was livid. I heard the rolling fanny-whacker cackle riotously, her laughter echoing throughout the arena. I locked eyes with her across the track and she winked at me and blew me a kiss. I furrowed my brow and opened my mouth to let fly a string of obscenities, but before I had the chance Stephanie Danielson—AKA Stormy Daze—ripped into her teammate like a tornado in a trailer park.

"Jesus Christ, Jabba!" she yelled. "What the hell is the matter with you?" Stormy turned to me and gently rubbed my arm. "Sorry, Jed. I know how much you like your milkshakes."

I stared at the banana-flavoured ice cream goodness as it continued to spill out of the cup onto the glossy grey concrete like a brother-in-arms bleeding out on the battlefield. I sighed deeply. At that moment the booty-smacking milkshake assassin completed another lap on the roller derby track.

"You got yourself some nice buns there, Butterfingers!" she hollered as she whizzed by and continued around the track for another lap.

"That's enough, Jabba!" barked Stormy, before patting my arm some more.

I finally snapped out of my milkshake mourning and focused. "Why do you keep calling her Jabba?" I asked.

"That's her name," replied Stormy. "Jabba the Slut."

"That's not really her name."

"Yes, it is."

"So if I looked at her driver's licence it would say 'Jabba the Slut?'"

"It may as well. This is roller derby, Jed. Our names are what empower us as warrior women and make us who we are. It's why, back when I used to wrestle, I was 'Stormy Daze,' but now when I hit the track I become the 'Amazombie.'"

Stormy put her hands on her hips and puffed out her chest proudly. I had met her eight months ago while unofficially working my first case. Her ex-boyfriend—and my former friend and pro-wrestling tag-team partner Johnny Mamba—had been murdered and my investigation led me to her. Although I briefly considered her a suspect in Johnny's death, it quickly became clear that she was a good woman who had loved him dearly. I'd not seen Stormy since Johnny's funeral. She left professional wrestling after Johnny died and I hadn't heard anything about her until she called the office that morning and asked to meet as soon as possible.

Stormy looked even better than I remembered, especially decked out in her roller derby gear. She was dressed in a pair of form-fitting, blue short-shorts and a red sports bra underneath a white baseball baby T-shirt that covered her curvy chest but left her taut midsection exposed. Her blonde hair was in pigtails, the tips dyed red and blue, while her symmetrical face was painted in white and black makeup, with drops of fake blood around her pouty, ruby-red lips to give her that oh-so-fashionable, sexy undead look. Finally, she wore retro, knee-high, striped athletic socks underneath a bedazzling pair of rainbow-coloured roller skates. With the extra three inches in height, for the first time we were standing nearly eye-to-eye.

With her gaudy outfit and lean, yet feminine muscular build, she looked like a walking-dead version of the Batman villainess Harley Quinn on steroids.

"Jabba the Slut and Amazombie," I said, shaking my head. "And I thought professional wrestling was overly theatrical."

"Never mind Jabba," Stormy said. "The one you really need to watch out for is 'Barracougar.' If she gets her paws on you, she'll make Jabba's spank feel like a love tap."

At this point the locker room doors slammed open and over a dozen women all dolled up in different outfits and makeup— and all wearing retro-style four-wheeled roller skates—charged toward the roller derby track and joined Jabba the Slut for warm-up laps. Stormy escorted me out of their way as they attacked the track with the ferociousness of rabid wolverines. Hoots, hollers, and war cries were spit out with both confidence and vitriol, and by the time I wrapped my head around the unusual sight before me, Stormy had guided me over to the players' bench and taken a seat. She tapped the hard plastic and motioned for me to sit. I slowly eased my aching bottom onto the unforgiving surface and joined her, still transfixed by the colourful swarm of skaters rolling around the track at varying speeds.

"You guys dress up like this for every practice?" I asked.

"No, usually only for games," replied Stormy. "But today is a sort of a dress rehearsal." I nodded as Stormy continued.

"So how about I tell you why I really asked you here."

"You mean it wasn't for an enormous woman on wheels named after a *Star Wars* villain to beat my ass like a rented mule?"

She smiled briefly before reaching out and squeezing my hand.

"I need your help, Jed." She waved her other glittery-gloved hand toward the roller skaters. "We need your help."

She let go of my hand and I shifted uncomfortably, my butt still stinging from Jabba the Slut's powerful smack. I glanced around the modest arena, a multi-purpose facility in the Greater Vancouver suburb of Coquitlam that, when not chock full of estrogen-charged roller-skating maniacs, was used for indoor soccer, box lacrosse, and ball hockey. Numerous purple and gold banners hung from the rafters, all sporting different years of championships won by the Coquitlam Adanacs, the local lacrosse club. I tried to ignore my aching rump and looked Stormy in the eyes.

"What can I do for you, Stormy?"

"We want to hire you."

"For what?"

"You're a real detective now, right?"

"Private investigator. And yes, I am, on a provisional basis under supervision until I log enough hours."

"Good. I told the girls I was pretty sure you were legit. After what you did for Johnny it didn't matter to me, but a few of the ladies insisted we hire a professional. I told them I knew just the guy."

"Hire me for what?"

"Our coach is missing. We're all a bit concerned, plus we have playoffs coming up and the team is nervous to take to the track without him."

"Has he ever disappeared for periods of time before?" I asked.

Stormy shook her head emphatically. "Not once. He lives for derby. He would never flake out like this."

"Can you think of any reason why he would leave town?"

Stormy let out a beleaguered sigh. "Well, maybe. You see, there are some rumours about him...."

"What kind of rumours?"

"Gambling."

"You think he might be in some trouble?"

Stormy shrugged. "I'm not sure. A couple times a guy with really big muscles came around to our practices and he and Larry would go off and have a chat. And one time Vicky Von Doom swears she heard some shouting."

"Larry, that's your coach's name?"

"Yes, but only I call him Larry. He goes by Lawrence. Lawrence of O'Labia."

It took everything I had not to smack my hand against my forehead.

"His real name, Stormy."

"His first name really is Lawrence. O'Labia is his derby name. I don't know his last name. Pippi Longstomping would know." Stormy slipped her index fingers into opposite sides of her mouth and let out a high-pitched sound so piercing you would have thought it came from a steam whistle. "Yo! Pip! Get over here."

A short, stout woman with fire-truck red hair hopped off the track and skated over to us. Her long pigtails flapped in the air behind her and, as she rolled closer, I noticed she had her face painted with over-the-top freckles the size of dimes.

"What's up, Cap?" she asked, before wiping perspiration from her brow with her matching red wristband.

"Pippi Longstomping, I'd like to introduce you to 'Hammerhead' Jed Ounstead. He's the investigator we're hiring," said Stormy as we both rose from the bench.

Pippi sniffed, wiped her palm on her shorts, and stuck out a stubby arm. I nodded and shook her hand.

"Nice to meet you, Jed. Think you can find Lawrence?" she asked.

"I know I can, but I need a surname to get started."

"Kunstlinger."

"Very funny."

"That's it, man."

I looked to Stormy for help but she just stared blankly back at me. Behind both Stormy and Pippi the rest of the team had started chanting while stretching and continuing to skate laps on the track. Jabba the Slut led them in the cheer.

"I'm the queen!" Jabba screamed.

"You're gonna die!" answered the team.

"Cross my path?" Jabba screeched.

"You're gonna fly!" echoed the roller derby women.

The ladies then broke into more whooping and war cries. I looked back and forth between Stormy and Pippi as my frustration bubbled up from within.

"Look, I want to help you guys. But I'm getting a little irritated here. My ass hurts like hell, my milkshake is history, and I've got whiplash from trying to keep up with all of your different roller derby names. I just need Lawrence's legal surname."

Pippi Longstomping looked stunned and glanced at Stormy before looking back at me.

"It really is Kunstlinger. I've seen it on his driver's licence."

"Lawrence Kunstlinger," I said, my voice tinged with disbelief.

"I think it's a German name," added Stormy.

I took a deep breath and glanced over at what was left of my banana milkshake. It had almost completely melted.

"Okay, then," I said.

"Thanks, big guy," chirped Pippi cheerily, before pulling a mouthguard from her shorts pocket and popping it between her teeth. She skated off and back onto the track to rejoin the other players.

"Do you have a picture of Lawrence?" I asked Stormy. She pulled out a black-and-white booklet and a pen from her back pocket.

"This is the program from our last game. It has pictures of Lawrence and the team and all of our bios inside. I glanced at the cover illustration of an anthropomorphic taco and a buff babe, both grappling one another while on roller skates. The large retro font read: *TACO KICKERS VS. SPLIT-LIP SALLIES* and underneath the date, venue, ticket pricing, team website, and Facebook page were all listed.

"Please tell me your team isn't the 'Taco Kickers,'" I pleaded.

Stormy giggled softly. I had forgotten how silky smooth her laugh was.

"We are not," she said.

"All right. I think I have enough to get started."

"I checked the rates on your website and I have a cheque in my purse for the retainer," she said. "Just hold on a second while I go to the locker room."

"Don't worry about that now. Besides, you're an old friend, so that means I'll charge you the friends-and-family rate our agency offers. Let's see what I can dig up first before we talk payment."

Stormy seemed relieved.

"Thank you, Jed. It took a lot for me to convince the entire team to go in on a private detective."

"How long has Lawrence been missing?"

"The last any of the girls heard from him was a week ago. He sent out an email to the team and since then no one has been able to get a hold of him. All calls go straight to voicemail."

"Do you have his phone number?"

Stormy plucked the program out of my hand and scribbled on the booklet.

"That's Lawrence's cell. I wrote mine down too," she said coyly. "Call or text me anytime. And if you could keep me updated as much as possible, I would really appreciate it. The girls and I are starting to get really worried."

I nodded and folded the program in my hands. Before I could say goodbye Stormy slowly rolled forward, cocked her head to the side, and gave me a soft, seconds-long kiss on the cheek. The rest of the Split-Lip Sallies wooed loudly from the track.

"I really appreciate this, Jed," she said, before spinning around and skating off toward her teammates. I turned and headed for the exit before my face flushed more red than the lipstick lingering on my cheek.

TWO

The mayor of tent city was holding court. He stood on a podium made of yellow milk crates and disseminated his edicts via a makeshift megaphone that, as far as I could tell, was nothing more than a rolled-up newspaper. He gesticulated wildly with his other hand, making long sweeping motions that seemed to imply, at very least, he was being inclusive to those he thought he governed. Of course, considering he was shirtless, wearing sunglasses, a bandana, and sporting a long ZZ Top-style beard, as well as the fact no one in tent city was giving his ramblings the time of day, I doubted any of his decrees would be heeded.

Although an injunction had caused the previous tent city in the Downtown Eastside's Oppenheimer Park to be dismantled and its homeless population forced to relocate elsewhere, the uncharacteristic heatwave Vancouver was experiencing in mid-to-late May had caused a new, smaller flare-up of portable shelters to appear at the same site.

A dozen or so orange, blue, and green tents—some inter-connected with long, overarching black tarps—were clustered together in the centre of the lot. A few homeless people milled about, either chit-chatting with one another or soaking up the sunshine in lawn chairs, but the majority of tent city's residents were either likely roasting in their portable homes or had found another way to beat the heat.

I slurped back what was left of my replacement banana milk-shake, switched off the air conditioning in my Ford F-150, and rolled down my window. It would probably only be a matter of days until these poor unfortunate souls were ousted from their tents yet again, but I found myself hoping that they might find themselves left alone for awhile. As my truck idled at the inter-section of West Hastings and Abbott Street, a skinny man with stringy hair charged my vehicle armed with a squeegee. He did a little happy dance when he saw me nod and then proceeded to do at best a mediocre job of wiping my windshield. I slipped him a ten-dollar bill as the light turned green and he was so surprised and thrilled he not only resumed his happy dance, but this time included some karate kicks and wielded and whipped his squeegee around his upper body like pair of nunchucks.

I drove another block and parked on the street. I eased my way out of my truck, certain a bruise was now forming on my behind, and walked with a slight waddle into the Emerald Shillelagh, the pub that my father had owned for years.

"You bloody wanker!" bellowed a familiar Irish brogue. "You're as useless as tits on a bull!"

My cousin Declan St. James towered over a short, disconcerted-looking young man holding a Guinness pint glass in one hand and a bottle of grenadine syrup in the other behind the pub's lacquered mahogany bar.

"What did I do wrong?" asked the kid, confused.

"You feckin' know what you did," snapped Declan.

"She ordered a black and blood," the kid said in defence.

"I don't care. We don't serve that sugary shite here."

"But it's what the customer wants," he pleaded.

"You're asking for there to be wigs on the green if you serve that bollocks, Boyo."

The kid adjusted his black, backward Kangol flat cap and seemed genuinely perplexed.

"I honestly don't have a clue what you just said," he said quietly, before continuing to make the abomination of pomegranate syrup mixed with a pint of Guinness.

Declan gritted his teeth and looked to me for support. "I'm gonna rip this dense dosser's throat out, Jed. I swear to Christ."

Considering my cousin was ex-IRA and possibly more deadly with his hands than he was with a weapon, I took his threat a bit more seriously than I would another man's.

"Take it easy, D," I said calmly, trying to keep my cousin's feisty temper from going from a simmer to a boil. "There's no need to go full *Road House* on him."

Declan smirked. "Aye, I suppose not," he conceded.

"Speaking of eighties cinema, instead of getting frustrated why don't you just send him to the back and have him watch *Cocktail* for a bit?"

"That's not a half bad idea, especially if it keeps me from effin' and blindin' 'til I'm all but knackered."

Just then the bartender trainee looked up after topping off the blasphemy that was a sweetened Guinness.

"What's *Cocktail*?" he asked.

Both Declan and I did a double take.

"The Tom Cruise bartending movie?" I replied, hoping for the kid's sake he had seen it.

"Never heard of it," said the bartending trainee.

Declan clenched his fists and I swear steam almost shot out of both of his ears like Yosemite Sam after losing a hand of poker to Bugs Bunny.

"*GET THE BLOODY HELL OUT O'ME PUB RIGHT NOW YOU SKAWLY SACK O'SHITE!*" Declan bellowed.

The former trainee almost jumped out of his skin and stared at us both in shock.

"He means it, Bub," I said, nodding toward the door.

The kid put down the black and blood Guinness he had yet to serve and bolted for the door. Although the place was mostly dead, the few customers scattered around the pub gawked at the commotion.

"And don't ever let me catch your stupid, mingin', kangaroo-cap-wearin' arse in here again!" Declan yelled after him. "You sicken me pish!"

I patted my cousin on the arm, feeling his hard, sinewy muscles taut with rage.

"Come on, let's have a pint of the black stuff. I'll pour."

I slipped behind the bar and selected two twenty-ounce, tulip pint glasses bearing the stout's name from the top shelf. I tilted the glass away from me at a forty-five-degree angle and filled it until it reached halfway up the iconic golden harp. I put down the pint to let the Guinness settle and repeated the process with the second glass.

Still seething, Declan slowly made his way around the bar, over to a bar stool, and sat down. I slid a bowl of mixed nuts in front of him and he started crunching salted cashews and almonds between his teeth with a vengeance.

"Let me guess … another film student?" I asked.

"Aye," Declan grunted. "Last time I let one o'those poncey muppets apply. I don't care how jammers we get around here because o'them no more."

Since it was a favourite watering hole for both students and staff of the Vancouver Film School, which was literally across the street, the Emerald Shillelagh had seen an uptick in budding filmmakers seeking to fill the part-time position the pub had recently posted.

With enough time passed, one by one I held the pints level and topped them off. I aimed to etch a shamrock in the foamy head of both, a true talent of a master pourer and something my cousin could do in his sleep. Unfortunately, my efforts left the foamy heads each looking like they had a squiggly letter Q carved into them instead.

"Damn it," I bemoaned before serving the pints.

"You'll get there," said Declan supportively.

I proceeded to tell my cousin about my encounter with Stormy and the Split-Lip Sallies, and how they had hired me earlier that afternoon to find their missing coach.

"Burly butt-slappin' broads and big-boobed babes on roller skates?" Declan asked. "You're takin' me to one o'their games, Mate."

"Maybe later. Right now I need your help."

I showed Declan the photo of Lawrence from the roller derby program and explained the gambling rumours.

"Lawrence of O'Labia?" he chuckled. "Jaysus, that's bloody priceless."

"They all have weird names. It's a roller derby thing. His actual last name is Kunstlinger."

Declan almost choked on his beer from laughter. "Quit takin' the piss."

"I'm serious."

Declan finished chuckling and took a closer look at Lawrence's photo from the program. In the picture the coach of the Split-Lip Sallies rocked a porn-star mustache and big, curly, 'fro-like hair, while his eyes were glazed over as if he were very stoned.

"So this pervy-lookin' git is a wee bit of a punter then, I take it?"

I gave my cousin an odd look. "I don't know if he frequents prostitutes."

"With a bazzer like that you can bet he does."

"Bazzer?"

"His haircut," said Declan, tapping his 'fro in the photo.

"What the hell are you talking about?"

"What the bloody hell are you talking about?"

"You just said he was a punter."

"Aye, you know, a gamblin' man."

"Punter means 'john' over here."

"Piss right off!"

"It's true."

"You goddamn Canucks. The only thing more dumb than your slang is your poutine."

"Watch yourself, D. It's a national delicacy."

"Cop on with ya, you big, hairy oaf."

"Can we get back to business here?"

"Aye," said Declan, before downing a big gulp of his Guinness. "So this Kunstlinger bloke, he likes his bets then."

"The girls weren't certain but it tracks. I think he may be into the sharks. And since I know how much you love to bet on your football—"

"Ya figured I could call me bookie and ask around," said Declan, finishing my thought. "Aye, I'll get on it right away."

Declan laid the program flat on the bar and snapped a pic of Lawrence with his phone. "Kunstlinger," muttered Declan under his breath, before chuckling some more.

We enjoyed some silent sips of Guinness before a middle-aged brunette with a pixie cut slid out of a booth across the pub and approached us.

"Excuse me, but I ordered a black and blood awhile ago and I'm still waiting...."

Declan slowly started to emit a low guttural snarl before I cleared my throat and walked back around the bar.

"I'm afraid we only serve our Guinness as Sir Arthur himself intended it, Ma'am," I said, trying to act as a buffer between the customer and my exasperated cousin. "How about a pint on the house for the delay instead?"

The lady nodded uncertainly and returned to her booth, her eyes lingering on the bottle of grenadine syrup still sitting on the bar where Kangaroo Kid had placed it. I left Declan to serve up one of his masterful creations of barley and hops, and after taking my pint to go, made my way into the hallway, past the restrooms, and up the spiralling staircase to the office on the second floor.

I used my key to unlock the door, shaking my head at the large engraved sign I still hadn't gotten used to. The brass plaque read OUNSTEAD & SON INVESTIGATIONS. My old man was so thrilled when I received my under-supervision private investigator's licence that he replaced the door and went all out on a new sign, which, with its jumbo font, seemed more like an entrance marker for a big-shot Hollywood film producer instead of a couple of local PIs working out of a modest office above a pub. In addition to the large sign, my old man had wanted to get a double-side partners' desk to face each other. Considering how in my face my father already was, a partners' desk would have been absolutely unbearable. Fortunately, I was able to convince him to stick with a single desk we could share and instead upgrade his archaic rotary phone and Windows PC with a conference phone and an iMac. In exchange for his technological progressiveness, I reluctantly conceded to my father's insistence that photocopies of both of our framed private investigator licences hang front and centre on the wall behind the desk. If it were up to me I would have kept mine in a drawer, but instead there they floated on the wall, the matching silver frames jumping out against the backdrop of the metallic blue paint. Several times I had caught my father gazing at the licences with the same look of pride you would see on a fishing enthusiast staring at a Haida Gwaii trophy salmon he had battled, caught, and mounted for display.

I slipped behind the cherry-red executive desk, fired up the computer, and logged into our joint investigative software. My old man had been working a fraud case for the Insurance Corporation of British Columbia the last few weeks and his logs revealed he was currently out on surveillance duty. Although ICBC had slowly cut back on the number of private investigators used for fraud investigations in lieu of their own cyber analysts, my father knew people within the company who preferred to have a retired Vancouver Police Department veteran work their cases instead of a bunch of selfie-stick-owning hacker twentysomethings who, while great at digging up a person's digital activities online, lacked the skill and subtlety it often took to catch a seasoned scam artist.

I started a new case file for Lawrence Kunstlinger, and after plunking in all the relevant info began the tedious task of scouring the web for any and all information I could find on the Split-Lip Sallies coach. Most of what I found was straight-forward enough. When not mentoring derby ladies, Lawrence worked as a delivery driver for a local auto parts shop. He was in his late thirties, had never married, and lived in a one-bedroom apartment in New Westminster, near the very hospital where he was born.

I sipped my Guinness as I started sifting through Lawrence's social media accounts, including Facebook, Twitter, and Instagram. His Instagram was the one in which he posted most often, and nearly all the pictures were taken at either roller derby games or practices. All of his accounts were public and shared the same profile picture, which was a close-up of Lawrence making a goofy face while Jabba the Slut kissed him on one cheek and Pippi Longstomping kissed him on the other. The last post he made was a snap of Lawrence leading the Split-Lip Sallies in a post-game cheer. It had been uploaded ten days prior, which fit with the date of his disappearance Stormy had given me.

I updated the case file with my notes. There was also nothing I could dig up on Lawrence that revealed him partaking in any gambling whatsoever. Not even a few random pics of him at a casino or even playing cards. Lawrence Kunstlinger may have been a betting man, but if he was he clearly went out of his way to keep that fact hidden. I left a yellow sticky note on the computer screen requesting my old man to call in a favour with one of his buddies at the VPD to run a full criminal records check on Lawrence, before jotting down his current address on another sticky and slipping the paper in my pocket. I finished the rest of my Guinness, locked up the office, then headed back downstairs only to find Declan behind the bar muttering to himself as he poured the bottle of grenadine into the drain in the sink. I told him I was headed to New Westminster to check out Lawrence's residence in person.

"Never show surprise, never lose your cool, Mate," he said with a smirk.

"Coughlin's Law," I replied, passing his test and correctly quoting back to him a line from *Cocktail*.

I left the pub with a smile on my face. Unfortunately it didn't last long.

THREE

A tugboat horn blasted as I walked down the hill and took a sharp left onto the sidewalk. I looked past the quay in the distance and while I couldn't see the little ship chugging along, the big riverboat the tugboat had in tow was visible, its bright red paddlewheel slowly turning as it was dragged up the Fraser River.

Lawrence's apartment complex was on the corner of Eighth and Carnarvon in New Westminster, just a block northwest from a Salvation Army Thrift Store. I loitered as casually as possible in front of the large, grey, rectangular building, hoping for someone to either exit or enter. After five minutes I had run out of patience and taken to buzzing apartments and answering "pizza delivery" when curious voices from the intercom inquired who I was. After three tries someone buzzed the lock and I slipped inside the building.

I took the stairs up to the fourth floor and then hoofed it to the unit furthest down the hall and on the right, facing the street. I slowed as I approached the door, noticing that it was slightly ajar. Upon closer inspection I saw that the lock was busted and the door frame was split. From the amount of damage done, it was clear that a crowbar had likely been used. The door hinges creaked ominously as I pushed it open and slipped into the apartment. The place had clearly been tossed. I had heard enough cop stories about illegal searches and B&Es from my old man to be able to recognize the difference between a professional and a sloppy search, and what had taken place in Lawrence's apartment was definitely the latter.

A table had been overturned in the hallway, the dingy carpet sprinkled with key rings, loose change, and red and white peppermints. The kitchen was to my left and the cupboards were all open and the floor littered with broken plates, pots, and pans. Both the freezer and refrigerator door were wide open, revealing nothing except empty ice cube trays and a ghost town of condiments. Either the intruders had been hungry or Lawrence Kunstlinger ate out a lot.

I kept moving until I reached the living room, which was as Spartan as a Buddhist monk meditating inside an oversized cardboard box. A modest flat-screen TV had been ripped off the wall and smashed, and a musty-looking chesterfield had been sliced open a dozen times, its white upholstery bulging from the slits like a scuba diver disemboweled by an outboard motor.

I crept cautiously toward the apartment's single bedroom. I poked my head into the room only to see more of the same. The mattress had been flipped and a dresser raided and turned over, while all of Lawrence's clothes had been pulled out of the closet and strewn about the room. Aside from having a penchant for bell-bottom jeans and bowling shirts, there wasn't much else in Lawrence's bedroom that told me much about him. His entire apartment was quite bland, and it appeared that someone tearing it apart was perhaps the most exciting thing to ever happen in the dreary living space.

Confident that I was alone, I suddenly realized I had been holding my breath in an effort to be as silent as possible. With stealth no longer a priority, I exhaled and began to move about the room and inspect the damage closer. Eventually I made my way to the window, which was open a crack. I pulled up the blinds and took in the view of Carnarvon Street as well as the New Westminster quay and Fraser River beyond it.

I spotted a man in a grey suit just as I finished scanning Carnarvon for the last time and was about to turn around. He was as motionless as a statue, standing by a parking meter directly across the street. He looked to be in his early forties, was of medium height, slender build, and, most peculiarly, was holding a black umbrella on an otherwise hot, sunny day. He also wore a bowler hat that perfectly matched the colour of his suit so he immediately reminded me of Chauncey Gardiner in the Peter Sellers film *Being There*, albeit with one significant difference.

The hairs on the back of my neck were standing straight up because this odd-looking, unnaturally static man was staring right at me. His beady black eyes betrayed no emotion. He continued watching me, his steely gaze slowly transforming into unnerving leering as the seconds ticked by.

I decided to make a run for it and try and catch up to the well-dressed watcher, however, the moment I resolved to do so I heard the first footstep. I had only turned halfway around when I caught a glimpse of the weapon coming at me, and despite ducking and using my forearm to absorb some of the blow, the blunt object caught me on the back of the head just behind my ear. I stumbled to one knee, the room spinning as I felt warm blood trickle down my neck. I managed to look up in time to see two twin attackers, but quickly realized I was seeing double. The attacker wound up again, his weapon now appearing to be a wooden stick. I dropped flat on the ground like a starfish and heard a whooshing sound as the stick flew by my head, nearly connecting. Knowing this was my only chance to get the upper hand, I rolled the dice and assumed the actual attacker was the one I saw on the left. I launched myself into a flying tackle and speared the man hard in his gut with my shoulder. He let out a cry and fell backward, falling awkwardly on the plastic and glass that was once a flat-screen TV. I heard the stick clatter to the floor, and as I struggled to get to my feet I saw the attacker roll off of the broken television and bolt for the door.

I forced myself to fight through the pain and disorientation and managed to climb to my feet. I leaned forward, holding my hands on my knees, and took in a few deep breaths. I exhaled, rolled back my shoulders, and started in pursuit. My footing was wobbly and the hallway seemed to be slowly spinning, but I doggedly ran after my attacker. I reached the stairs and was more grateful for the four flights of handrails than an out-of-shape marathoner for a water station. My balance and coordination started to return as I raced down the stairway and when I burst out of the front door, I spotted my assailant. He was sprinting down Eighth Street toward the quay's River Market and had just made it to an overpass stairway that went over a pair of train tracks and led to the waterfront emporium.

I gave chase. I had gotten my wind back and was flying. I started gaining on my attacker, who was nearing the other side of the pedestrian overpass. He was still running fast, his long, stringy brown hair flapping underneath his backwards Vancouver Canucks baseball cap. Suddenly he dropped out of sight again as he descended the staircase toward the pier. I bounded up the stairs and shot across the overpass before coming down the other side. I reached the pier and paused, unable to relocate my assailant. I scoured my surroundings as I stood on the old wooden planks, between a decommissioned tugboat converted into a playground and a thirty-foot toy soldier that served New Westminster proudly as a "tallest-in-the-world" tourist attraction. Sunlight glinted off of the toy soldier's glossy red jacket forcing me to squint and avert my eyes, but when I opened them again I spotted him. He was no longer running, but walking briskly, checking back over his shoulder as he left the pier and entered an organic market.

He didn't see me. I charged after him and was moving so fast the automatic doors nearly didn't open in time. I was suddenly enveloped in pungent scents of fish and handmade soaps, along with an aromatic whiff of hot basmati rice. Canucks Hat was standing next to a table where a hipster in an orange apron was giving out samples of fresh cold-pressed juices, but when he saw me both his jaw and the cup of whatever green concoction he was drinking dropped. The juice splattered on the floor and Canucks Hat turned and dashed out of the market, past several toy store kiosks and up an escalator to the second floor of the River Market.

I was right behind him. When we reached the second floor we found ourselves surrounded by some kind of board game tournament. Forty people or more were seated around a dozen tables, all deeply immersed in a variety of different games. Canucks Hat was caught off guard and tried to pivot and run the other way, but before he had the chance I leapt across a bench and tackled him into a table. Little plastic figures of knights on horseback and game cards depicting the Holy Grail, Excalibur, and Saxon warriors went flying in all directions as we rolled off the table and onto the floor. I straddled Canucks Hat's chest, grabbed a handful of his shirt, and cocked a fist.

"Don't hit me! Please!" he begged.

I hesitated, and then looked around to see dozens of board gamers staring at me in shock. I slowly lowered my duke and got off of my assailant. He dusted himself off and sat up. He made no effort to rabbit and simply waited there on his bum until I made my next move. Just then a pimply-faced, bespectacled teenager took a half step forward and pointed at the overturned gaming table.

"Dude ... you just ruined our game of *Shadows over Camelot*."

I looked at the kid, then at Canucks Hat, and then back to the kid.

"Just call me Lancelot," I replied.

I grabbed Canucks Hat by the scruff of the neck and yanked him to his feet. He barely came up to my chest and was much shorter than I had realized.

"Let's take a walk," I said forcibly.

"Okay, man, whatever you say," he replied.

We left the board gamers staring at the carnage in dismay and rode the escalator back down toward the organic market.

"Why did you attack me?" I asked.

"Why did you trash Lars' pad?"

"I didn't."

Canucks Hat was stunned. "But then—why were you there?"

"I'm a private investigator. Lawrence's roller derby team hired me to find him."

Canucks Hat took of his cap and ran his fingers through his stringy hair.

"Shit, man," he said, before securing the cap back on his head. "I had no idea. I'm, like, totes sorry."

"Totes?"

"Yeah. Totes. Like as in short for 'totally.'"

I felt the adrenaline slowly fading from my system, although it was immediately replaced by irritation that this guy thought dropping a few letters from a word was a time saver.

"Let's go back to Lawrence's apartment," I said, as we passed children playing on the tugboat playground, and started marching up the stairs toward the giant toy soldier's head and the pedestrian overpass. Canucks Hat nodded obediently and we walked the rest of the way in silence. When we reached the apartment complex Canucks Hat whipped out his keys and unlocked the door.

"You live here?" I asked.

"Yeah, man. I'm Lars' neighbour. I live across the hall."

We took the elevator to the fourth floor and walked until we were back inside Lawrence's humble abode. Canucks Hat shoved his hands deep into his jeans pockets and slouched against a wall. I ripped a few sheets of paper towel off of a roll on the kitchen floor and used them to dab the cut on the back of my head. The wound was small and had clotted, so I was pretty sure I didn't need stitches. I caught Canucks Hat's eye as I wiped the remaining blood off my neck and he hung his head as if in shame.

I moved to the living room and found the weapon he had used to attack me—an old-school, wooden lacrosse stick. I used the stick to scoop up a small-framed photograph near the broken television. In the team picture Lawrence stood proudly behind the Split-Lip Sallies. I placed the photo on the kitchen counter-top bar.

"That's the only thing they didn't mess up," said Canucks Hat.

"What's that?"

"His roller derby stuff."

Canucks Hat pointed above me on the hallway wall. I had missed it before due to its height, but a large floating shelf hosted a variety of roller derby memorabilia. Framed photos, a yellow helmet covered in spandex with two black stars on it, and numerous trophies all hovered safely over the rest of the trashed apartment.

"That picture must have fallen off or something," reasoned Canucks Hat.

I slung the lacrosse stick behind my neck and with both arms on opposite ends used it to stretch out my chest and back.

"What's your name?" I asked.

"Troy Whitlock."

"What do you do for a living?"

"I work at Safeway. Produce department."

"How long have you known Lawrence?"

Troy shrugged. "Couple years, I guess? He was already living here when I moved in."

"Do you have any idea who could have done this?" I asked, motioning toward the massive damage.

"I wish, man."

"When did this ransacking take place?"

"Must have been this morning. His place was locked up tight when I got in last night."

"Have you seen anything else suspicious around here lately?"

"No, man. Look, if we're going to play twenty questions do you mind if I at least have a puff? You scared the shit out of me back there."

"Have at it, Bub."

Troy dug in his pocket and pulled out a slim, black vape pen. He pressed a button, inhaled deeply, held his breath, then blew out a blueberry-scented cloud of vapour. I leaned the lacrosse stick against the wall and waited for him to take another hit before continuing my questioning.

"Is that nicotine?" I asked.

"Weed oil," said Troy, grinning.

I nodded. "Better?"

"Much."

I took a step forward and crossed my arms.

"Do you know if Lawrence had any gambling debts?" I asked.

"Nah, man. I mean, not that I know of. But he did like to gamble."

"On what?"

"Sports mostly. NFL, NBA, NHL, even some MLB in October. Sometimes we used to talk strategy before he placed his bets."

"Talk strategy?" I asked skeptically.

Troy chuckled and took another hit from his vape pen. "Well, as much strategy as a cold beer and some Mary Jane will provide," he answered earnestly.

I nodded and moved on. "When's the last time you saw Lawrence?"

"About a week ago. We usually smoke a bowl and watch sports on Sundays, but he never showed. I tried knocking on his door a few times, but there was no answer. And he hasn't responded to any of my texts." Troy took a long drag on his vape pen and blew vapour rings when he exhaled.

"Has Lawrence ever disappeared like this before?" I asked.

"Not since I moved in. And not without telling me. I'm the one who feeds his fish when he goes away."

"What fish?"

Troy looked around the apartment.

"Whoa…" he said, in a manner so dumbstruck Keanu Reeves himself would have been impressed. Troy's cannabis-laced vapour must have been kicking in something fierce as he kept staring at the countertop bar that divided the kitchen and the living room as if in a trance.

I snapped my fingers a few times. "Troy? Troy!" Troy rejoined the land of the living and looked at me with a confused expression. "Yeah?"

"What fish?"

"Carlos."

"Carlos?"

"Larry's Siamese fighting fish. That's where his little tank usually is," he said, pointing to the bar countertop. "He's gone, man." The short stoner frowned. "I liked that fish," he said sadly.

"Troy?"

"Yeah?"

"If the fish or its tank isn't here, then I'm sure it's okay."

"Oh man, I hope so. I really liked that fish."

Realizing I was reaching a point of diminishing returns due to Troy's puffs of Mary Jane, I decided to wrap up my inquiry.

"Last question. Have you ever seen a man in a grey suit around here before?"

"What, like a professor?"

"A professor?"

"Yeah, man. Don't professors wear grey suits?"

Troy was fading and fading fast.

"I mean like a slim guy in a nice suit, with an umbrella and a bowler hat."

Troy started laughing.

"What's so funny?"

"Bowlers don't wear hats, man," he said, snickering some more.

I decided to throw in the towel. I gave Troy my card and told him to call if he remembered anything else that might be useful in tracking down Lawrence. I escorted him out of Lawrence's apartment and back to his own. He was still giggling as he opened his front door.

"Bowler hats," he chuckled to himself as he rode his high back into his apartment.

Twenty minutes later I was halfway to my pop's pub and three quarters of the way through a large banana milkshake when my phone chimed.

I opened my text messages and saw a single sentence from Declan.

Found Mr. O'Labia's bookie, Mate.

FOUR

The thoroughbred whinnied loudly, then stood on its hind legs and reached for the sky with its front hooves. The white stallion's mane rippled as a gust of wind suddenly passed by and it took all the restraint I had not to hoist my large banana milkshake in the air and shout *"Hi-Yo, Silver! Away!"* The steed's front hooves landed back on the track and in a flash it began to kick up dirt as the horse took off like a shot around the oval raceway, while the little jockey stood up in the saddle, kicking his heels and coaxing the magnificent beast to run faster.

Sunlight suddenly broke through a shifting cloud and lit up Hastings Racecourse. The sun had been playing peekaboo, as was often the case in Vancouver, and the weather had been in flux.

I turned my back to the track and bounded up a stairway until I reached the man sitting by himself in the tenth row. The rest of the stadium was empty, save for the few horses and jockeys warming up on the racecourse.

The man wore aviator sunglasses and a crisp navy-blue blazer over a pair of khaki pants, and his jet-black hair was slicked back. He looked calm and comfortable as he sat with his legs crossed and held a small, reddish, dachshund in his lap, slowly, and repeatedly stroking the little dog's floppy ears.

"Sykes?" I asked.

"Mr. Ounstead, I presume," he replied, still watching the horses.

"How do you know who I am?"

"My colleague, whom I understand regularly takes wagers from your cousin, alerted me that I would likely be receiving a visit from you soon." Sykes turned his head and looked at me, giving me the once over. "I have never cared for professional wrestling. Its scripted storylines make it a pointless event on which to bet. At least with boxing there remains an element of unpredictability."

"I don't wrestle much anymore."

"That is not what I have heard."

"It's a bit … complicated."

I motioned to the red plastic seat next to him. "Do you mind?"

Sykes considered my request for a moment before nodding and returning his gaze to the track. The dachshund was skittish and jumpy in Sykes' lap as I took a seat next to him. Sykes continued to stroke the nervous little dog and stare out toward the racecourse. I took a big sip of my banana shake before speaking.

"Nice wiener dog," I said finally, breaking the silence.

"I loathe that term," replied Sykes. "Napoleon here is a pure-bred dachshund. He comes from a long line of hunting dogs that were experts at flushing out badgers and other burrow-dwelling animals. Referring to him as a wiener dog is an insult to his lineage."

Sykes was stroking the dog all the way from its head to its mid-back now. The cute canine looked proud and stared at me as if it knew its owner was defending its honour.

"No offense intended," I said.

Sykes let out a big sigh and exhaled forcefully.

"It is not your fault. I blame pop culture for branding these amazing animals with such a silly name."

"I would imagine one doesn't usually find dachshunds at horse races," I said.

"Unless it is summertime in Vancouver."

"How's that?"

"The annual Dachshund Championships."

"A dog show?"

"Racing, Mr. Ounstead."

"You mean these little wien – I mean, dachshunds, actually race each other?"

Sykes smiled, revealing a mouthful of bright white veneers.

"They do indeed. Top prize this year is a ten-thousand-dollar purse, and that is in addition to any wagers I may take. Napoleon is set to make me a lot of money."

As if on cue the dog yipped and sat up in Sykes' lap. Sykes hushed the pooch and as it sat back down he produced a treat from his pocket and fed it to the racing hound.

"I take it you are not here to place a bet on my little friend?" Sykes asked as he resumed stroking the dog.

"I'm here about Lawrence Kunstlinger," I replied.

Sykes' face lit up again. "Lawrence," he said, dragging out the pronunciation of his name. "One of my favourite clients. Always pays his debts. Always pays them quickly."

"He's gone missing."

Sykes removed his aviator sunglasses and clipped them to the white polo shirt he was wearing underneath his navy-blue blazer. His ice-blue eyes sparkled as a smug smirk crept across his face.

"Perhaps he simply does not want to be found," said Sykes slyly.

"You know where he is, don't you?"

Sykes returned his gaze to the racecourse. More chestnut-brown horses ridden by jockeys trotted out onto the track.

"I do not. But I may have a way to contact him."

"How? He hasn't been answering his cell phone in over a week."

"No, he simply has not been answering that particular cell phone in over a week."

I mulled over the nugget of information Sykes had offered. After a moment, I figured it out.

"Lawrence is using a burner," I said, now realizing what my missing roller derby coach was up to. "The son of a bitch is still placing bets with you, isn't he?"

Sykes' mouth formed into a smug smirk again as he nodded slightly. I was a bit stunned. It dawned on me that because of the trashed apartment and creepy, grey-suited peeper, I'd been leaning toward the possibility that Lawrence may have been caught up in some kind of foul play. Instead, for whatever his reasons, the guy had booted it out of Dodge of his own volition.

"I need the number for that burner," I said.

"And I need you to listen to a proposition first," replied Sykes.

I hesitated before answering, wondering just how cautious I need be with a character like Sykes. After a moment, I responded.

"Go ahead."

Sykes took a deep breath and gave Napoleon another treat. The little guy gobbled it up out of Sykes' hand faster than a duck being offered a piece of bread.

"Unfortunately, the mother of an associate of mine recently had a stroke. As a result, this associate is out of commission for the time being. However, I still need the services he typically provides and I need them now. If you were able to help me with said service, I would gladly compensate you for your efforts with the number for Mr. Kunstlinger's new mobile phone."

"You want to use me as an enforcer."

"I want you to simply collect some money that is owed to me."

"I'm not a goon-for-hire."

"I never said you were. But let us be honest, a man with your size, smarts, and wrestling ability—well—surely you have the skill set required to coerce a stubborn individual into squaring away his debt."

"Don't try and butter me up, Sykes. Who owes you this money?"

"A man by the name of Dale Forrester. He is a longshoreman down at the Port of Vancouver. A foreman, actually. Needless to say he makes very good money."

"Good money that translates into wagers with you."

"Exactly. Forrester, well … he works hard, then he lives hard."

"And you'd like me to have a chat with him?"

"I would like you to collect from him. This Friday is his payday. And on the following day, as he does every second Saturday of the month, he visits a certain club, engages in a variety of activities, and more often than not blows through the bulk of his paycheque."

"And you want me to collect the debt he owes you before this happens."

"Indeed."

I slurped back the last of my banana milkshake and watched as a jockey hopped off his steed and comforted his nervous horse, momentarily spooked by a car backfiring in the parking lot. I contemplated Sykes' offer before finally making my decision.

"How much does he owe?" I asked.

"Forty-two hundred," Sykes replied.

"And he'll have that on him?"

"He will."

"When and where?"

"The Graf Zeppelin nightclub in Gastown this Saturday. Anytime after 9:00 PM. Forrester always stays until closing."

I reached out a hand slowly and gave the dachshund's head a scratch. He looked up at me with big brown eyes then licked his chops, apparently having grown accustomed to my presence.

"Have Lawrence's number ready," I said, before standing up and walking toward the stairs.

"Mr. Ounstead?" said Sykes.

"Yes?"

"This particular club … well … it is safe to say it caters to a certain type of clientele. I encourage you to proceed with caution."

I nodded confidently toward Sykes, despite wondering what kind of situation I was entering.

FIVE

Declan lit a cigarette and tossed the blackened matchstick over his shoulder. The charred thin strip of wood landed on top of the dark green whiskey barrel at the feet of the infamous Gassy Jack, but the statue of Vancouver's founding father remained as taciturn as ever.

We walked through Gastown's Maple Tree Square and along the red brick road up Carrall Street when Declan asked a question I knew was coming.

"Pint o'the black stuff?"

"I'm working, D."

"Well I'm sure as shite not." Declan checked his watch. "C'mon, don't be a narky wanker. We got a half-an-hour to kill so let's have a craic at least."

"Just one," I said, relenting.

Declan stomped out his cigarette butt before we stopped off at the Irish Heather gastropub and sidled up to the bar. The bartender took one look at Declan before nodding and pouring our pints without a word. All but a legend in Gastown, everyone knew nobody served a better pint of Guinness than my cousin.

To this day I still don't know exactly where he gets the kegs of Guinness used to pour pints at my old man's pub, and if you try and ask Declan about it, he gets all cagey and changes the topic.

When our pints were finally ready the bartender slid them in front of us.

"No bloody shamrocks, Jeff?" asked Declan, staring at the smooth, creamy heads on our stouts. Jeff shrugged apologetically before slipping off down the bar to tend to a sudden influx of patrons. "This is bollocks, Mate. Any self-respecting Irish pub etches goddamn shamrocks into the top o'their Guinness."

"Let it go," I said. "I need you calm."

"Aye, then let me get me drink on, already."

I nursed my pint while Declan knocked back his and ordered another.

"So tell me what kind o'club is this again?"

"I'm not exactly sure. Apparently every second Saturday it's rented out for special events. Sykes suggested I proceed with caution, and rolling in to an unknown location with you by my side in order to collect forty-two hundred from a longshoreman with a gambling problem is about as careful as I know how to be."

"I should o'brought me gun."

"No, you shouldn't have. There's no reason to think this won't go smoothly."

"Aye, well there's every reason to think I'm going to kick some serious arse if it doesn't."

"Fair enough."

We drank some more and Declan recapped how his favourite striker from the Galway United Football Club had scored a stunning overtime goal in a League of Ireland soccer game earlier in the day. I listened dutifully and after finishing most of my Guinness we settled our tab, exited the gastropub, crossed the road, and made our way down Cordova Street until we reached the entrance of the Graf Zeppelin club.

A wide, beefy, and hairy-chested man in a V-neck T-shirt sporting earlobe spacers and spiky blonde hair stepped forward as we approached. Before he could raise a hand to motion us to halt his bouncer partner patted his shoulder and instructed him to stand down.

"Easy, Paulo. I know this character."

"Pistol Pete," I said, extending my hand and shaking his. "Since when did you leave the Roxy? That's a plum gig."

"Oh, I'm still there," he replied. "I just pick up extra shifts here once in awhile."

"You mean for special events like tonight?" I asked.

"Exactly," replied Pistol Pete.

While nowhere near as large as his fellow spiky-haired bouncer Paulo, Pistol Pete was no slouch in the size department. He was nearly as tall as me and was easily a solid two bills and change of tight bodybuilder muscle. Having worked the door together at numerous clubs over the years, before I became a private investigator, I had seen firsthand the guy more than hold his own against all kinds of drunk and rowdy club-goers.

"Pistol Pete?" said Declan. "Ain't that the name o'some Yankee basketball fella from the seventies?"

"It certainly is," I replied. "It's also what we started calling Pete after he single-handedly took down an armed patron outside of Brandi's a couple of years back. What was that punk carrying, a revolver?"

"Thirty-eight snub," said Pistol Pete proudly.

"That's right," I said, remembering the night fondly.

"While I'm pleased as punch you two fannies are havin' a lovely stroll down memory lane," said Declan. "How about me *Col Gaolta* and I head into this club already?"

"*Col* what?" asked Pete.

"It's Gaelic. For cousin," I replied.

"You two are related?" asked Pete, surprised.

"Aye, we are indeed, Mate. So unless you're not done feedin' biscuits to a bear, I suggest you let us in."

Paulo suddenly stepped forward, puffing out his chest like he was Arnold Schwarzenegger taking the stage at his first Mr. Olympia competition.

"Whadda you mean by 'bear'?" Paulo asked angrily. You calling us queers or something?"

"It's just an old Irish expression, Bub," I said. "No one is calling anyone anything."

Declan had reached his limit. "Jaysus, Jed. Now this pointy-haired ponce is gonna start olagonin'? I ain't got all night," he snapped.

Paulo's eyes darted back and forth between me and my cousin, his face scrunched up in an expression of total and utter confusion.

"I don't—what—what the hell is he saying?" stammered Paulo.

"Everybody chill," interjected Pistol Pete. "Paulo, why don't you go do a lap inside, make sure everything is copacetic."

"Copa-what?" snapped Paulo.

"Just make sure everything's cool, okay?" said Pete soothingly.

Paulo glared at Declan and me before heeding Pistol Pete's instructions and heading inside.

"You should really get that guy a thesaurus," I said.

Pistol Pete chuckled. "Same old Jed," he said. "Still a shit disturber."

"It's a gift."

"Seriously, why are you here?"

I explained how I was working a case and needed to have a conversation with Dale Forrester.

"Look, Jed, you and I—we go back," said Pete. "I want to help you out. But you can't enter the club dressed like that."

Declan and I glanced at each other's outfits—he was in boots, blue jeans, and a flannel shirt while I wore a Henley over a pair of black pants.

"What the bloody hell is wrong with our clothes?" asked Declan.

"Do you guys even know what kind of place this is?" asked Pete.

"One that caters to a certain clientele?" I responded.

Pistol Pete took a step forward and lowered his voice. He glanced up and down the sidewalk to ensure no one was within earshot.

"This is a kink club, Jed," he said. "A full-blown BDSM party."

"Get the fuck out o'here," said Declan, smirking.

"Even if I let you in, unless you're dressed in fetish wear you are going to get tossed immediately. They have staff and security inside and are very strict."

"Look, Pistol, I don't care if Richard Gere himself is in there having a gerbil-jousting tournament. I need to have a quick chat with Forrester. Tonight. Then I'm gone."

Pistol Pete scratched his stubbly chin and I could see the wheels turning in his head. He examined our outfits again before letting out an exasperated sigh.

"Goddamn it. Okay, Jed. Give me a minute and I'll see what I can do. Watch the door while I'm gone and don't let anyone in. Just make them wait until I get back."

Pistol Pete entered the club and closed the door behind him. Declan and I did a one-eighty before standing shoulder-to-shoulder guarding the entrance to The Graf Zeppelin. I could feel my cousin staring at me and when I looked at him he had a big smile plastered across his face.

"What?"

"A feckin' kink club, Mate."

"Yeah, yeah."

"Do you even know what BDSM stands for?"

"Bondage, Domination, and Sadomasochism?"

"Jaysus. Somebody's been reading their *Fifty Shades of Grey*."

"Look, D, however this plays out, just watch my back in there, okay? I don't need some leather-clad pal of Forrester's sneaking up from behind and choking me with a chain or something."

"Aye, don't you fret your pretty little head. I got you covered, Boyo."

Just then Pistol Pete reemerged from the Graf Zeppelin carrying a stack of clothes. "All right, this should be enough to get you guys in," he said.

Pete handed me a black and red rubber blazer that I slipped on over my shirt. I struggled with the form-fitting garment, and it literally felt like I was sliding giant condoms onto my arms, but once I was wearing the uncomfortable jacket he gave me a pat on the back and a nod of certainty. He then tossed me a dog collar with large chrome spikes that were bigger than a great white shark's teeth and motioned for me to put it around my neck.

"You've got to be kidding," I said.

"You want to talk to this guy of yours or not?" asked Pete.

I sighed and fastened the dog collar around my neck, being careful not to make it too tight. Declan started laughing so hard he almost peed himself.

"This is bloody fantastic," he said, holding a hand on his stomach.

"Not so fast, buddy," cautioned Pete. "At least Jed has black pants. You need to wear these."

Pistol Pete whipped out a pair of black leather chaps, complete with cut-outs in the bum, and adorned with frilly tassels up and down both legs.

"Get up the yard ya Bombay Shitehawk," snarled Declan.

"Do you want in or not?" asked Pete.

Declan looked at me in desperation. Except now it was my turn to laugh. "Maybe there's a mechanical bull inside that you can ride," I quipped.

Declan spat out a litany of Gaelic curse words as he slid the leather chaps on over his blue jeans. Pistol Pete pointed to Declan's flannel shirt.

"Take that off and wrap it around your waist. With these chaps and your undershirt you should be able to skate by for awhile."

Declan did as instructed and whipped off his shirt and wrapped it around his waist, which conveniently covered the blue jeans peeking through the cut-out areas in his rear. With his shirt removed, wearing only a white undershirt, Declan's lean and sinewy muscular biceps and triceps were revealed. When Pistol Pete saw my cousin's orange, white, and green IRA tattoo, accompanied by two colourfully inked sleeves that ran all the way from his shoulders down to his wrists, he smiled.

"You should have told me you had tats," he said. "You'll definitely fly under the radar now."

"Must be me lucky day," sniped Declan, before crossing his arms over his chest.

"You guys ready?" asked Pete.

Declan and I shared a nervous glance. It was a rare thing, seeing my cousin out of his comfort zone, but I'll be damned if I wasn't enjoying seeing his relentlessly sarcastic ass all dudded up in a pair of frilly black leather cowboy chaps.

"As we'll ever be," I said.

And with that, Pistol Pete opened the door and we entered into a world of kink.

SIX

Once inside the Graf Zeppelin we walked down a dark hallway and toward a purple-velvet curtain that led into the club. A coat check girl with a large floral chest tattoo, dressed in a red corset, black panties, a garter belt and stockings, sat in a chair behind a counter filing her nails while chomping and popping a mouthful of bubblegum. She glanced up at us briefly, before nodding toward Declan.

"Nice ink," she said to my cousin, blowing a large pink bubble.

"Right back at ya, Lassie," replied Declan, winking at the girl.

As we neared the velvet curtain all I could hear was the distinct sound of scrunching leather.

"Your chaps are rubbing together awfully loud," I said.

"You tell one bloody soul about this I swear I'll cut you off from drinkin' at the pub for life," he warned.

"I think it's the leather tassels making most of the noise. Maybe you could reduce the sound if you walked a little bow-legged. You know, like a real cowboy?"

Declan gritted his teeth and fumed while I had a good laugh.

"You're a real gammy bastard sometimes, you know that?"

"Pistol Pete did call me a shit disturber," I said.

"Aye, and then some," agreed my cousin.

I pulled back the curtain and we entered into a cornucopia of kink. Four giant glass cubes in each corner of the room, illuminated with a kaleidoscope of colours, housed topless male and female dancers. A lady DJ wearing aviator goggles and a skintight, steampunk, Catwoman costume bopped her head to the beat as she spun the latest techno music. The dance floor was peppered with an abundance of fetish-clad individuals—chains, chokers, leather, lace, vinyl—you name it, someone was wearing it, and provocatively at that.

A man dressed as a clown, but with a creepy white-latex mask with a zipper mouth, twerked on the dance floor while his effeminate dance partner, wearing nothing except for an oversized diaper and pink pasties on his nipples, groped the eerie jester's buttocks. A blonde woman in a golden bikini, her skin spray-painted the same colour head to toe, walked a man with mermaid and shark tattoos all over his back around the club on a dog leash. The submissive acted like a canine by panting excessively and yipping whenever his master yanked on his collar. A sultry lady dwarf in a pink corset, sporting a pair of butterfly wings twice her size, was being hand-fed grapes by a portly woman in a rainbow tutu and suspenders, while sitting in an oversized throne chair adjacent to the dance floor. The dwarf licked the woman's fingertips after every nibble of fruit, and she appeared orgasmic after each bite. The dance floor itself was stuffed fuller than a tin of sardines, the air thick with the scent of sweat and musk of dozens of BDSM enthusiasts, all gyrating their bodies to the pulsing music. Finally, we heard the chime of a bicycle bell as a mime in face paint, decked out in a top hat, a tailcoat, and checkered black-and-white spandex shorts rode by on a tricycle toward the bar on the far left side of the club.

I stole a glance at my cousin, whose jaw was nearly on the floor.

"Jaysus, Mary, and Joseph," he said incredulously. "It's bloody Xanadu."

"Come on," I said, and almost had to drag Declan over toward the bar, his bulging eyes staring at the dance floor and its strange inhabitants. I flagged down the bartender and a heavy-set woman with shaved head and the biggest pair of breasts I had ever seen walked over to us.

"What'll it be, newbies?" she asked.

"That obvious, eh?" I replied.

"'Fraid so."

"Just a bottled water, thanks."

"And your handsome friend there?"

I nudged Declan but he was still in a trance watching the dance floor.

"He'll have a beer," I said. "Something craft and local."

Declan focused and turned around only to find himself face-to-face with our well-endowed bartender, whose shiny silver bra was so taut with tension I thought it might snap at any moment and unleash her mounds of bosom with enough force to knock my cousin unconscious.

"Janey Mack!" exclaimed Declan. "Look at the size o'those thrupenny bits!"

"What the hell did he just say?" asked the bartender, as Declan continued gawking at her chest.

"Please ignore him," I replied. "He's a bit overwhelmed by this place."

"He wouldn't be the first," said the bartender, before snapping her fingers in front of Declan's face to catch his attention. "Look, Cutie, I don't mind you ogling Greta and Gertie—that's what they're there for—but don't be callin' them any funny names."

"Greta and Gertie?" inquired Declan.

The bartender slipped both hands under her left breast, lifted it up, then dropped the massive mammary down on the bar.

"Greta," she replied, before repeating the same action with her right breast. "Gertie," she said and then wiggled her chest, which caused her enormous cleavage to jiggle like a bowl of Jell-O during an earthquake.

Declan looked up from the bartender's bosom and a huge grin spread across his face. "Aye, that I can do, Love."

The bartender returned his smile, slid her boobs off the bar, and left to get our drinks. Declan turned to me and I could see the sparkle in his eyes.

"I don't think I've ever been this happy before, Jed."

"That's great. But I've got a job to do."

"Greta and Gertie," mumbled Declan, losing interest in what I was saying as his gaze drifted back to the dance floor as if pulled by a magnet.

The bartender returned with our drinks. However, since one of her hands was full of empty pint glasses and the other my bottled water, she had tucked the bottle of Red Truck Ale in between her breasts. She whistled at Declan as she appeared before us and his face lit up like a kid on Christmas morning.

"Here you go, Honey," she cooed, before Declan reached out and plucked his beer free. "First round's on me."

"What's your name?" I asked.

"Trixie. Trixie Titties."

"I think I love you," blurted out Declan.

Trixie blushed and puckered her lips.

"Control yourself, D. Trixie, may I ask you a couple of questions?"

"Sure thing, Sugar."

"Miss Trixie Titties," interrupted my cousin, "I just want to give a grand lady like yerself a proper thank you for the way you've been mollycoddlin' our lucky arses. And I'd be lyin' if I didn't admit that right now all I can think about is banging away on those babies like bongo drums," he added, nodding at her jumbo bust.

"For God's sake, Declan!" I snapped. "Just drink your beer and let me talk to her."

My cousin grumbled in Gaelic before gawking at the dance floor. Trixie was still giggling from Declan's proposition.

"He's a hoot," she said.

"You have no idea,' I replied. "So I'm looking for a guy...."

"Plenty of those here."

"He's a regular. Name's Dale Forrester."

"I just know faces, not names. And the ones I do know are kinky ones. Not a lot of real names used in a place like this."

"Makes sense."

"What's this Dale look like?"

"I don't know. But apparently he's a big spender."

"Then you're in the wrong place, Hon."

"He's not here?"

"Oh no, if he's a regular and a big spender, he'll be here all right. But you won't find him on the dance floor. You want the dungeon."

Declan spun around faster than a figure skater during the finale of a free skate.

"Dungeon?" he asked giddily.

"No way," I said, shutting him down. "You stay here with Trixie. I got this."

Declan sulked and took a pull of his beer. I nodded toward my cousin.

"Keep an eye on him for me, will you?"

"Absolutely," purred Trixie.

"How do I get to this dungeon?"

"Go down that hallway past the restrooms. There's a spiral staircase at the end that leads downstairs. And if you need any help just ask one of the purple shirts."

"Purple shirts?" I asked.

"You'll see."

I followed Trixie's directions to the spiral staircase. Another bouncer I didn't know patted me down before granting me access. My boots made a racket on the metal steps as I wormed my way down and around the twisting stairway until I reached the bottom. There was only one direction to go so I walked down the hallway until I reached yet another bouncer, this one guarding a large red door. He gave me the once over, then nodded silently, and opened the passageway.

I stepped through the red door and into the dungeon, and the world as I knew it would never be quite the same again.

SEVEN

The lights were dim. Candles were mounted on the walls
throughout the great room, their flickering light glinted off of
the metal components of assorted bondage equipment. A nearly
naked, skinny, bespectacled man was held hostage in the middle
of the room, his head and wrists locked in wooden stocks. He
had an orange ball gag in his mouth and alternated between
moans of pleasure and jerky, spastic movements as a dominatrix
towered over him, while running a chrome pinwheel up and
down his back and bum.

To my left, a naked woman hung in the air inside an octagon
suspension frame. Thick ropes tied around her torso and ankles
kept her floating five feet above the floor. Her hands were cuffed
behind her back, and she had a blissful smile on her face while
she slowly rotated within the suspension frame, like a wind chime
absorbing a light breeze.

Across the room from the hanging woman, a man tightly
gripped an A-frame as his male partner stood behind him, tick-
ling his backside with a long, thin stick with a feathered tip. Near
the back of the room a small Asian woman lay on a padded table

while two hulking men, both twice her size, massaged her supple skin. A half-dozen other active bondage stations were spread about the room, including a hoist, a swing, a gurney, and more stocks. Despite the menacing nature of the equipment, the entire room had an odd sense of tranquility about it. Synthesized music played softly in the background as the BDSM patrons went about their business calmly and matter-of-factly.

I was cocking my head to the side, trying to make out the facial expression of a man in leather underwear hanging upside down on an inversion table when a spritely blonde girl with her hair in double buns approached me.

"Can I help you?" she asked.

I looked at the girl and noticed her purple shirt, the word STAFF in all caps printed across the front. She also wore matching purple examination gloves on her hands. One of five dungeon staff present, she and her colleagues floated throughout the room, from station to station, discreetly monitoring the bondage sessions.

"Quite the place," I said.

"Best and safest dungeon in the province," she said proudly. "Are you looking to play?"

"Not today."

"I see. Well, we have a strict no spectator rule, so if you aren't going to engage in any erotic activities, then I'm afraid I have to ask you to leave."

"There's someone here I need to see. Dale Forrester."

The girl looked at me suspiciously.

"Do you know him?" I asked.

"I know a Dale, yes, but why do you need to see him?"

"It's an urgent family matter. I can't really say any more."

"Oh. Well, I suppose that's okay. He's actually about to start a session in the VIP room. I could go and get him—"

"If it's all the same, I'd rather just pop in there myself if you don't mind. I'll only be a few minutes."

The girl considered my words for a moment before nodding.

"Very well," she said. "It's the door on the left side in the back, just past the smother box."

Not wanting to know or even imagine what the hell a smother box could be, I thanked the girl and she wandered off to supervise a woman in a rubber dress about to apply a nipple clamp to her shirtless male partner.

I kept my eyes low as I walked past multiple bondage sessions toward the back of the room. I saw a large square wooden box with a hole cut into the middle against the wall and figured it had to be the smother box. Once passed it, I found the door to the VIP room, paused a moment, took a deep breath, opened the door, and slipped inside.

The VIP room was brighter than the dungeon. There was a queen-sized bed against a red-brick wall, with the image on the black and grey gothic bedding of a moonlit metal gate in the shape of a skull. The ensuite bathroom door was only open a crack. Across from the bed, in the middle of the room, stood a large square rack, not that dissimilar from one you might see at a gym where people performed squats. However, instead of a barbell and plates, this rack was only equipped with ropes and cuffs. A short, hairy man was restrained inside the rack, his wrists and ankles bound and pulled in four different directions, making his entire body look like a large letter X. The hairy man—Dale Forrester I presumed—was wearing nothing save for thong underwear and a blindfold, and he was excitedly humming and wiggling his fingers and toes. A few feet behind him, on a dozen coat hooks, hung a collection of riding crops, floggers, whips, paddles, and chains.

"Hurry up, you dirty slut!" Forrester suddenly snapped.

I looked around the VIP room. We were all alone, although when I heard a toilet flush I realized Forrester's kinky friend was in the bathroom.

"Yeah, yeah, here we go," said Forrester. "I need it bad you filthy whore."

Forrester was now wiggling his bare butt cheeks excitedly. I heard boots on tile and when the bathroom door opened a statuesque dominatrix with black hair in a bob cut, in a corset and fishnet leggings, walked into the room. She paused when she saw me and stared curiously. Before she could open her mouth to speak I put a finger to my lips and silently shushed. I held up my hand and mouthed the words, "I need five minutes." I then slowly pulled out my wallet, counted out one hundred dollars in twenties and offered it to the woman. The dominatrix looked at the cash in my hand and then back to me. She put one hand on her hip and held up two fingers with the other. Not wanting to haggle, I quickly pulled out another two fifties and gave her the money. She folded the cash, tucked it into the top of one of her knee-high leather boots and then strutted right up to me. She leaned her head forward until her lips were nearly touching my cheek, and I could feel her warm cinnamon breath on my ear when she spoke.

"The safe word is *pistachio*," she whispered.

And with that she turned on a dime and walked out of the VIP room, quietly closing the door behind her.

"What the fuck is taking so long, bitch?" asked Forrester. "Get over here and give me what I paid for."

I started walking toward Forrester. Hearing my footsteps approaching, he got even more worked up.

"Yeah, yeah," he said, still wiggling his ass. "That's it, you slut. Come give it to me. Give me what I goddamn need."

Now, normally in a situation like this—not that I had ever been in a situation even remotely like this—I would take a more diplomatic approach, try and reason with the person, and generally avoid as much confrontation as possible. But because Forrester was a crude and vile little troll, I adopted a different method of engagement.

I picked up a riding crop, felt the weight of it in my hand, then used it to slice through the air, creating a whooshing sound.

"Yeah, that's it," said Forrester.

I placed the riding crop back on the hook and selected a flogger—the ol' cat o'nine tails. I snapped the flogger in the air and the multi-tailed strips of leather cracked loudly.

"Ooooh, you're such a fucking tease. Take out your tits. Take out your tits and rub them on me."

I snapped the flogger again, this time flicking my wrist more. The mop-like leather strings cracked even louder this time.

"Mmmm, yeah! Yeah! Listen, I know the rule is no sex stuff but I will pay you an extra three hundred dollars to blow me after my punishment."

I placed the flogger back on the wall and walked over to the last hook on the right. I picked up a regulation cricket bat and spun the handle in my hand, watching as the long, wide, rectangular wooden blade twirled.

"Five hundred!" he blurted out, as he writhed in anticipation. "Five hundred bucks for you to suck me off!"

I lined up the cricket bat, dropped into my best batting stance, and started my windup.

WHACK!

I swung the cricket bat with all my strength and landed a powerful blow directly to Dale Forrester's naked ass.

"*AAAAIIIIIIIIIEEEEEEEE!*" shrieked Forrester.

I slung the cricket bat over my shoulder and walked around to the front of the rack until Forrester and I were face to face. He was still blindfolded and his face was contorted in pain.

"*Pistachio! Pistachio!*" he yelped. "Jesus Christ, pistachio!"

Forrester squirmed desperately in his restraints, hopelessly trying to soothe his throbbing bottom. Then he started to cry and peed himself.

"*Fuck me, that hurt so bad. Jesus, why would you do that? Oh, does that hurt.*"

Forrester went limp in his restraints and fell forward slightly, continuing to cry. I waited until the last of his urine dribbled down his leg and his cries turned to whimpers.

"I need the forty-two hundred you owe Sykes, Dale."

Forrester whipped his head from side to side as if he was either trying to see or shake off his blindfold. He was unsuccessful in both attempts.

"Wh—wh—what? Who are you? How did you—"

"Do I need to use the paddle again?"

"No! God, please no. I have the money. It's in my pants in the bathroom."

I retrieved Forrester's thick roll of cash, removed the elastic and counted out forty-two hundred dollars. I paused, then plucked two more hundreds for myself to make up for the bribe money I gave the dominatrix. With the bills safely tucked away in my pocket, I returned the cricket bat to the hook on the wall and headed toward the door. I hesitated before grabbing the doorknob, then turned back toward Forrester, still hanging limply in his restraints above a puddle of urine and whimpering softly.

"You might want to try talking a bit nicer to the ladies in the future," I suggested.

I exited the VIP room and, as I was walking quickly through the dungeon, the girl with the double hair buns ran up to me.

"Is everything okay in there?" she asked.

"Yes, he'll be okay. I just gave him the news about a death in the family."

"Oh my," the girl said, putting a hand over her heart.

"You should give him a moment. He's in a lot of pain."

The dungeon staff girl nodded. By the time I had reached the main floor of the club, Steampunk Catwoman was spinning some godforsaken and blasphemous dubstep remix of AC/DC's "Thunderstruck." I made my way back to the bar where I found Declan enjoying his beer and hand-feeding baby carrots out of a bowl to a very attractive blonde woman dressed up as a white bunny. The woman's costume consisted of a plastic headband with long rabbit ears, a fuzzy white top that also showcased some spectacular cleavage, a fluffy tail attached to her white short-shorts, and a little plastic nose complete with whiskers and buckteeth.

"Jed! You have got to meet me new lady friend!"

"Hello," I said, nodding at the bunny woman.

The bunny woman tucked her wrists, pressed them against her cleavage, hopped over to me, and gave me a quick peck on the cheek. She hopped back to Declan, shook her fluffy tail, and began nibbling on another carrot that he offered.

I sighed deeply and shook my head. "I don't even want to ask."

"She's a kinky furry, mate!" said Declan, excitedly.

"A what?"

"A furry! They get all done up as their favourite animals and make'em all human-like and shite. Ain't that right, Darlin'?"

Bunny woman hopped once in place and nodded her head so vigorously her bunny ears almost slid off her head.

"I'm done, D. I need to get out of this place."

"C'mon, the night is still young."

I turned my back on my cousin and headed toward the exit.

"Bollocks!" I heard Declan shout. "I sure do got the glad eye for ya, Lassie, an' I promise I'll call soon. But I've to go with me Cuz. Give me a snog for the road."

I glanced back over my shoulder to see Declan kiss his bunny babe goodbye before he caught up to me and grabbed me by the arm.

"Jed, wait—"

"Declan, I collected the money, I'm dog-tired, and I've seen enough weird shit tonight to last me a lifetime. I'm leaving."

"Aye, that's fine and dandy and I'm coming with ya. But you've got to let me get me painting first."

"What painting?"

Declan darted back to where he had been sitting and Trixie handed him an eleven-by-seventeen canvas from behind the bar and then blew him a kiss. Declan caught up with me at the coat check station where I was returning the rubber blazer and studded dog collar.

"Sorry, Mate, but I couldn't leave without this," he said, clutching his painting like a newborn baby. "Did you know there's a bloody penis painter back there? The mental fella actually dips his willy in paint and uses it as a brush!"

"That's disgusting."

"Nah, Mate. It's incredible."

"I never should have brought you along tonight."

"Are you right banjanxed? This has been one o'the best nights o'me life!"

Declan ignored me and held up his new prized possession for both the coat check girl and me to view. The painting was a collage of colourful circles of various sizes.

"It just looks like a bunch of dots from bingo dabbers," said the coat check girl, popping her bubblegum.

"Aye, this is one o'his newest ones. It's from his line o'nutsack paintings."

"He did all that with just his balls?" the coat check girl asked, impressed.

"Damn right, he did. The man's mad as a box o'frogs."

I left Declan and the coat check girl and headed outside.

"Wait up, Jed! I still need to take off me chaps!"

I exited the club and thanked Pistol Pete again for getting me inside. Despite all of the Caligula-level visual stimuli I had just witnessed, as I strolled along the sidewalk back toward my old man's pub, all I could think about was what could have possibly been bad enough to cause Lawrence Kunstlinger to bail on his beloved roller derby team when they needed him the most.

EIGHT

Napoleon was taking a dump. I had never seen a wiener dog
poop before, and due to the dachshund's elongated torso, I guess
I assumed its waste would be long and thin. Instead, Napoleon
stared me directly in the eyes as he proudly excreted a soft, swirling, triangle-shaped turd that was so perfectly formed all it was
missing to make it look exactly like the poop emoji was a pair of
googly eyes and a grin.

"Very well, Napoleon," said Sykes. "Return to your mark."

Napoleon heeded his master's command and scampered off
the green artificial turf and back onto the red oval track at Simon
Fraser University's Terry Fox Field. Sykes remained seated in his
deluxe lawn chair, but made no motion to clean up the dog poo.
The little pooch stopped on a white start line, then slowly lowered
itself into a stance. Sykes readied a stopwatch in his hand before
raising a starting pistol above his head and firing.

The second the diminutive dachshund heard the shot, he took
off like a bolt of lightning, rocketing down the track until he
crossed the hundred-metre marker. Sykes clicked the stopwatch,

checked the time, and then nodded approvingly before whistling with his fingers, summoning Napoleon back toward him.

"He's pretty fast," I commented.

"Napoleon is just warming up," replied Sykes. "He is still working up to his top speed."

The speedy hound made it back to his mark, and lowered himself into his stance again. Sykes fired off another shot from the gun and Napoleon darted off even faster than before.

A women's soccer team funnelled out of an exterior cement hallway and took to the field, but Sykes was so focused on Napoleon's sprinting he paid them no mind. One of the soccer players stepped on Napoleon's still steaming deposit as she jogged by, however, when she turned to reprimand us, she immediately bit her tongue upon seeing Sykes. Instead the soiled-shoed soccer player simply lowered her head, did her best to scrape off the feces off of her cleats, and then joined her teammates. I still didn't know a lot about Sykes, but one thing was sure—the man clearly had some clout.

"Pretty nice digs for training a dog," I said.

"Training a champion," said Sykes, correcting me.

Having had my fill of wiener dog race training for the day, I dug in my pocket and retrieved Forrester's forty-two hundred dollars, while Napoleon trotted slowly but confidently back toward his master.

"Here you go."

For the first time since I had arrived at the track Sykes made eye contact with me.

"Well done, Mr. Ounstead. I am curious, did procuring this debt cause you much trouble?" he asked, as he took the elastic-wrapped wad of bills and tucked them into an inside pocket in his tan blazer.

"Just a cousin who now treasures a testicle painting and has developed a sudden furry fetish," I replied.

Sykes smiled. "From what I know of the venue that you visited, that is a small price to pay."

"The burner number, Sykes," I said, having grown impatient with pleasantries.

"Yes, of course."

Sykes slipped a hand into his blazer's breast pocket and slipped me a Post-it Note with a 778 area code phone number written in impeccable penmanship.

"Tread lightly, Mr. Ounstead. I am not certain what kind of trouble Mr. Kunstlinger may be in, but I can say that I have never known him to be so nervous. A single call may be all that you get."

"But if I speak to him and he tosses the burner, won't he just buy another to get in touch with you to place more bets?" I asked.

"Most likely," said Sykes with a smile, as Napoleon sidled up to him for a well-deserved scratch behind the ears and a gourmet dog treat.

"Which means you could give me the number again," I continued.

Sykes stole a moment away from praising his precious pup to glance up at me. As if on command, his silver-tinted aviator sunglasses slid down the bridge of his nose and I looked directly into his icy blue eyes.

"Yes. But for a price, of course," he said firmly.

And with that I turned around and left a bookmaker, a dachshund, and two-dozen cleated co-eds to their training.

NINE

Declan stood in front of the Emerald Shillelagh's great
mahogany bar with his arms crossed. He opened his mouth to
speak, and then closed it, stroking his chin for a long while. After
some more hemming and hawing, he finally spoke.

"Aye, that's the bloody perfect spot." He put his hands on his
hips and looked at me proudly. "Don't you agree?"

I sighed as I stared at the multi-coloured, testicle painting
which now hung above the bar, replacing the framed document
that had been there for years.

"Where are you going to put the health department operating
permit?" I asked, motioning to the large letter A on the bar top.

"Who gives a shite? Look at that glorious thing. Folks are
gonna come from all over just to see it."

"It's not the Mona Lisa, D. A guy just dipped his balls in
some paint."

"Ah, to hell with ya. It's true what they say. Some people
just don't get art."

I pulled up a stool at the bar and took a big sip of my
Guinness. I retrieved my phone from my pocket and entered the

burner number Sykes had given me as a new contact for Lawrence Kunstlinger. When I finished I put my phone down, spun around on the stool, and started slowly tapping my fingertips together like my grandfather used to do while thinking. I stared across the pub at the Emerald Shillelagh's Irish wall of fame.

I shifted my gaze upward from framed photos of Oscar Wilde and Conor McGregor delivering a robust left hook to a bloodied opponent until my eyes zeroed in on a picture of Bono crooning into a mic while standing back-to-back with the Edge jamming on his axe. The song "Mysterious Ways" popped into my head and played while I wondered if perhaps I should simply call Lawrence. If I did it seemed likely that he would screen the call and not answer. But if he actually picked up, what would I say? He might not be too happy someone managed to track him down while he was off the grid, get spooked, and hang up on me before I was able to explain who I am. If that happened Lawrence would most certainly toss his burner and get a new one, which would leave me having no choice but to trudge back to Sykes for another potentially unsavoury task. I shivered as the image of a near-naked and hairy Dale Forrester wiggling excitedly in his restraints flashed in my mind. No, I couldn't risk a call. I needed to send Lawrence a text. That was the safe play, and if I made it clear that I had been hired by his roller girls, all of whom were collectively concerned about his well-being, then odds were he would be more inclined to respond to me, or at the very least, give me a message that I could relay to them.

I spun my stool back around and reached for my phone—only to find it gone. I immediately looked behind the bar and saw Declan sipping a Guinness with one hand and holding my phone to his ear with the other.

"What the hell are you doing? I snapped.

"Calling this Kunstlinger bloke."

"Declan, put it down now!"

"Keep your panties on."

I jumped off my stool and lunged across the bar but it was too late.

"Aye, is this Kunstlinger?" asked my cousin. "I got a fella here who needs to have a wee chinwag with your underground arse." I held my breath and glared at my cousin, furious yet desperately awaiting his reaction to what he had just said.

"Aye, that'll do. And Kunstlinger? With a name like yours I'd say ya bloody well missed your callin' as a porn star, Mate."

I shot daggers with my eyes at Declan as he reached across the bar and handed me back my phone. I took a deep breath and held it to my ear.

"Lawrence?"

"Who the fuck is this?" he barked. "And how did you get this number?"

"Sykes."

"Sykes? How did you even find out about him?"

"I'm very resourceful."

"You know what? Fuck you! I'm hanging up, this is some kind of trap—"

"Stormy Daze!" I blurted out suddenly. Seconds ticked by, and I fully expected to hear a click at any second. After a moment, he spoke.

"What about her?"

"She hired me to find you. In fact, your entire roller derby team did."

More silence. Then I heard something I didn't expect. Lawrence started chuckling. "Those goddamn crazy broads," he said.

"My name is Jed Ounstead. I'm a private investigator."

"How are my girls?" he asked, with great concern.

"They're fine. But they are all very worried about you."

"Tell them I'm okay."

"I can do that for you, Lawrence. But I can also do more. I can help you with whatever trouble it is that you're mixed up in that made you skip town."

"You can't help me with this."

"Don't underestimate me."

"You don't understand, man. I'm in some deep shit."

"I've tangled with the baddest of the bad before and come out on top," I replied.

Lawrence paused again. I heard him take a deep breath. "Who are these bad people?"

"Do you remember that big biker gang shootout on the Lions Gate Bridge last October?"

"What about it?"

"I did that. I took them down. By myself."

Declan frantically snapped his fingers at me and then exasperatedly threw his hands in the air. He had killed one of the gang members himself in self-defence before being shot when they had raided the Emerald Shillelagh and was none too pleased that I wasn't giving him his deserved credit.

"Bullshit. Some tough old cop killed those guys," said Lawrence.

"That's my father. He took the heat for me so I could dodge the legal ramifications of taking out four guys in four minutes with a couple of unlicenced guns." Lawrence was silent for a moment. "I also have backup," I said. "Good men who are deadly in a fight."

Declan pounded his fist on the bar top, nodded proudly, and resumed drinking his Guinness.

"You really took down the Steel Gods?" asked Lawrence.

"I did. I'll deny it if asked about it, for self-preservation, but between you and me, I'd be happy to tell you the whole story over a beer. And then maybe you could share with me your current problem so I can help you solve it and get you back where you belong, coaching the Split-Lip Sallies. They miss you and need you."

More silence. Ten seconds went by. Then fifteen. "I have to think about all of this," he said. "I'll call you back at this number in a few days." *Click.*

I sighed and clicked off my phone. Declan shook his head as he killed the last of his Guinness. "You should have told him about the nutsack painting," he chastised. "If ya did I bet the frightened lad would o'been here lickety-split."

TEN

I had never been hit with a sack of potatoes before, and despite getting my forearm up to absorb some of the blow to the side of my head, it hurt a hell of a lot more than I expected it to. The impact knocked me to my knees, at which point I took another smack point blank on my lower back and hip that flattened me out on the mat.

My opponent, "Spudboy," strutted victoriously around me in the ring, swinging his sack of starchy tubers with one hand and flipping off the angry, booing crowd with the middle finger of his other. I rolled on my side and caught my wind, then waited for my cue. Spudboy riled up the crowd some more, milking the heat, before turning his back on me as planned. The sack of potatoes dangled at his side. I hesitated until I saw the pre-cut hole in the orange mesh bag, and then made my move. I dove forward, slipped my fingers into the hole, and ripped the bag open. Potatoes showered the mat as they fell everywhere, but before Spudboy could mourn the loss of his weaponized taters I picked up two russets, sprang to my feet, and used the spuds to box his ears—a perfectly legal move in our no-disqualification match. Spudboy sold it beautifully, and we both fell back to the mat feigning pain and exhaustion before dragging ourselves to separate corners of the ring to recover from the mutual potato pummelling we received.

The crowd at the Bill Copeland Sports Centre in Burnaby broke into a "THIS IS AWE-SOME" CLAP-CLAP-CLAP chant as Spudboy and I both dramatically struggled to climb to our feet in our respective corners like Rocky Balboa and Apollo Creed at the end of *Rocky II*. With the way the ringside seating had been configured for the evening, the two-thousand-seat arena had been able to add nearly another two hundred seats, all of which were filled to capacity. Once the referee had finished sweeping the potatoes out of the squared circle, Spudboy and I charged one another and locked up in the middle of the ring.

"Irish whip into a bulldog?" he whispered into my ear.

I grunted my approval before I let Spudboy slip out of my grip, knee me in the stomach, grab my wrist, and slingshot me into the ropes. I bounced off and rebounded back to the centre of the ring where Spudboy performed a one-handed bulldog by grabbing me by the back of my neck and jump slamming me face first to the mat. Spudboy rolled me over and went for the pin. The ref's hand slammed the mat repeatedly as the crowd counted along:

"ONE-TWO—"

Moments before the third count I shot a shoulder up off of the mat. The crowd let out a collective cheer and sigh of relief. Spudboy threw a tantrum and screamed at the ref, who was holding up his index and middle fingers and turning around in a circle to show the crowd it had only been a two-count. I rolled on my side and saw a fan in the third row standing on his chair, mimicking the referee by waving two fingers around to his fellow wrestling fans, taking great pride in thinking he was providing a valuable service.

"Get up, Hammerhead!" bellowed a fan in the front row.

"You have to get payback for what he did!" yelled a woman from the other side of the ring.

Spudboy and I had been engaged in an ongoing feud ever since he interfered in my big return match eight months ago, costing me a victory over El Guapo, the current XCCW Heavyweight Champion. Bert Grasby, the owner of X-Treme Canadian Championship Wrestling, the promotion for which I had started wrestling again, had decided to keep the strap off of me for now because I was a part-timer at best. Instead, he concocted a main event-level feud with their hottest heel, Spudboy, a very talented young wrestler who was definitely going places. While he had the usual height of a couple of inches shy of six feet, Spudboy was definitely heavier than your typical cruiserweight. However, with his speed, flexibility, and high-flying aerial maneuvers, he sure moved like one. It was a bit of a challenge for me to keep up with him, as I was more of a classic grappler, which is why my traditional big man, in-ring style was more similar to pro-wrestling legends like The Rock, Triple H, and Stone Cold Steve Austin.

I rolled onto my back and prepared myself for the next spot. Spudboy had finished berating the ref and saw me in position. Closing in for the kill, he began one of his most popular and signature moves—Rolling Thunder. Spudboy bounced off the ropes, did a somersault on the mat, then jumped up and performed another forward roll mid-air, before landing on my chest and splashing me with his sweaty back. It's a brash, acrobatic, and aggressive move, but Spudboy pulled it off perfectly.

I've always hated receiving splashes, and since Spudboy landed square on my sternum, the Rolling Thunder literally knocked the wind out of me. The best way I can describe receiving an in-ring splash is to imagine jumping off a diving board for the most unforgiving, painful, belly flop you could ever perform. As a result, I crawled toward the ropes legitimately wheezing while Spudboy taunted the crowd yet again.

That was when I saw him.

Standing by a concession cart over a dozen rows back near the entrance to the locker rooms was the man I had dubbed Chauncey Gardiner, the same stoic-faced, grey-suit wearing, bowler-hat sporting son of a bitch I had seen staring at me from the street while I was in Lawrence's apartment. He peered at me with the same unnervingly lifeless eyes as before, his face a creepy, blank canvas.

I sprang up suddenly, before breaking kayfabe and instinctively sliding out of the ring in pursuit. Spudboy gawked at me quizzically, wondering what the hell I was doing. It took me a moment to collect myself outside the ring, but before I could pursue him, I glanced back up and saw that my persistently peculiar voyeur had vanished. I started down the aisle after him, but I had gone only a few rows when Bert Grasby, my pudgy, red-faced, comb-over sporting, pro-wrestling employer, headed me off.

"What are you doing, Ounstead?" he snapped in a hushed tone, followed by a fake grin flashed to the confused spectators around us. He sidled up to me and gave me a phony pat on the back, which I think he intended to be reassuring.

"I saw someone," I said weakly, clutching a hand to my still stinging sternum.

"So sign an autograph for them after the show," spat Grasby, between gritted teeth. "This is the main event for Christ's sake. Finish the goddamn match."

I took a deep breath and accepted the fact that the creepy bastard who had now spied on me twice was long gone. I turned around and lumbered back into the ring, barely beating the ten count the referee had been calling out since I had slid through the ropes. I saw Spudboy exhale a sigh of relief before realizing it was on him to lead up to the finish of our match. He charged at me, but I stopped him in his tracks with a facebuster. He stumbled about, dazed, before I booted him in the gut, slipped his arm into a shoulder lock, bent his arm against his back, slipped him into a front facelock, and then finally dropped him to the mat with a Hammerlock DDT, my signature finishing move. I rolled up Spudboy for the three count and the crowd went wild. I staggered about the ring, exhausted, before reaching my corner and retrieving my weakened two-by-four piece of Western red cedar. The audience was going nuts at this point, and after swinging the two-by-four around in the air a few times, my celebratory custom, I broke the piece of wood over my forehead and split it in two. At that point every wrestling fan in the building was on their feet, and the guy ringside who rang the bell started tossing me cans of Hell's Gate Lager while my entrance music played. Jeff Beck wailed on his electric guitar, playing his instrumental tune "Hammerhead." I cracked the beers and chugged them while climbing the turnbuckles and towering victoriously over the crowd. I couldn't help but scan the entire sports arena looking for any sign of the man who had recently made a habit of watching me.

There was none.

ELEVEN

"What the hell was that?"

"I messed up."

"You broke kayfabe!"

"I know."

"Do you?"

"It won't happen again."

"I sure as shit hope not. Things have changed, Ounstead. These past months have been incredible. XCCW is on the map in a way it's never been, and is even slowly morphing into a de facto feeder system for NXT, man! Aspiring wrestlers from all over the world are reaching out to me, wanting a shot. I know that's mostly because of you—I do—but that is also why you of all people can't be breaking character and going off script like some rank amateur. You're my goddamn golden goose."

"I hear you, Grasby. It was a momentary lapse in judgment."

"Why?"

"What?"

"What made the most professional and best wrestler who's ever worked for me get distracted to the point he almost tanked a main event match?"

I pulled the towel down from around my neck and wiped the sweat from my face. We were alone in the locker room, Grasby having banished the handful of wrestlers who were hanging out waiting to congratulate Spudboy and me on our match, which up until I botched the finish, had been outstanding and incredibly well received by the crowd. Grasby stood with his hands on his hips while his bowling-ball belly hung over the thick waistband of his black velour tracksuit, something Grasby essentially considered formal wear, due to the embroidered leopards on its lapels and on the back of his zip-up jacket. Grasby always trotted out his nicest tracksuits for the big XCCW shows. I snapped the towel back around my neck and hung my head.

"Someone was watching me."

"Yeah, two thousand people," replied Grasby.

"No, I mean, this guy has been stalking me."

"Stalking? Jesus Christ, Ounstead. Why didn't you tell me? I could have had security on you like that," he said, snapping his fingers.

"I can take care of myself."

"And I can't afford to have my top-draw in danger. Who the hell is this son of a bitch, anyway? Some obsessed fan?"

I waved Grasby away. "No, I think he's connected to a case I'm working somehow. Don't worry about it, I'll be fine."

"I don't know why you bother with that goddamn PI stuff," bemoaned Grasby. "Come work with me full time, already. Think of the cheddar we could make!"

"Grasby," I warned in a serious tone.

"All right, sorry, I know the rule, no trying to upsell you on wrestling more than you want to do."

"Speaking of cheddar…."

"I got it right here. And holy shit did we ever have a good night," he said, before handing me an envelope filled with cash. "That includes your take from the merchandise sales from tonight, too. Your new T-shirt is selling like hotcakes."

The shirt he was referring to depicts a muscular arm clutching a two-by-four piece of wood with the words "*Hammerhead' Jed*" written above and "*The Thunder With Lumber*" inscribed across the back. I opened the envelope and thumbed through the thick wad of bills. Grasby was right, it had been a good night.

"You better not be shorting me," I cautioned. "You know Pocket will tell me if you are."

Pocket was a loquacious dwarf pro wrestler I had befriended back when I first investigated XCCW as part of my first case. He also had a diploma in accounting, and since being sidelined with an ankle injury, he'd been running the ever-expanding merchandise table. He'd even started helping Grasby balance his books. Grasby had become a new man since I joined XCCW part-time, and unlike years past, was determined to keep his suddenly lucrative promotion legitimate and above board.

"I know, I know," said Grasby. "So can I pitch you what I think should come next with your Spudboy feud?"

"I'm going to take a rain check," I replied. "It's been a long few days."

Grasby nodded, his jowls jiggling as he conceded. "Okay, well I better get back out on the floor then. Those new pyrotechnic guys are fucking retards and the last thing I need is them shooting themselves in the face with fireworks while packing up and then trying to sue me."

Grasby headed toward the locker room exit. "Grasby," I called out, as he pulled the door open. He stopped, glanced back, and I looked him in the eye. "I'm sorry about the finish. It won't happen again."

Grasby nodded, satisfied, and suddenly I was alone. I got up off of the bench and went to my duffel bag in the corner of the room. I unzipped it and rooted around inside until I found what

I was looking for—another envelope. However, this envelope was empty and had an address written on it. I slipped the cash out of the one envelope and transferred it to the other. I licked it sealed, then read the address I had written on the front: *Spinal Cord Injury BC, 780 SW Marine Drive, British Columbia, V6P 5Y7*.

There was no return address and I would slip it through the mail slot on my way home, long after the office had closed for the day, as was my routine. I donated in cash because I didn't want the organization to have a record of my name. I didn't want the tax deduction receipts, I didn't want their emails in my inbox, and I didn't want their flyers in my mail. I didn't want anyone else learning of the tragedy that had caused me to walk away from professional wrestling just as my career was booming and my celebrity was about to explode. All I wanted was to give them every dollar I made working with XCCW. Nothing could ever change what I had done. But at least by making these donations it was easier for me to live with myself. I could wrestle a little again. I could move on with my life and help people as a private investigator. For the first time in a long time, I owned my penance—it didn't own me.

My phone rang, snapping me out of my self-reflection. I dug through my duffel bag until I found it. I glanced at the caller ID—it was Lawrence Kunstlinger. It had been nearly a week since I had spoken to him and I was giving up hope that I would hear back from him at all. I answered the call as quickly as possible.

"Hello?"

"You lying sack of shit."

"Excuse me?"

"You're not a detective. You're a goddamn professional wrestler."

"I used to be a pro wrestler, Lawrence." I caught my shirtless reflection in a mirror, and the image of my shiny, black, knee-high boots and black spandex pants compelled me to be as truthful as possible. "And to be honest, I still do occasionally wrestle as a hobby. But I am a legitimate PI and have nearly completed the two thousand hours as an 'under supervision' investigator required to become a licenced, unrestricted, private investigator in the province of British Columbia."

Silence. Seconds ticked by. Finally, he spoke.

"Can you really help me?" he asked meekly.

"Yes."

"Let's meet tomorrow. I'll text you the time and address."

He hung up. I tossed my phone back in my duffel bag, and then realized that I was clutching the envelope full of cash for Spinal Cord Injury BC in my other hand. I laid the envelope flat on a bench, smoothed out the creases, then slipped it into my bag, for the first time wondering if I could actually back up the bravado I had boasted about to Lawrence with real results.

TWELVE

The sun was shining and the air was balmy, so Lawrence had chosen for us to meet at an outdoor patio. The Lamplighter Public House, established in 1925, had long been a staple in Vancouver's historic Gastown. Located at the corner of Water and Abbott, the Lamplighter had seen resurgence since being purchased by the Donnelly Group, a corporate juggernaut that had spent the last twenty years buying up all manner of public houses, cocktail taverns, and nightclubs across Vancouver. The Lamplighter's patio was one of my favourite in Gastown, with two rows of tables in front of rustic red brick pillars and framed black windows that gave a view to the inside of one of the city's oldest and liveliest watering holes.

I nursed a pint of Guinness with Declan at the Emerald Shillelagh while waiting to head out for my afternoon meet, and as I walked down Abbott Street past Blood Alley, I found my mind wandering and pondering the legendary passageway's history, including the abundance of blood the old-time butchers used to pour into the infamous street, and that the strip's square was once used for public executions. I thought about the men I had killed while rescuing my father eight months ago, and felt a lingering, white-hot tip of burning anger deep within my chest that the bastards had come so close to ending my father's life—and mine. I silently promised myself that I would be cautious as I prepared to help Lawrence Kunstlinger and possibly paint another bull's eye on my back for some seriously bad people.

I focused as I neared the Lamplighter, reminding myself that Kunstlinger was still jumpy, and that I needed to keep him calm if I was going to be any kind of help to him. I spotted Lawrence when I was about thirty feet away from the patio, and he was seated at a rear corner table by himself. He wore dark sunglasses and a plaid shirt with the sleeves rolled up, and his curly, 'fro-like hair was even bigger and wilder than it was in his picture in the roller derby program. He was texting on his phone, and, almost as if he sensed me, glanced up in my direction. I nodded and he returned the gesture, before he suddenly whipped off his shades and his eyes bulged out so far I thought they might pop out of his head. The sound of screeching tires and a revving engine roared behind me and I spun around just in time to see the shiny metal and chunky bull bar attached to the front grill of a black GMC Vandura fly past me. My clothes rippled from the gush of wind the vehicle left in its wake. Time seemed to slow down as the van suddenly veered to the right, hopped the curb, smashed through the thin metal patio fence, and hit Lawrence Kunstlinger, driving his body back against a red brick pillar. People screamed in terror as the other Lamplighter patio patrons desperately scrambled away to safety. I started sprinting toward Lawrence and the van, and as I got close the sight was more gruesome than I could have imagined.

Lawrence's lower torso and legs had been completely crushed in between the muscular vehicle's front bull bar and a brick pillar, and the rest of him was flopped forward on the hood of the van with his arms outstretched. I stole a glance through the passenger-side window and saw that the driver's side door was open, the operator of the vehicle nowhere to be seen. Steam from the van's radiator hissed as it escaped from under the hood. I over-heard someone behind me calling 911 when Lawrence lifted his head and looked at me, his dazed eyes taking a moment to focus.

"Hold on, Lawrence. An ambulance is on the way."

He tried to say something. "J-J...."

"Try not to talk. You're going to be okay," I said, knowing I was lying. "Just hold on."

He reached out a hand and I took it in mine. He squeezed it, then continued his laboured efforts to speak. "Jam ... J-J ... Jim ... errr...."

"Jim who, Lawrence?"

"Pan ... paaant...," he gurgled, before a stream of blood pooled and spilled out of the side of his mouth.

"Pants?" I asked, confused.

Lawrence locked eyes with me and nodded, before resting his head on the hood of the van. "Eeeeeeeee..." he said, one more time, before his hand withered in mine and went limp. I watched him exhale his last breath as the life slipped out of his body. I took a step back, and, when my heart slowly stopped pounding in my chest, realized how shaken I was. I took a moment to compose myself, and only then did I notice the throng of spectators who had gathered around the smashed van and damaged patio.

"Is he dead?" asked a skinny guy in a poncho with his hair in a man bun.

I ignored Man Bun and took a step back to examine the van. The front grill was a complete wreck wrapped around Lawrence's body and the red brick pillar like an accordion. I walked around to the driver's side. The door was ajar, the vehicle's keys dangled back and forth, still in the ignition. I turned to face the crowd.

"Anybody see the driver?" I was answered with blank stares and hushed chatter. "Anyone?" Still no response. I gave up on any outside help and leaned inside the van.

"You shouldn't do that, man," hollered Man Bun. "It's like, uh, a crime scene."

Sirens began to wail in the distance as I looked around the van's console and dashboard, then in the rear of the vehicle. Nothing. I leaned in further and caught sight of something sticking out from underneath the passenger seat. I slid my sleeve over my fingertips, grabbed the object, and pulled it out from under the seat. My heart skipped a beat and my stomach lurched when I recognized the item I had found.

It was a grey bowler hat.

THIRTEEN

The police had cordoned off a couple of blocks on Abbott
Street, as well as a portion of the intersection by the Lamplighter,
however, there was still enough room on Water Street for cars
to continue heading west on the one-way, red-and-black brick
road. Locals and lookie-loos tried their best to peer past the
collection of emergency response vehicles and take in the spec-
tacle, but the combination of how the trucks were parked and
the perimeter the VPD had set up made it difficult for them to
see much of anything.

I sat on the bumper of a fire engine and watched as a tow
truck slowly pulled back the black GMC Vandura from the pillar it
had wrapped its front grill around. Lawrence Kunstlinger's body
collapsed as the van moved backward a few feet, but the coroner
and one of his assistants were on either side of the corpse and
caught Lawrence under the armpits before he had a chance to
fall lifelessly to the ground. The coroner and his team then slid
Lawrence's remains onto a spinal board, before lifting the body
up and over toward a waiting body bag that was on a gurney near
the coroner's van.

Declan appeared beside me and took a long drag off a cigarette. I had texted him an update while waiting to give my statement to the lead detective, who had yet to arrive on scene. I glanced at my cousin, but his amber-tinted aviator sunglasses prevented his steely eyes from betraying any emotion. Instead he just stared at the crime scene, pulled a flask from inside his jacket, unscrewed the top, and took a swig of what was most certainly Jameson Irish Whiskey. He wiped his lips on his sleeve and handed me the flask, then put a hand on my shoulder and gave it a squeeze. A few moments later he was gone, on his way back to the Emerald Shillelagh. I wondered momentarily how Declan had managed to slip through the perimeter the police had set up, but given his unique skill set and ex-IRA pedigree, I was hardly surprised.

I took a pull on the flask and continued watching the flurry of emergency responders go about their business. Uniformed cops took statements, EMTs tended to a few patio patrons who had suffered scrapes or were still in shock, and a pair of techs in matching navy-blue windbreakers from the VPD Forensic Identification Unit began examining the GMC Vandura's interior. I had left the bowler hat in the van where I found it, but I couldn't stop thinking about it.

That creepy, Peter Sellers-dressing, voyeuristic bastard drove the van and used it to commit vehicular homicide. Because there were no airbags in the Vandura due to its age, it meant the impact could easily have been significant enough to send his hat flying off of his head. Perhaps he was injured in the crash? He was certainly stealthy and seemingly smart enough to know better than to leave any potential evidence behind, but since I found his hat partially underneath the passenger-side seat, he must have missed it when scrambling to flee the scene. Chauncey clearly had picked up my trail after spotting me earlier at Lawrence's apartment, and again at the XCCW show, so there was no doubt he knew me. Which meant he could easily have tracked me to the Emerald Shillelagh and Ounstead & Son Investigations.

Although I checked for a tail before leaving the pub, I had seen no sign of Chauncey Gardiner or anything suspicious. How had he known I was meeting with Lawrence? Did I somehow miss him surveilling me from afar? I took another hit of whiskey from the flask when the strong and smoky voice I had been waiting a long time to hear again spoke to me.

"Are you seriously drinking at my crime scene?" she asked.

I snapped out of my reflective trance only to find her standing in front of me, her arms crossed, looking down at the silver flask in my hand. I screwed the top back on and tucked it into my pocket. "Declan brought it for me," I said, in a pathetic attempt to excuse getting caught swilling hooch at a murder site.

Detective Constable Rya Shepard either didn't buy what I was selling or didn't care. We last spoke right after I had rescued my old man from the biker gang eight months ago. While my father took the heat for my actions, and the VPD eagerly lapped up the story about one of their own taking down a crime syndicate, Rya was the only cop sharp enough to figure out the story that we were slinging was bullshit. She had kept it to herself, most likely out of respect and loyalty to my father, her former mentor, but the fact that I had engaged in a rescue without reaching out to her had left her bitter and angry with me. I didn't really blame her.

Rya sighed and took a seat next to me on the bumper of the fire engine. She watched the FIU techs as they combed the GMC Vandura for evidence before snapping her fingers. It took me a moment to catch on, but I clued in and slipped her the flask. She took off her light black blazer and used it to cover the container of whiskey on her lap. She unbuttoned the top of her crisp, white, linen dress shirt, rolled up her sleeves, checked her surroundings, then popped the top of the flask and took a furtive sip. A light gust of wind passed by, causing Rya's dark, wavy hair to flutter near my face. She smelled like lavender with a hint of whiskey, and in that moment I found her more beautiful than I ever had before. She subtly handed me back the flask.

"It's good to see you, Rya."

"You've lost weight," she replied, matter-of-factly.

I patted my slowly-but-surely tightening mid-section. "I've been wrestling again. Need to keep my conditioning up if I'm going to main event matches."

"How's Frank?"

"The old man is good. Working a lot of fraud cases lately."

Rya nodded, seemingly satisfied. "So are you going to tell me how the hell you're involved with what happened here?"

I proceeded to explain how Stormy Daze and her roller derby team had hired me to find their missing coach. I glossed over the details of my arrangement with Sykes, skipped ahead to the part where I secured Lawrence Kunstlinger's burner phone number, and convinced him to meet. Then I told Rya about the rumours of Lawrence's gambling, how he'd said he was in deep trouble, Chauncey Gardiner and the two instances of him spying on me, and finally the bowler hat that was inside the GMC Vandura.

"It all adds up that this dapper creep is Lawrence's killer, right?" I asked.

"So far it sounds … promising. But what's the motive?"

"I was hoping to find that out this afternoon."

Rya nodded, then pulled a small leather-bound notepad from her pocket, clicked open a pen, and started jotting down notes. I gave her time and returned my gaze to the FIU techs by the van, who were now bagging and tagging the bowler hat.

"Jed, if what you say is accurate, then you pretty much led this guy in the bowler hat right to Kunstlinger."

"No."

"No?"

"I mean … maybe. I don't know."

"It sounds to me like you served him up on a platter."

"I didn't—I, uh … it makes the most sense I guess. But I really did look for a tail before heading out to meet Lawrence today."

"Apparently not hard enough."

That snipe cut deep. Rya noticed, and I could feel her immediately regretting it.

"Listen, Jed…."

"There should be some hair or DNA in the bowler hat," I said, pressing forward. "And the make and where they are sold could give you something to go on. I've only seen the beady-eyed bastard twice, but he's always impeccably dressed and well put together."

Rya jotted down some more notes. "Duly noted," she said.

An awkward silence hung in the air. Neither of us knew exactly what to say. I could feel the emotional conflict emanating from within her, just as it was from within me. Nevertheless, sitting next to Rya, even after all of these months, felt like the most natural thing in the world. I was exactly where I wanted to be, circumstances be damned. And I had a feeling that she felt the same. After awhile, she slowly slipped her hand into mine. My heart started racing. I mustered the courage to look her in the eye, only to see her smiling softly back at me.

"I've missed you, you know."

My heart swelled in my chest. I smiled back at her, wanting to say so much, but unsure of where to start. I opened my mouth to speak when I heard my name being called.

"Jed!" exclaimed Stormy Daze, standing at a nearby barricade, waving at me frantically. Stormy tried to muscle her way past a couple of uniformed VPD officers who weren't having it. "Jed!" she hollered again.

Rya withdrew her hand and stood, put on her blazer, and transitioned back into work mode. She waved at the beat cops to let Stormy through. They did as instructed and seconds later Stormy heaved herself at me, her buxom cleavage pressing hard into my chest as she held me tight and sobbed. Rya instinctively took a few steps back as I tried my best to soothe Stormy.

"I can't believe he's gone," she said, sniffling into my shoulder.

"I'm sorry."

She nuzzled deeper into me, like a vulnerable animal cub would into its mother's chest. I held Stormy close as she cried. I tried to make eye contact with Rya, but Stormy's colourful, puffy ponytails obscured my vision. I sighed and gritted my teeth, frustrated that my moment with Rya had slipped away. I had called Stormy to update her not long after Lawrence was murdered. I advised her to stay by the phone and let me come to her later with a proper update, but she was adamant that she wanted to meet me at the scene of the crime. Client or not, had I known how the timing of her arrival would play out, I would not have called her.

I slowly peeled Stormy off me, despite the fact she clung like plastic wrap. "Take some deep breaths," I suggested. Stormy followed my advice. Once she had composed herself, Rya stepped forward to speak to her.

"Hello, Ms. Danielson," she said. "I wish we were meeting again under better circumstances." Rya knew Stormy from when she was briefly considered a potential suspect in the murder of my late pro-wrestling friend Johnny Mamba. Once she had been cleared of suspicion, Rya graciously and quickly had Stormy released from VPD custody.

"Detective," said Stormy, who although was no longer hugging me, had her arms clutched around one of mine and rested her head on my shoulder. Even though she was leaning against me, Stormy's Amazon-woman frame still allowed her to tower over Rya's much smaller height and slighter build.

"Can you think of anyone who had a grudge against your coach?" asked Rya.

Stormy shook her head. "All any of the girls had ever heard were the rumours of his gambling."

Rya jotted down a few words in her notepad. "I'd like to speak some more with you and some of the players on your roller derby team who knew Mr. Kunstlinger best."

"Of course," replied Stormy. "You should come by a practice sometime when we are all there."

Rya nodded and requested Stormy's phone number. After writing it down, she snapped her notebook shut. Stormy clung tighter to my arm and Rya uncomfortably shifted her gaze away.

"I have everything I need for now," she said. "I'll be in touch soon, Ms. Danielson."

Stormy nodded and Rya spun on her heel and walked toward the FIU techs who were still completing their examination of the GMC Vandura. I managed to pry Stormy off of my arm and faced her.

"I can't believe this is happening," she said.

"I'm truly sorry for your loss, Stormy. But I have to get to work."

"Work?"

"Yes."

"But you did what we hired you for. You found Larry."

"It's more complicated than that. I need to find out who did this."

"Isn't that Detective Shepard's job now?"

"Yes, but … let's just say that as a PI I can do things she can't. As a cop, she has to follow proper procedure to find Lawrence's killer. I don't."

"Like you did with Johnny's murder," Stormy said, understandingly.

"Did Lawrence know anyone named Jim?" I asked.

Stormy thought for a moment. "Not that I can think of. I can ask some of the girls, I suppose. Why?"

"It was something he said as he was dying. His last words."

"What were they?"

"Something about a Jim. And pants."

Stormy scratched her head, perplexed. "That's weird."

"He was pinned against a wall and dying in excruciating pain. He was probably just delirious."

Stormy pulled me close into a hug. "This is all just so horrible." I patted her back as she wept softly on my chest. After a few moments, she composed herself. "I have to tell the girls," she said, determinedly.

"And I need to talk to Detective Shepard. I'll check in with you soon, I promise."

"Okay, Jed," she said, before sniffling and wiping a tear from her eye. Stormy abruptly leaned forward and kissed me quickly on the lips. I was caught off guard by the intimate gesture and froze. "Be careful," she cautioned, before walking away from the crime scene. It took me a moment to regain my bearings. I glanced over at the GMC Vandura and saw Rya quickly turn her head away from me toward the van. I was certain she had just seen Stormy kiss me. I used my thumb to wipe away the strawberry lip gloss I could feel and smell on my lips as I approached the vehicle. Rya saw me coming and headed me off.

"I'll need to debrief you a bit further about your investigation into Mr. Kunstlinger's disappearance," she said.

"Uh—yeah, sure," I stammered. "Listen, Rya—"

"I'm busy, Jed. Time for you to go."

"But—"

She stepped in close to me, quickly and confidently, and lowered her voice an octave before speaking. "And just so we're crystal clear, this will not be like last time. You did your job as a PI and found that roller derby team's coach just as you were hired to do. Kunstlinger was not your friend and this isn't some murder in the pro-wrestling world that you think you're better equipped to investigate than the cops. This is a vehicular homicide of a victim whom you didn't know. So if you have any ideas about poking around my case I suggest you drop them right here and now. You're a witness. That's it, that's all."

She stared at me long and hard, and I knew better than to push back. "Okay, Rya. I'll be around when you want to talk more about how I found Lawrence."

Satisfied, Rya gave me a curt nod before returning to the side of one of the forensic techs. I left the crime scene and started walking back to the Emerald Shillelagh, my mind consumed with the ramifications of inevitably ignoring Rya's warning.

FOURTEEN

Dairy Queen had slowly but surely upgraded their franchise
locations all across British Columbia, and with each renovation
I found myself feeling more and more melancholy. While growing up as a kid in Greater Vancouver I had two great joys in
my life—watching Canadian pro-wrestling legend Bret "The
Hitman" Hart electrify as the "Excellence of Execution" within
the squared circle, and going to Dairy Queen Brazier locations
for frosted treats with my parents. The name "Brazier" origin-
ated in 1957 when one of DQ's franchisees set out to develop a
standardized food system. After witnessing flames rising from
an open charcoal grill (AKA a brazier) at a New York City eatery,
a visionary man named Jim Cruikshank had found his concept.
As a result, Dairy Queen Brazier franchises were born and had
been a staple of my youth. However, since the early to mid-aughts,
they've slowly been replaced with either "DQ Restaurants" or
"Dairy Queen Grill & Chills." The problem with these corporate
makeovers was that not only were the vintage DQ signs updated
with current, modernized, uninspired Dairy Queen logos, but
the iconic 50s and 60s-style malt shop interiors and exteriors

were replaced as well. My pop was particularly choked when his favourite Dairy Queen Brazier on Main Street and 13th in Vancouver was overhauled into a DQ Grill & Chill. As a result, the retro, red-bubble roof my father loved was swapped out for a bland, rust-coloured rectangular one that looked like every other generic strip mall building popping up across the city at an alarming rate, robbing small and quaint neighbourhoods of their nostalgic charm and historical significance.

I had gone for a drive to clear my head after witnessing Lawrence's murder and then warmly, if awkwardly, interacting with Rya at the crime scene. My mind replayed the gruesome death over and over until I found my Ford F-150 idling in front of an empty lot in East Vancouver at the corner of East Hastings and Lakewood Drive. There had been a Dairy Queen Brazier at this location since 1969, but I had forgotten that it had been scheduled for demolition a few months ago in order to make way for the construction of a six-storey rental building.

I slammed my palm against my steering wheel in frustration, then continued east on Hastings until I had driven past Playland amusement park, which had just opened its gates for the season. Even with my window rolled up I still could hear people screaming excitedly as the infamous Wave Swinger spun its giant, umbrella-like top, whipping its forty-eight, chain-suspended seats outward and in circles with increasing velocity. I ploughed down Hastings Street, and over the Cassiar Tunnel until I had officially left Vancouver, before barrelling my way through the municipality of Burnaby's trendy neighbourhood known as The Heights. A few minutes later I passed the Admiral Pub and pulled into a parking lot for a DQ Restaurant. Since they had no drive thru, I hopped out of my truck, entered the store, and, since there was no line, walked right up to the till.

"Welcome to Dairy Queen. May I take your order on this fine day?" asked an overly chipper teenage boy with an unruly mop of hair. "Large banana milkshake to go, please."

"Absolutely, Sir! Would you like whip on your shake?"

"Excuse me?"

"Would you like your shake topped with whipped cream?"

"That's ridiculous."

"It's free of charge."

"It's blasphemy. When did you start doing that?"

"For quite awhile now, Sir. I tell you what, I'm going to just go ahead and put a teeny bit on for you try. I promise you'll love it."

"No, I goddamn won't!" I snapped. The kid jumped in his skin. The Dairy Queen fell silent as all customers stopped eating their meals and ice cream treats and stared at me. "I'm sorry. Just a large banana shake, no whip." I handed the kid a twenty-dollar bill. "Keep the change." I stepped out of the line and headed to the washroom. I washed my face with cold water, but couldn't bring myself to look at my reflection. The sound of the Vandura's screeching tires and its front grill crushing Lawrence's body into the brick and cement pillar kept playing in my head over and over again on a loop. I took a few deep breaths, exited the washroom, then picked up my waiting milkshake—hoping that the kid hadn't spit in it—and hustled to my truck before firing up the engine and heading back toward Vancouver.

I found a spot directly in front of the Emerald Shillelagh, parked, then tossed my empty banana milkshake cup into a curbside garbage can. Happy hour had yet to begin, so the pub was quiet, save for a group of film students in a booth huddled over numerous storyboard pages. I pulled up a stool at the bar and Declan brought over two glasses and a bottle of twelve-year-old Glenfiddich. We didn't speak until after we each had finished three-fingers' worth of single malt.

"I feel like shit," I said.

"Aye."

"I looked for a tail before I left here, you know."

"Not hard enough."

"You're the second person to say that to me today."

"That's because it's bloody well true."

"You think I don't know that?"

Declan opened his mouth to speak, but hesitated.

"What?" I asked.

"Nothing," he replied.

"Say it."

My cousin slammed his empty glass down on the bar, startling me. "You kind o'got that Kunstlinger bloke killed, Jed."

I felt like I had just taken a sucker punch to the sternum. "Excuse me?"

"Look, it probably would o'happened anyway due to the kind o'heat the fella had brought onto himself, but you sort o'went and made it easy for them."

"There was nothing more I could have done," I said defensively.

"That's bollocks and you know it."

"Jesus Christ, D. Tell me how you really feel."

"We both know Frank's trained yer arse well enough to spot a tail a mile away."

"Spotting a tail isn't foolproof," I countered.

"Oh, piss off with ya. You knew you were being watched by that rawny chancer in the bowler hat. And since he'd evaded you twice, you also knew what a stealthy little bastard he is. You should have been dog-wide and extra cautious, but you weren't."

"You're really kicking me while I'm down here, don't you think?" I snapped, angrily.

"You think I enjoy layin' boots to ya? This has been a long time coming given the way you've been acting the maggot lately."

"Oh, so now I'm an asshole too?"

"A wee bit, yeah. Don't think I haven't noticed how you've been walking around town like you're a shaper who thinks his shite don't stink. Ever since you took down those bikers, got your PI licence, and started solvin' cases lickety-split you've turned into a bit of a cocky caffler."

Declan slung a bar towel over his shoulder, crossed his arms, and glared at me. I couldn't believe what I was hearing. My cousin had always had my back. He'd always been in my corner, no matter what. I was stunned that he was attacking me, especially when I realized he was doing a better job of beating me up than I was myself. My blood was boiling. I was drowning in a sea of guilt, betrayal, and anger. The emotions were too much and even though I knew I would regret it, I lashed out anyway.

"Fuck you, Declan," I growled, sliding off my bar stool and knocking it over onto the ground with one hand. I stormed out of my family's pub, not once looking back.

FIFTEEN

Nestled right on the waterfront of Coal Harbour, Cardero's
Restaurant never lacked for customers looking to dine on some
of Vancouver's finest food while overlooking the best marina in
the city. The pier-side eatery was also surrounded by dozens of
flashy, glamorous boats and yachts, docked and moored. The
patio lights burst to life as the sun set, dusk arrived, and the
bright light shimmered and danced across the ocean water as
far as I could see.

I stared through the blinds of my front window, trying to
work up the motivation to walk across the street and grab a bite at
the bar, but I simply couldn't muster it. I wasn't even that hungry
anyway. Instead I crushed the empty can of Moody Ales Affable
IPA in my hand, threw it into my recycling bin, then replaced the
can with another from my fridge. I flopped into my large La-Z-
Boy recliner and sipped the beer slowly while sitting alone in the
dark. Sometime and several beers later, there was a knock at my
door. I checked the peephole and was surprised by who was on
the other side. I stifled a burp and opened the door.

Frank Ounstead stood before me, his massive bulk filling up most of the door frame and blocking the light from the street lamps behind him. I stepped aside and the old man let himself in with a grunt. He stumbled slightly when a big boot of his hit the first stair that led up and into my townhouse.

"Turn on some goddamn lights, for Christ's sake," he commanded. I did as I was told. "That's better," he said, before putting down the two Dairy Queen milkshakes he was carrying and taking off his triple-XL jacket. My father slung his coat over the stairway banister, slipped off his shoes, then headed upstairs, and seated himself at my dining room table. I followed behind and took a seat across from him. He slid a large banana milkshake across the table. I pushed aside my beer and took a long sip of my favourite beverage. Silence hung in the air for what felt like an eternity, and I avoided my old man's powerful gaze. There was no hiding from it, however, and eventually I caved and made eye contact.

"Place looks good," he said.

"Thanks," I replied.

"I still can't believe you can afford to live here."

"Professional wrestling does have its perks."

"You're wasting your money having this place clear title. You should sell, move somewhere reasonable, and invest the rest."

"I like it here."

The old man grunted again. That was it for the small talk. Never one to mince words, my father got right to the point. "You need to apologize to your cousin."

"I know."

"He was right to call you out like that."

"I know, Pop."

My father took a big sip of his milkshake, which was most likely root beer, although he had been experimenting with the DQ menu lately. He seemed pleased with how things were going so far.

"Part of this is my fault," he confessed.

"What are you talking about?"

"I should have been around more instead of ass-deep in all of these fraud cases lately. I should have noticed you getting too big for your britches. I mean, my God, after what you pulled off on the Lions Gate Bridge, how could you not?"

"It wasn't that big of a deal."

"No son, it was. I don't know any other man who has the skills, the smarts, and the stones to do what you did. You outwitted and eliminated dangerous, seasoned criminals, and saved my life in the process. Afterward, I was just so damn proud of you, and the fact that you finally got your PI licence and joined the family business, I figured you earned the right to pat yourself on the back a bit."

"None of this is on you, Pop. I should have played it safe and assumed I was being followed closely by a professional before meeting Kunstlinger. I know how to shake a tail properly. I was just so eager to sit down with him and close another case that I figured I was fine and half-assed it."

My father nodded. "Still, I should have worked with you more these last eight months. You just took to PI work like a fish to goddamn water so I wanted to give you space to work your own cases. That's the quickest way to becoming a great investigator."

We sipped our shakes in silence. After awhile, my father spoke. "It happens to everyone, you know."

"What do you mean?"

"You work enough cases, you put away enough bad guys, you help enough people—it can be addictive. Empowering. Makes you feel like you're invincible."

"I guess, yeah. I just—I don't know. Working as a private investigator, even wrestling part-time … it's nice to have purpose in my life again. I didn't have that for a long time. I guess I kind of let it go to my head."

My father grunted in agreement. He sucked back on his milkshake until it made a slurping sound. I knew my old man could pack away frosted treats, but I don't think I'd ever seen him knock one off this fast before.

"Did I ever tell you about my time in ERT?" he asked.

ERT, or the Emergency Response Team, was the Vancouver Police Department's version of SWAT. My father had served on the Team back in the day, before transferring into the Major Crime Section.

"You've shared a few stories over the years."

"This is back in the nineties. You were just a young fella and we still had your mother in our lives—God bless her soul. Anyway, I had just made the Team. Passed the training and tests with flying colours. Even set a department record or two on the obstacle course and pull-ups. Needless to say, I thought I was a big deal. After a few months in ERT and numerous successful operations, I was on top of the world. We'd run a bunch of warrants, barricades, even a couple hostage rescues. You name it, we handled it. So one summer evening we get a call. Shots fired in a neighbourhood in Kerrisdale. Buddy's holed up in a house with a nine-millimetre."

"Buddy?"

"Cop talk. For a suspect." I nodded and my father continued. "So me and the rest of our crew show up on site and relieve patrol of the inner perimeter. We're getting set up and waiting for the Duty Officer to show up. No movement or sounds from inside while we wait. The Duty Officer arrives and confers with the Negotiator and our ERT sergeant. The Negotiator tells him there's been no luck making contact with the suspect and agrees with taking next steps. Since I was our Breacher and it was my job to get the squad inside, Sarge calls me over and tells me to kick things off with a SWAT rock to try and get Buddy's attention."

"What the hell is a SWAT rock?"

"It's a rock, son."

"You mean you just found any old rock?"

"In the neighbour's yard, actually. But since I was the number five man on the Squad, it became my job to throw it at the house to try and get a response."

"What did you do?"

"Chucked it through the front window."

"And?"

"Nothing. So a few minutes later we move onto step two."

"Which is?"

"Doorknocker."

"I'm assuming that's code for something other than strolling up to the front door and wrapping your knuckles?"

"There ain't no flies on you, boy. A 'doorknocker' is a KO1 round fired from an ARWEN gun. Just a hard plastic projectile. So we launch one of those babies straight at the front door and it makes a hell of a bang. That got Buddy's attention. Next thing you know, he's screaming bloody murder and yelling at us to fuck off or he might shoot himself. Now that we got him engaged, the Negotiator makes another attempt to talk, but Buddy makes it clear he doesn't want to. The Duty Officer authorizes the use of tear gas and the Sarge directs me to go to the back of the Suburban to get some expulsion grenades."

"What are those?" I asked.

"It's tear gas, but it's flameless—we call it 'cold gas,' so there's no chance of fire, which was especially important given that the house looked like it was on the verge of being condemned."

My father leaned back in his chair and stroked his bristly salt and pepper mustache, losing himself in his memory. I waited patiently, silently sipping my banana milkshake, as my old man sat there with a solemn expression on his face. After what seemed like minutes, he leaned forward and put his elbows on the table.

"We only had five of our Squad on the call that night so I was going to be throwing one of the canisters into the house through the window I had busted with the SWAT rock. It was dark and with my adrenaline pumping I quickly grabbed the canisters and legged it back over to my Squad. Two of my Squad mates took turns lobbing cold gas into the house before Sarge gave me the nod. I tossed a canister straight through the middle of the front window. We were waiting for Buddy to surrender when it happened."

"What?"

"House lit up on fire."

"But you said there was no risk of fire."

My father shook his head. "My canister was hot gas. In my rush to raid the inventory I accidently grabbed a pyrotechnic grenade. They look close enough. Anyway, next thing we hear is screaming and Buddy charges out the front door waving a gun around. We yell at him to drop it but he's still screaming and then he turned and levelled the weapon at us. That was it."

"He was killed?"

My father nodded. "Shot dead on the front lawn. To this day I wonder if I had thrown the right canister if that guy would still be alive."

"He still could have charged out wildly from the cold tear gas," I said.

"Maybe. Or maybe the reason he panicked was because of the fire. Maybe I'm the one who got him killed. That's something I have to live with every day."

We sat in silence for awhile as my old man's words hung in the air. Eventually, my father got up, headed toward the stairs, and started putting on his jacket and his shoes. I followed him to the front door.

"Were you reprimanded by the Department?"

"My brothers had my back. It was ruled an honest mistake, not negligence. But I knew that I was better than that."

I reached out a hand and placed it on one of my father's football-size shoulders. "You couldn't have known what would happen," I said.

My father reciprocated the gesture and slapped one of his giant gorilla mitts down upon my deltoid, and the joint felt like it had just been saddled with a twenty-pound weight. "Neither could you today, son," he said. "After that night, I made myself a promise. I vowed to never again let my guard down. To never be anything but vigilant, at all times. And most importantly, no matter what great achievements I might accomplish, to never let my ego affect my ability to perform my job."

I nodded silently. My father pulled me into a bear hug, and he squeezed me so hard that for a moment I couldn't breathe. Once he let me go I put on my boots and hoodie, and then grabbed my keys from the hook on the wall.

"Going somewhere?" asked my old man.

I looked him right in the eye. "I've got work to do."

SIXTEEN

There were two New Westminster Police Service squad cars parked outside of Lawrence Kunstlinger's apartment building on Carnarvon Street. I caught a lucky break and followed an elderly lady who had just opened the door to the building. If my not being buzzed in properly had bothered her, she certainly didn't show it. I took the elevator to the fourth floor and made the familiar trek down the long hallway toward Lawrence's end unit.

A uniformed NWPS officer stood just inside the open doorway, talking to dispatch through his shoulder-mounted mic. My gaze lingered past him a bit too long, however it allowed me to spot a plain-clothes detective from the VPD Homicide Unit, whom I recognized, inside the apartment chatting with another uniformed NWPS officer. Just as the officer in the doorway took notice of my nosiness, I made a sharp left turn, and knocked on Troy's door directly across the hall. I could feel the uniformed officer's eyes staring at the back of my head as I rapped on the door a second time, and even though marijuana was legal in Canada, I still really hoped that the little lacrosse-loving stoner didn't answer the door with a giant blunt dangling between his lips. A moment later Troy swung the door open and, for better or worse, greeted me.

"Dude!" he said loudly and enthusiastically before pulling me into a big hug. "The 'za is on its way, Brah! You ready for some tits and dragons?"

"You know it," I replied, before slipping inside the apartment. Troy nodded at the officer a few feet away and the policeman gave a little nod back. As soon as Troy closed the door he spun around victoriously as if he had just outwitted Death during a chess match, before executing a vigorous fist pump.

"*Dude!*" he bellowed excitedly. I put my finger to my lips and made a shushing sign. Troy caught on, and then walked past me, waving me over toward a beat-up couch and musty recliner. He motioned for me to take a seat and after a moment I deemed the couch the lesser-of-two evils and sat down.

Troy flopped into the recliner and threw his arms up in the air. "Bro, am I a good actor or what?" he asked proudly.

"Nothing like a casual *Game of Thrones* reference to make one seem legit."

"Damn right. That show is tight!"

I nodded in agreement, and even though I was a few seasons behind, I figured that since Troy's entire apartment reeked like a weed dispensary the odds of him sharing spoilers for the program were low. Troy picked up the biggest bong I had ever seen in my life off the circular wooden coffee table between us and fired up his Zippo lighter. I watched him curiously and after a moment he snapped the Zippo shut and shamefully placed both it and the bong back on the table.

"Shit, man. I'm sorry," he said.

"No worries," I replied, grateful that the pint-sized pothead had the presence of mind to realize that unlike last time I would prefer to chat with him before he was completely baked.

"Where the hell are my manners?" he asked, shaking his head, before sliding the bong and Zippo toward me.

I waved off what to Troy must have been the most incredibly generous gesture possible and leaned forward. "No thanks, kid. And if you don't mind not taking a hit until we're done talking, I would really appreciate it."

Troy nodded heartily. "You got it, Bro."

"I assume you heard about Lawrence?"

"Yeah. It's so messed up. Cops told me what happened when they knocked on my door earlier to interview me."

"What did they ask you?"

"Basic questions. How long has Lars been gone, had I heard from him, did he exhibit any strange behaviour recently, do I know of anybody that wanted to harm him, et cetera."

"What did you tell them?"

"The truth."

"The truth?"

"Hell, yeah. Except, well, I left out the actual part about people who might want to harm him. I've never trusted the cops, man, not since my Daddy got pinched on charges for smackin' my Mama around years ago even though the lippy bitch deserved it."

I did my best to appear appreciative. "Hold on. You're saying that you know of someone who might have wanted to do Lawrence harm—but that you kept it from the police and didn't mention it to me when I talked to you before?"

"Damn straight," he said proudly.

"So you were just going to sit on this lead and potentially let your friend's murder go unsolved?" I asked incredulously.

"Hell, no. I have your card. I was going to give you a call once the cops left."

"Geez, kid," I said. "You should have told them. This isn't a game."

"Hey, cut me some slack, all right? I wasn't sure what kind of dude you were when we first met. And for the record, I had just cracked you over the head with a lacrosse stick. Forgive me for being cautious." Troy picked up his bong and held it up toward me. "Just one little puff?" he asked meekly.

I nodded and tried to brush aside Troy's multiple manipulations and focus on the matter at hand. "Who is this person you think wanted Lawrence dead?" I asked.

Troy flicked open the Zippo with his thumb, lit the bong, and then took a massive hit off of the impressive yellow-coloured glass apparatus and smiled. "You're gonna want to brace yourself for this," he sputtered, before pulling the bowl out of the stem and inhaling the remaining smoke in the chamber.

SEVENTEEN

A short, stocky, balding man worked a pair of battle ropes with ferocity. Meanwhile, an attractive, middle-aged lady grunted excessively as she performed box jumps, while a very pale twenty-something punk with overdeveloped, tribal-tattooed deltoids, biceps, triceps, and chicken legs cranked out repeated reps of clean and jerks, ending each set by clanging the embarrassingly light barbell on the ground and shouting out a "*Wooo!*" so loud even Ric Flair himself would have been impressed. As far as I could tell this was par for the course at BossFit YD in Coquitlam, which was the sixth largest city in British Columbia and one of the twenty-one municipalities that comprised Metro Vancouver. While I don't make it out this way often, I had spent some time in the Tri-Cities growing up with a never-ending series of minor hockey games and tournaments, so I was familiar with the area.

After getting a little taste of his herbal panacea, Troy had filled me in on the person he was convinced wanted Lawrence Kunstlinger dead. In addition to being the sole proprietor of Coquitlam's largest BossFit gym, a man known as "Yogi Barrels" was also a rival roller derby coach whose team had lost a hard fought battle for the crown of best Women's Flat Track Derby Association team in all of Vancouver to Lawrence and the Split-Lip Sallies. Although not his legal name, Barrels was best known by his roller derby moniker because he taught hybrid yoga classes and lifted, squatted, and rolled actual wooden barrels around his gym when not coaching at the track. He was also well known as a notoriously fierce competitor, with a win-at-all-cost temperament that Troy had seen firsthand at the Split-Lip Sallies championship match last year. According to Troy, Barrels regularly slipped into fits of rage featuring vehement displays of some seriously unsavoury language while coaching during derby games.

However, it was not the most important piece of information that Troy had shared with me before I allowed him to finish smoking a bowl. A few weeks earlier he heard a skirmish across the hall and knocked on Lawrence's door to see if he was okay. There was some more banging, thrashing, and grunting, but eventually Lawrence answered the door. He was dishevelled, out of breath, and sweating, and it was clear to Troy that he had interrupted a fight between Lawrence and Barrels. Barrels stormed out of the apartment, and Lawrence remained tight-lipped about the nature of their quarrel despite Troy's best efforts to get him to open up about the incident in the following weeks.

With a history as bitter roller derby rivals, an established record of Barrels being a hothead, and now a recent physical altercation, it stood to reason that Barrels could have had a motive to want Lawrence Kunstlinger dead. If that was the case, Lawrence must have realized that Barrels had crossed a line and put out a hit on him, otherwise he wouldn't have skipped town. But where did Chauncey Gardiner fit into all of this? Was the fashionista also a professional killer Barrels had employed? Or perhaps he was a friend or confidant who had criminal experience? I had more questions than answers and talking to Yogi Barrels was the only way I was going to make any headway on solving Lawrence's murder.

I wandered around the gym under the premise of being a potential customer who wanted to check out the facility until I found Barrels in the rear of the building, putting a variety of dumbbells back into numerical order on the rack. I knew it was Barrels because Troy had mentioned he would be easy to identify from a prominent, black Nike swoosh tattoo on his neck. Barrels sensed me and tensed up as I approached him from behind. He gave me a cursory over-the-shoulder glance before continuing to rearrange the dumbbells.

"Can I help you?"

"Maybe. I have a few questions."

Barrels racked the last of the dumbbells and marched past me without even looking at me, bumping one of his muscular deltoids against my arm with a tough guy nudge as he walked by. "Ask them somewhere else," he snapped.

Troy was right. This guy was a dick. I followed Barrels over toward a squat rack where he again had his back to me, this time stripping forty-five-pound plates off of an Olympic barbell and racking them.

"You know Lawrence Kunstlinger?"

"Who?"

I sighed. These roller derby folk took their names more seriously than pro wrestlers did. "Lawrence of O'Labia."

"What about him?"

"Did you know he was murdered yesterday?"

Barrels froze. After a moment, he slid a plate back onto the Olympic barbell. He rolled his shoulders back, flexed his traps, and then turned to face me. Although he was only five-foot-nine, Barrels was powerfully built with a thick torso, arms, and legs. He was clad head-to-toe in Under Armour workout gear, and I was pretty sure even his socks were made of material that wicked sweat away. Meaty blue veins the size of earthworms bulged out of his plump forearms and calves. He took an aggressive step forward.

"Who are you? What the fuck are you talking about?"

I studied Barrels' expression closely but his inherent prickliness made him hard to read. "My name is Jed Ounstead. I'm an investigator looking into Lawrence's death. Someone drove a van onto a sidewalk yesterday and crushed him against a brick wall. He died almost instantly."

Barrels ran a hand over his shiny bald head as he considered what I had told him. He stared at the floor. After awhile I continued my line of questioning.

"Word is that you two had quite the rivalry. What were you fighting about at his apartment recently?"

That question snapped Barrels out of his trance. "What the fuck did you just say to me?"

This guy sure liked his F-bombs. But at least now I had his undivided attention. "I know about the tussle that you guys had at his apartment a few weeks ago. What were you fighting about?"

"That's none of your goddamn—wait, you think … you think I killed him?" he asked incredulously.

"No, actually, I don't. But that doesn't mean you didn't have a motive to want to see him dead. By the way, how do you feel about bowler hats? I find them to be dated and kitschy myself, but I'm sure one would do a hell of a job of covering up your shiny scalp there."

Barrels instinctively ran a hand over his head. "What?" he asked.

"Come on, Yogi. Look at that dome," I said, jabbing a thumb over my shoulder toward the floor-to-ceiling mirrors behind me. "You're just two bushy white eyebrows and one hoop earring away from being able to star in Mr. Clean commercials."

Barrels lunged forward with the speed and power of a panther and shoved me hard on the chest with both hands. I didn't see it coming and the force of the push was so great it sent me stumbling backward, nearly causing me to fall on the floor.

"Get the fuck out of my gym!" he bellowed. Barbells, dumbbells, and other BossFit equipment clanged and banged to the floor as everyone dropped what they were doing, fell silent, and stared. Barrels stormed off toward an office, slamming the door, and drawing the blinds behind him.

I regained my balance and steadied myself on my feet. I knew I may have overplayed my hand with Barrels, but considering how cagey and uncooperative he was being, I had decided to roll the dice and try and elicit a reaction. And boy, was it effective. I wasn't sure what it meant yet, but there was definitely some fire to the relationship between Barrels and Lawrence. I wanted to see his renowned temper in action. Mission accomplished.

Back in my truck I slid the key into the ignition but stopped before turning it over. The afternoon sun popped out from behind a grey cloud, its rays beamed through my windshield, and lit up the truck's interior. I grabbed a pair of Ray-Bans from the console, slid them on, flipped down the visor, then leaned back in my seat. I had lectured Troy at his apartment about sitting on a lead, and here I was doing the same thing. Maybe Barrels was involved in Lawrence's death or maybe he wasn't, but now I was trying to do Rya's job for her, while she and the VPD were still in the dark about the existence of a viable suspect. I contemplated calling Rya, but decided to hold off for just a little bit longer until I thought things through. I took a moment to review the facts I had uncovered so far, and in doing so quickly realized that in order to investigate Yogi Barrels thoroughly I would need his actual legal name. I figured the best place to start would be with Stormy Daze, then cursed myself when it dawned on me that my recent bout of self-pity had prevented me from updating her since seeing her at the crime scene yesterday. I dug out my phone and called. She answered on the second ring.

"Jed, thank goodness. I was starting to worry. Are you okay?"

"I'm fine. I'm sorry for taking so long to get back to you. I've been working through some stuff and following up a lead."

"On Larry's killer?"

"Potentially. What can you tell me about Yogi Barrels?"

"What do you want to know?"

"Were he and Lawrence enemies?"

"Well, I don't know if I'd say enemies, but they certainly didn't like each other."

"What about his temper?"

"It's pretty bad, that's for sure. But he would get just as angry with Lawrence as he would at other coaches, players, or refs. He really hates the refs."

"What about the championship bout last year between Barrels' team and yours?"

"It got pretty nasty. He and Larry were at each other's throats a few times. Both coaches ended up being ejected from the game."

So far everything tracked with what Troy had said and my encounter with Barrels. Still, what the hell would have caused him to show up at Lawrence's apartment and physically attack him? There had to be some kind of escalation that I was missing.

"Jed?"

"Yeah?"

"Do you think Yogi Barrels killed Lawrence?"

"I don't know. But there's more to their rivalry than roller derby, I can tell you that. Do you know his legal name?"

"Actually, I do. I trained at his gym for a few months after I left XCCW. He's the one who first encouraged me to try out for derby. His actual name was on the membership contract that I signed. I still remember it because it was so uncommon."

"What is it?"

"Yosef Dillon."

"Anything else you can tell me about him?"

"He's married with two kids. His wife Veruca Assault used to be a star for the Eves of Destruction—that's Yogi's team—until they got married. Then he made her quit. She stopped coming out to games to see the girls, and Yogi wouldn't even allow us to come visit her or meet her babies. He made her stay at home and raise their kids. According to the girls, he's a real controlling bastard, both on and off the track."

While I still had much more of his background to dig into, so far there was no doubt about it—Yosef Dillon was shaping up to be a grade-A asshole across the board.

"One last thing—have you ever seen a guy in a suit and a bowler hat around your roller derby practices or games?"

"Umm. No, never."

"Okay. Thanks, Stormy."

"When will I see you again?"

"I'm not sure. I've got to see a few things through first."

"You never said anything about yesterday."

"Yesterday?"

"When I left the crime scene."

"Oh," I mumbled, suddenly remembering the kiss she had planted on me.

"I'm sorry, Jed. I guess with Larry having just been killed my emotions got the better of me."

"No!" I blurted out. "I mean … it was nice."

There was a pregnant pause. After a moment, she replied. "It was, wasn't it?"

I took a moment to consider my options. Stormy was clearly interested in me. With Rya not wanting me within ten miles of her or her homicide investigation, and the way things were with my cousin at the moment, I figured a little company might be exactly what I needed. Despite having a renewed purpose, I was still working through guilt over my role in Lawrence's death. Something told me Stormy would likely lend a sympathetic ear.

"Would you like to go to dinner with me tonight?" I asked finally.

"I'd like that a lot."

"Okay, I'll give you a call a bit later and we can…."

I trailed off, sat forward in my seat, and pulled off my sunglasses to get a better look at the person hustling out of the BossFit gym in a hurry.

"Jed?"

"I'm sorry, Stormy, I've got to go. I'll be in touch soon."

I clicked my phone off and watched as Yogi Barrels sprinted toward a bright yellow Mazda Miata with a black racing stripe in the parking lot, jumped behind the wheel, fired up the engine, and peeled out. I started my truck and followed in pursuit.

EIGHTEEN

Once Yosef Dillon sped through the intersection of North Road and Lougheed Highway on the border of Coquitlam and Burnaby, I had a pretty good idea where he was going. I had to do twenty kilometres over the speed limit just to keep up as he tore down East Columbia Street alongside the Fraser River, which was calmer than usual, save for a rogue log boom that had broken loose, and was floating aimlessly in the waterway. Dillon cranked a hard right onto Eighth and parked haphazardly in a loading zone across the street from Lawrence Kunstlinger's apartment building. He sprang out of his Miata like a man possessed and bolted toward the entrance.

What happened next I did not expect. Instead of randomly buzzing apartments, or pacing back and forth until someone entered or exited the building, Dillon instead dug a large ring of keys out of his pocket and used one of them to enter the building.

Why the hell did he have a key to Lawrence's building? I racked my brain for some explanation as I did a U-turn on Carnarvon and pulled up to the curb in front of a preschool, one building over from Lawrence's apartment. I thought about following Dillon inside, but quickly decided that the smart play would be to sit back and wait. Regardless of whatever he was doing in Lawrence's apartment, Dillon had to return to his douche-mobile at some point and, when he did, I would be there.

I drummed my fingers impatiently on the steering wheel while I waited. Two preschool teachers and a dozen toddlers, dressed in neon green-and-yellow reflective safety pinnies, exited the preschool and marched in tandem side-by-side down the sidewalk toward the quay. I checked my watch. Dillon had been inside five minutes. I exhaled and tried to summon an explanation for why he had a key to Lawrence's building. Did he steal it? What was so important in Lawrence's apartment that he needed to leave his gym and race across town? What about my visit had spooked him so badly?

I barely had time to ruminate when Dillon exited the building, carrying a cardboard storage box in his arms. He crossed the street quickly, popped the Miata's trunk, placed the box inside, and slammed the trunk shut. He put his hands down on the trunk, and leaned forward, sighing deeply. I still didn't know what he was up to, but I did know I wanted to find out what was in that box. Dillon walked around to the driver's side of his car and opened the door, but hesitated to get into the car. After a moment he closed the door, marched across the street, and made his way back into Lawrence's apartment building.

Now I really had no idea what the hell was going on. I did, however, see an opportunity. I popped open my glove compartment and dug around until I found the trusty lock-picking kit my old man had given me, tucked it into my jacket pocket, hopped out of my truck, and crossed the street. Carnarvon was still quiet and the early-morning traffic was light. I went about picking the trunk lock on Yosef Dillon's Miata, opened it, retrieved the cardboard storage box, and returned to my truck. I placed the box on the passenger seat and searched inside. The contents were lackluster. A couple of roller derby medals and trophies, a few beat-up paperback novels, and a collection of Blu-ray discs. However, the box did contain one item of interest—a Sony Handycam flash memory camcorder. I fumbled with the camcorder, trying to figure out how to turn it on. Just as I was able to power up the device, sirens blared, and a New Westminster Police Service squad car careened around the corner at Eighth and Carnarvon before screeching to a halt directly in front of Lawrence's apartment building.

I tossed the camcorder back into the box and jumped out of my truck. Two uniformed NWPS officers stormed into the building. They hit random buttons and identified themselves before being buzzed in. I took off after them, and was able to reach the front door to the building before it closed and locked behind the cops. I ran into the lobby, only to catch a glimpse of them headed up the stairway. Just then an elevator door dinged open. I hurried inside and hit the button for the fourth floor. When the elevator arrived the doors opened just in time for the cops to run past me on their way to Lawrence's apartment. I ran out into the hallway in time to see both officers trying to pull Yosef Dillon off of Troy, who was curled up in the fetal position, trying to protect himself from the savage beating he was receiving at the hands of the unhinged BossFit coach.

It took both officers to subdue Dillon, who grunted and writhed as they struggled to put the cuffs on him. One of the officers clubbed him on the back of the head with his baton, dazing him enough for police to drop him and restrain him. I ran to Troy's side, past an elderly lady in a bathrobe standing in her apartment doorway holding a cordless phone she must have used to call the police. Troy had a few cuts and welts as well as a nasty goose egg on the side of his forehead. I darted into his apartment, opened his freezer, and rummaged through boxes of Pizza Pockets and popsicles until I found an ice pack. I ran back to Troy's side and pressed it against the small mountain that was growing near his temple.

"Ahhh!" yelped Troy, as I knelt beside him. I put a reassuring hand on his shoulder.

"Hang in there, Bub. You're going to be okay."

One of the officers called for an ambulance and joined me by Troy's side.

"Who are you?" asked the cop.

"A friend," I replied. I gently helped Troy sit up. He had a bloody, fat, bottom lip, but considering Dillon's strength and power I thought the kid got lucky.

Troy looked up and it took a moment for his eyes to focus on me. "Hey, Bro," he said weakly.

"What happened?" asked the officer.

Troy shrugged. "Dude knocked on my door and when I opened it he started yelling at me. Asking if I had talked to Jed and how he wanted to know exactly what I had said. I told him everything but he was still super pissed. I tried to tell him to chill and even invited him in for a chat and some purple kush, but then he grabbed me, yanked me into the hallway, and threw me against a wall. Then poor Mrs. Hankle came out of her apartment to tell him to leave me alone and the bald bastard screamed at her and said, 'Fuck off you old bitch!' That's when I got really mad and shoved him. Mrs. Hankle's a saint, man. She bakes me pies."

"Troy?" I said, trying to get the kid to stay on track.

"Yeah?"

"What happened next?"

"Well after I shoved him the guy just snapped and went all Brock Lesnar on my ass. I tried to run away, but he grabbed me and started pounding on me so I turtled up as best as I could until you guys got here."

"Just sit tight, both of you," the officer said, before going to confer with his partner, who was kneeling on top of Dillon's back.

"Did he say anything else while he was attacking you?" I asked.

"Just to keep my mouth shut or else he'd kill me."

"Keep your mouth shut about what?"

"I have no idea, man."

I helped Troy move over a few feet so he could sit with his back to the wall. I told him I'd return in a minute and headed back down the hallway. The cops were still preoccupied with Dillon but eventually noticed me leaving the scene.

"Hey, where do you think you're going?" hollered one of the cops after me.

"I'll be right back," I said, but since Dillon was still squirming, swearing, and twisting on the ground, the officers had their hands full.

I made it back to my truck and picked up the camcorder Dillon had retrieved from Lawrence's apartment, popped open the viewing screen, and pressed play. After watching and fast-forwarding through a few minutes of footage, everything I thought I knew about Lawrence Kunstlinger changed.

NINETEEN

I followed the EMTs and Troy out to the ambulance and
wished the kid well. I told him everything was going to be okay
and promised him that Dillon would never bother him again.

"How are you going to do that?" he asked.

"Trust me, kid. Just go get checked out and get yourself on
the mend. You're going to want to be back on your feet if you're
going to be sitting ringside during my main event match at the
Commodore in June."

Troy's eyes widened and he perked right up. "For real?"

I nodded and the little stoner gave me a big hug. I patted his
back and smiled. "Go on now. I'll be in touch."

Troy climbed into the back of the ambulance. The last thing
I heard before one of the EMTs closed the rear doors was Troy
asking a question.

"Yo, Bro, do you think you could let me turn on the sirens?"

I smirked as the ambulance drove away and turned around
to see one of the cops who had responded to the assault walking
toward me. He was a fit, twenty-something officer named Kirsh,
and he suggested that since the New Westminster Police Service

headquarters were literally a block away he would escort me on foot to the station to record my statement while his partner drove Dillon in the squad car. I thought it was a good idea and during the short walk Kirsh was quite chatty and was unfazed when he learned I was a private investigator. It was a nice change for me. When I rubbed elbows with cops outside of the VPD (where I was well known and my old man was a legend) they usually responded with either indifference or distaste upon learning of my new vocation. Kirsh became particularly inquisitive as we waited at a crosswalk for the pedestrian signal.

"I swear I know you from somewhere," he said aloud for the second time. "It's driving me crazy."

Since I was being held hostage on a street corner by a glowing orange hand I gave in. "You like pro wrestling, Kirsh?" I asked.

He stared at me for a moment before I saw a light bulb above his head turn on. "Are you shitting me? You're *the* 'Hammerhead' Jed Ounstead?" he asked excitedly.

"In the flesh."

Kirsh grabbed my hand and pumped it vigorously. "Where's your goatee? Damn it, that's why I didn't recognize you."

"Shaved it off," I replied, amazed that yet again even the slightest change to my appearance from my former pro-wrestling days often confounded fans. Mercifully, the pedestrian signal changed and I tuned out Kirsh as we crossed the street while he began blabbering like a giddy schoolboy about some of his favourite matches of mine. It was always the big, flashy, pay-per-view matches people like Kirsh remembered, instead of the underappreciated efforts in the squared circle that I used to turn in week in and week out. Just once I wanted a fan to remember my personal, all-time favourite match—a simple yet stellar one-on-one affair years ago in front of an especially dead crowd in Greensboro, North Carolina, on an episode of Monday Night Raw. In my opinion, that epic match featured the payoff of a months-long feud in addition to outstanding in-ring technical work. Despite the crowd being out of it at first, the performance by me and my opponent Artemis Artifice not only reanimated the lifeless arena, but by the conclusion everybody was on their feet giving us a minutes-long, standing ovation. Forget the steel cages, the gimmick matches, the tables, ladders, and chairs. As far as I was concerned, completely winning over an unengaged crowd in a limited amount of time was the essence of what professional wrestling was really all about.

Kirsh escorted me past the NWPS front desk and back into the bullpen. He set up a couple of chairs next to a vending machine, before taking my order and darting off to get drinks and donuts. He returned less than a minute later with a couple of old-fashioned glazed, a bottle of water, and a root beer for himself. I thanked Kirsh and took a sip of my water while he dove into his donut and pop like a kid at a carnival.

"My partner's just finishing processing the perp," said Kirsh, taking a seat beside me. "Then we'll take your statement and you can be on your way."

I knew Kirsh didn't need his partner for that, but decided to let it go. I had a strong feeling he wanted to talk more about wrestling, but before he got the chance I steered the conversation in a different direction.

"What specifically is Dillon being charged with?" I asked.

"As of now, just assault," Kirsh replied. "Possibly making threats as well. Personally, I don't see a way the Crown doesn't prosecute the bastard for doling out such a savage beating, especially since you, my partner, and I were all eyewitnesses."

I thought of the box I had retrieved from Dillon's trunk. Although his Miata was still parked across the street from Troy's apartment building, Dillon had no idea that I had lifted his prized possessions. I remembered the camcorder and its footage. However his legal situation played out, Dillon was going to be in a rush to get out of police custody as fast as possible in order to retrieve, and most likely destroy, that video.

"How long until he posts bail?" I asked.

Kirsh exhaled and checked his watch. "There's a chance it could be later this evening, but in all likelihood he'll be spending the night in a holding cell."

"Can you give me a call when he's about to be released?"

"We're not really supposed to do that," he said dourly, like Charlie Brown after missing a kick at a football.

"Listen, Kirsh—"

"Stan."

"Okay, Stan, I've got my hands full with my own ongoing investigation. That being said, keeping the kid safe is my top priority. All I want to know is if and when Dillon is set loose on the streets that you'll personally give me a heads-up. I'm sure I'm just being overly cautious, but considering how unstable the guy appears, I don't want my little buddy to get blindsided again."

Kirsh hummed and hawed for a bit before caving. "All right. But let's keep this between us, okay?"

I slipped Kirsh my card. "I'm main-eventing a show at the Commodore Ballroom next month. It's a local indie promotion, but it's entertaining and high-quality wrestling. There will be two tickets at will call with your name on them if you want to attend."

Kirsh's face lit up brighter than a Nebraskan homemaker on *The Price Is Right* being told to come on down to Contestant's Row.

I gave my statement, texted Stormy, set a time for our date later that evening, and walked back to my truck. Dusk was approaching as I drove west on the Trans-Canada Highway, the purple and blue lights of the Grand Villa Casino illuminating the hotel tower that overlooked the congested route. I exited the highway and instinctively started driving toward the Emerald Shillelagh before remembering how I had left things with Declan. I checked my dashboard clock, realized there wasn't enough time to square things with my cousin before my date, so I elected to head home instead.

Once there, I showered, shaved, and cleaned myself up. I picked out a pair of dark blue jeans and a slim-fit burgundy button-down shirt. Although I used to rock the long locks back in my wrestling days, after officially partnering with my old man, I relented and started cutting my hair in a manner he approved. While I was far from looking like a marine, I did now have much shorter hair and was not yet used to the style. I threw a dab of gel in my hair and mussed it around. I stopped off at a liquor store, bought a bottle of a limited edition Vintage Ink red blend wine, then drove to Stormy's condo, where we had first met, when I interviewed her as a potential suspect while working my first case. Her building, the Mondeo, was as nice as I remembered. I made my way to her second-floor unit and knocked twice. A moment later the door swung open and Stormy stood before me. She was dressed in a chic green-and-black, diagonally striped dress, which featured a thick, black, high-waisted belt with a gold buckle. She wore tan pumps that gave her five-foot-ten frame extra inches and brought us nearly eye-to-eye, and her formerly wavy, red-and-blue coloured hair was now straightened and dark blonde. She was an absolute knockout.

"Hi," she said softly.

"Hi," I replied. We stood in silence for a few moments until it dawned on me the longer it went on the more awkward it would become. "You look gorgeous," I gushed, offering her the bottle of wine. She blushed slightly, took the gift, and eyed the label.

"Whisky-barrel-aged wine?"

"I don't know if you remember, but last time I was here we got into the Johnnie Walker a little."

"Oh, I remember," she said coyly. "But I don't really drink spirits anymore."

"Well then this is the best of both worlds. The guy at the liquor store recommended it. Said the whisky barrel gives the wine a nice smoky oak flavour."

"Should I pour us each a glass?"

I checked my watch. "Actually, we should probably get going if we want to make our reservation."

"You made a reservation?"

"I hope that's okay."

Stormy smiled and placed the bottle of wine on her kitchen counter. "Let's go."

I always enjoyed the drive up Burnaby Mountain, and this night was no different. A brief drizzle had left the endless succession of Douglas firs, hemlocks, yews, and other conifers lining the hill's roadway with a light dusting of raindrops and their evergreen needles shimmered in the light from the street lamps. I turned off Burnaby Mountain Parkway and onto Centennial Way, following the darkened, winding road as it snaked its way toward the restaurant. Although we exchanged a little chit-chat on the drive, Stormy mostly looked out the window, taking in the abundance of foliage around us. I was grateful for the lack of pressure to fill the ride with non-stop conversation, because ever since Stormy opened her door, my heart had been racing, and my hands had become clammy. I had always found Stormy an attractive woman, but had only ever seen her in casual wear, wrestling attire, or roller derby gear. The woman who sat next to me now looked stylish, sophisticated, and stunningly beautiful.

We drove past Burnaby Mountain Park's Japanese totem poles, better known as the Playground of the Gods, before I found a parking spot near the restaurant. Stormy surprised me by holding my hand as we walked past a flower garden bursting with vibrant red, purple, and yellow blossoms and up the stairs to Horizons Restaurant. We were seated at an intimate table beside a large window. The view was spectacular, and the window-wrapped dining room allowed us to see Greater Vancouver in all its glory. I had ordered a bottle of Okanagan Valley wine, and Stormy raised her glass in a toast.

"To Larry," she said solemnly.

I nodded and clinked my glass to hers before we both enjoyed a sip of the Syrah-Malbec.

"This is really nice, Jed," said Stormy.

"Couldn't agree more," I replied earnestly.

A suave Persian waiter named Reza appeared at our table and informed us about potential food pairings with our wine and the evening's specials. We decided to delay ordering entrées, but agreed to have a cup of the seafood chowder and split an apple and squash pumpkin seed appetizer salad. Reza left to place our orders. I was perusing the entrées and trying to decide between the rack of lamb or the wild salmon when Stormy caught me off guard.

"I'm different now, you know."

"I'm sorry?"

"I'm not the same person I was when Johnny died. You have to remember how things ended between us. He really hurt me by cheating. And it definitely brought out the worst in me. It doesn't excuse my behaviour at the time, but I just wanted you to know that I'm not like that anymore. I left wrestling, cut back on drinking, joined derby, and went to counselling. I guess what I'm trying to say is that I created a new life for myself. A better life. Hell, I even managed to get a job as an aesthetician at Chi."

"Chi?"

"The luxury spa at the Shangri-La Hotel. It's the best in the city. You wouldn't believe the number of celebrities I've given mani-pedis to."

I took a sip of my wine and leaned forward. "Stormy, you don't have to justify anything to me. I've liked you since I first met you."

"You have?"

"Yes. And that was before I saw you in this head-turning number that you're wearing tonight."

Stormy smiled brightly and blushed. After a moment the smile faded. "That night when you came to my condo, I made a drunken pass at you. And you shut me right down."

"I did that because my friend had just been murdered and, even though you two had broken up, it didn't feel appropriate to respond any other way."

"So it wasn't me?" she asked sincerely.

"Of course not. It was just bad timing. Ex-girlfriend or not, I couldn't have done that to Johnny right after he was killed."

"I'm so embarrassed I acted that way. I was in a lot of pain," she said, before becoming a bit emotional. She sniffled and dabbed a tear from the corner of her eye. "I'm sorry, Jed. I just wanted to have a clean slate between us. So we can start fresh."

This time I was the one to reach out and hold her hand. "I appreciate that. And we can. But first, I have something that I really need to share with you."

"What is it?"

"It's about Lawrence. I discovered something … significant."

"How significant?"

"Something that he was definitely trying to hide."

I told Stormy about my visit to Yosef Dillon's BossFit gym and his subsequent street race to Lawrence's apartment, assault on Troy, and the storage box he confiscated and stowed in the trunk of his Miata.

"What was in the box?"

"A few knick-knacks, some personal items, and a camcorder."

"A video camera?"

"Yes. And the footage on that camera is exactly why Dillon was in such a frenzy to retrieve it."

"What was it?"

I took a sip of my wine and lowered my voice. "A sex tape."

"Oh my God! Of Yogi Barrels?"

"Yes."

"I don't understand. Why would Larry have had that? Who was Yogi cheating on his wife with?"

I leaned forward and looked Stormy directly in the eyes. "Lawrence."

Stormy stared at me as if I had just spoken to her in Klingon. "Wait, what? No, that can't be right. He wasn't gay."

I shrugged. "Maybe he was bisexual. All I can tell you is that I got an eyeful when I played back that camcorder footage and saw those two going at it."

Stormy took a big sip of wine and shook her head. "No, Jed, you don't understand. His derby name was 'Lawrence of O'Labia' for crying out loud. Everybody knew what a womanizer he was. He had a reputation."

I dug my iPhone out of my pocket, opened my videos, muted the device, and handed it to Stormy. Anticipating her reluctance to accept the truth, I had recorded ten seconds of footage as proof. Stormy hit play, then gasped loudly, and covered her mouth as she witnessed her roller derby coach on the receiving end of some very aggressive homosexual coitus.

"That's why Dillon assaulted Lawrence's neighbour Troy. Because a few weeks ago the kid heard Lawrence and Dillon thrashing around from across the hall, so he knocked on the door to make sure everything was okay. When Lawrence opened the door he was out-of-breath, dishevelled, and sweaty. Troy assumed they were having a fight. Except they weren't. They were having rough sex. And Dillon was so paranoid about their tryst being discovered that, after retrieving the sex tape from Lawrence's apartment earlier today, he went back and beat the ever-living hell out of Troy as insurance."

Stormy placed the phone on the table, screen down, as if she were getting rid of a hot potato. "I can hardly believe this. So this means that Yogi Barrels killed him."

I paused for another sip of wine. "Actually, I don't think he did."

"But they were bitter rivals who were also secret lovers. That's a recipe for murder if I've ever heard one."

"Fair point, but think about it. If Dillon killed or had Lawrence killed, why would he wait to retrieve the sex tape? He only hotfooted it over to Lawrence's apartment after I visited his gym and told him Lawrence had died. Not to mention that whoever tossed Lawrence's apartment while he was on the lam didn't find the camcorder. Which means wherever it was in the apartment it was hidden. Only Lawrence and Dillon knew where."

Stormy shook her head in disbelief. "This is all so crazy."

"I'm determined to find the person who killed Lawrence, Stormy. But it's not Yogi Barrels."

Stormy got up from the table, walked over to me, and gave me a soft but deep kiss. I didn't put up a fight. She cupped my cheek as our lips parted. "I'll be right back," she said, before grabbing her black clutch and walking toward the restrooms.

I leaned back in my chair, took in a whiff of the Syrah-Malbec's big nose, enjoyed the scents of blackberries and honey, before emptying my glass. I glanced across the restaurant and saw Reza looking at me while setting another table. He flashed a big smile and gave me a nod. I nodded back in return. Things were looking up and I was starting to feel better.

My phone vibrated on the table. I picked it up and saw it was Rya calling. My first instinct was to answer. My finger hovered over the touchscreen, but I hesitated before answering. I put the phone back down and let it go to voicemail. A few moments later, the phone vibrated again. "Damn it," I muttered to myself, before answering the call and bracing myself for what I was sure was going to be a prickly conversation.

"Psychic hotline. You have the wrong number."

"You rat bastard."

"Rat bastard's a bit harsh. I prefer mousy troublemaker."

"Don't play cute with me, goddamn it, unless you want to see your balls spit-roasted over a fire and then blended into one of your beloved banana milkshakes."

"Okay, come on now. Don't bring banana milkshakes into it. That's offside."

Rya's voice lowered and she spoke slowly in a seething, gravelly tone. "I warned you to stay away from my case."

"What makes you think I haven't?"

"For starters, that a New Westminster police officer, who seems to be particularly charmed by your doofus ass, couldn't stop talking about how he met a celebrity pro wrestler while responding to an assault."

"Why were you talking to the NWPS?" I asked.

"Because I was looking into Kunstlinger's family and friends when I discovered that his next-door neighbour had been assaulted by a rival roller derby coach. And don't try and turn this around on me, Shitbird. I'm the one asking the questions."

"You're really on fire with the insults tonight."

"What the hell are you up to, Jed?"

I sighed and leaned back in my chair. "Look, Rya, I'm not trying to get in your way, I swear. But whoever killed Lawrence, well, I accidently led them to him."

"So what? That doesn't give you the right to start poking around an active homicide investigation of mine. Why didn't you call me when you had a lead on Dillon?"

"I meant to. I just—I don't know. With how things have been with us lately…. "

"Don't you dare try and play that card with me. We both know the reason why I distanced myself from you, and I think we can both agree that it was because of your actions, not mine."

"Can we?"

"You asshole."

"I just—I really wish things had played out differently between us."

"So do I, Jed."

"Do you remember when we were at the crime scene the other day? When you held my hand and told me you'd missed me?"

There was a long pause before she responded. "Yes," she said.

"I've missed you too, Rya. More than you know."

The line went silent. Ten seconds went by. Then fifteen. I was holding my breath. Finally, she spoke.

"Jed, I—"

"May I top up your wine?" asked Stormy, as she returned to the table. "It's not whisky-barrel-aged, but it's still pretty good, wouldn't you say?"

I clenched my teeth. I heard Rya take a long, slow, deep breath. "Is that Stormy Daze?"

"Yes."

"Are you … are you on a date?"

I hesitated before answering. "Hey, you called me."

Click. The line went dead. I switched off my phone and slid it into my pocket.

"Is everything okay?" asked Stormy.

"Yes, just work stuff," I said, before rubbing my tired eyes. It had been a long day and the wine was only helping it catch up with me.

Stormy frowned. "Don't fizzle out on me now, Jed," she said, before slipping off a shoe underneath the table and running her foot up my leg. "The night has just begun."

She wasn't kidding.

TWENTY

Stormy Daze was a spooner.

Usually I enjoy lots of space when I sleep so I can toss and turn until I get comfortable. But this morning I awoke to find the statuesque roller skater who had been my date the night before wrapped around me like a besotted boa constrictor. I tried to peel one of her arms off me, but it was slung over my chest with her hand tucked under my ribs. She moaned softly as I tried to free myself, then dug her hand deeper into the mattress under my ribs, rolled me onto my back, and nuzzled her way up my chest until she sleepily kissed me on the lips. I was relieved I elected to go with the salmon over the garlic-crusted rack of lamb at dinner the night before.

"Good morning," she purred.

"Hi there."

She kissed me again. "That was really something last night."

"It was. Reza is without question the best waiter I've ever had."

She slapped my chest playfully. "I'm talking about after dinner."

"Oh."

"I mean … that many times?"

"I'm sorry, that's never happened to me before. I must have been tired."

Stormy chuckled and slapped my chest again. "That's from *Ace Ventura.*"

"So you're sweet, beautiful, and can quote lines from cheesy nineties movies? Be still my beating heart."

Stormy giggled and kissed me some more. Things were progressing quickly when my phone rang.

"Let it go to voicemail," she urged.

I rolled over and saw it was from a number I didn't recognize. "I'm sorry, I have to take this," I said, before sitting up in bed and answering the call. "Hello?"

"'Hammerhead' Jed," said a voice I couldn't place.

"Who's this?"

"It's Stan." I blanked. "Stan Kirsh. From the NWPS."

"Yes, of course, Stan. How's it going?"

"Just giving you a heads-up that Yosef Dillon is about to post bail."

I scrambled out of Stormy's bed and started picking up my clothes, strewn about the bedroom floor. I glanced at her bedside clock: 9:57 AM. Stormy sat up in her bed, covered herself with a sheet, and mouthed, *"What is it?"* I put up an index finger for her to give me a moment.

"Jed, are you still there?"

"Yeah, Stan, just getting dressed. If a car was parked illegally on the street overnight by your station where would it be towed?"

"Oh, that'd be Anna's Towing. They're literally just down the street." A few moments went by while I slid on my socks and buckled up my pants. "Why?"

"Dillon's car. He parked it in a loading zone before assaulting Troy."

"Wait a minute, you're not planning to confront him right now, are you?"

"I need to speak with him, Stan. It's about a case I'm working."

"No, no, no, no, no. Shit. Shit! I knew I shouldn't have done this."

"Stan—"

"Damn it, Jed, if you two get into it right now, I could catch so much heat."

"Listen to me. I give you my word. No matter how my confrontation with him goes down, the NWPS will not be called. I promise you that."

"I'm not sure if that's a good thing or a bad thing."

"It's going to be fine. I just need a word with him."

"This is my ass on the line here, man."

"Trust me, your department won't get wind of it. I'll see you at the upcoming XCCW show. And be sure to show security the VIP stamp on the back of your ticket so you can come backstage and have a beer with me and some of the other wrestlers after the show. It's the least that I can do for you helping me out."

"Okay, Jed. Just make sure whatever you're up to goes down as promised."

"You got it, Bub."

I ended the call and started buttoning up my shirt. I was in such a rush to get to the tow yard I had almost forgotten about the lovely but confused woman sitting in bed waiting for an explanation.

"You're going to see Yogi Barrels?" asked Stormy.

"We need to have a chat."

"Be careful, Jed. He's bound to be extra hot after spending a night in the slammer."

"The slammer?" I asked, amused by her choice of words.

Stormy shrugged. "I like to read Mickey Spillane paperbacks when not watching cheesy movies."

I finished getting dressed and sat on the edge of the bed. I leaned in to give Stormy a long, passionate kiss. "I'll see you soon."

Twenty-five minutes later I was leaning against the hood of Dillon's bright yellow Mazda Miata, parked in a long row of towed vehicles in the yard of Anna's Towing, when the muscle-bound miscreant walked toward his impounded ride. He stopped dead in his tracks when he saw me. After a moment he balled his fists and started storming my way.

"I hear there are a lot of break-ins around here at night. It'd be a shame if someone left any valuables in the trunk of their car." I could see Dillon losing steam as he considered the meaning of my words.

"What are you talking about?" he snarled.

"That box of items in your trunk. I took them. Wouldn't have wanted them to fall into the wrong hands."

Dillon's shoulders slumped. He put his hands on his head and looked like a guy who had just blown ten grand at a craps table.

"You saw the video?" he asked quietly.

"I saw enough."

He crossed his arms across his chest and looked up at me with sad, puppy dog eyes. "You can't tell anyone," he pleaded. "Please, I'm begging you."

"As long as you answer my questions I don't see any need to."

"Okay."

"I saw you when you charged into Lawrence's apartment complex yesterday. Couldn't for the life of me figure out why you of all people had a key to his building, but now it all makes sense. How long had you and Lawrence been lovers?"

"On and off for nearly a year."

"So you got together after your team lost the roller derby championship to Lawrence and the Split-Lip Sallies?"

"Yes. That was the night it first started."

"The affair? Wait a minute. You—a well-known hothead—lose a fiercely contested championship game, in which you shout and scream at the rival coach to the point where you are both ejected, and afterward you deal with that loss by hooking up with each other for the first time?"

"It wasn't planned. We'd both been booted from the bout and were still yelling at one another back in the locker room. Emotions were charged, and, well, it just sort of happened."

"Right there in the locker room?"

"Yes."

"You weren't worried about getting caught?"

"We weren't thinking. We just … gave in."

"To what? Carnal desire?"

"Pretty much. It was intense. It was always intense with him."

"Did you love him?"

Dillon sighed and thought long and hard about the question. After a bit he answered. "In a way, yeah, I think so."

"How did you know that Lawrence was gay or bisexual?"

"I didn't know for sure. I just had a feeling."

"But he had a reputation as a womanizer. His roller derby name was Lawrence of O'Labia."

Dillon chuckled slightly. "That was all for show. Lawrence was cagey. And he was big on misdirection. He coached that way too. Sneaky plays, junk offences, intentional theatrics track-side—but he always knew what he was doing. He was always in control."

"Does anyone else know about you two?"

"I thought maybe just that kid who interrupted us."

"His name is Troy. And you beat the ever-loving shit out of him for something he didn't even know, you bastard."

"You know what? Fuck you. I couldn't take the chance that he did."

"Why's that?"

"Because I'm married with two kids. If my wife found out, she'd divorce me like that," he said, angrily snapping his fingers.

"From what I've heard you've got your wife under your thumb. Even made her quit roller derby to raise your children."

"She's a devout Christian. And she comes from money. How do you think I got my BossFit gym up and running? Look, I may have her domesticated in some regards, but if she knew that I fucked guys on the side, she'd nuke my family like Hiroshima and I'd hardly ever see my kids again."

"So, just to be clear, you're secretly gay then?"

Dillon scoffed at me. "Why do you think I married someone so religious?"

I was silent for a few moments as I processed what Dillon was telling me. I decided not to ask anymore follow up questions about why a gay man would willingly choose to stay married to such a pious woman or why he wouldn't just simply come out— that was his business. But it all tracked with what I had learned so far about Lawrence and was making a lot of sense.

"Do you know what kind of trouble Lawrence was in? Or with whom?"

Dillon shook his head. "We didn't talk a whole lot. And when we did, it was always about derby."

"Did Lawrence ever speak about a slim, well-dressed man in a bowler hat?"

"What? No. What is it with you and bowler hats?"

"Can you think of anyone who would have had reason to want Lawrence dead?"

Dillon shoved his hands in his pockets and chewed his bottom lip. After a few seconds, he said something that surprised me. "Maybe."

"Maybe?"

"It's a long story."

"And you're going to share it with me."

"Fine," he said, glancing around behind him. "But can we go somewhere else?"

"Why?"

"If I'm going to get into all of this, I'm gonna need to sit down and do it right. There's a lot to tell."

I eyed Dillon cautiously. He seemed genuine, but given the guy's recent behaviour, I trusted him about as much as I trusted my cousin not to boast to customers about the colourful testicle painting currently hanging above the bar of my old man's pub.

"Okay, Dillon. I know a place nearby. Follow me there. I'm driving the black Ford F-150 parked out front."

Dillon nodded obediently. I got up off of his Miata and started toward my truck. I was halfway to the tow yard exit when I heard him holler behind me.

"Hey!" I spun on my heel and looked back at the man better known as Yogi Barrels. "I do this—you'll give me back that video camera, right?"

Suddenly I heard my cousin's voice in my head reciting that quote from the Tom Cruise movie *Cocktail*—*"Never show surprise, never lose your cool."*

"We'll see," I replied, before turning my back and walking.

TWENTY-ONE

Despite being an updated Grill & Chill location, the Dairy Queen on Sixth Avenue in New Westminster maintained a certain degree of quaint charm. Nestled on the corner of an alleyway next to a No Frills produce market and a European deli, the tiny DQ franchise was unique in having only three tables and an eight-to-ten person seating capacity. However, since summer was on its way and it was turning into an especially warm day, an additional three tables and chairs had been placed on the sidewalk in front of the ice cream shop. I bought a banana milkshake and then joined Yosef Dillon outside. He had declined any beverage or frosty treat, and instead sat on an angle, staring blankly at the Royal City Centre shopping mall directly across the street.

I took a seat across from Dillon, and greedily slurped my large banana milkshake. Dillon glared at me with disgust.

"Do you have any idea how many calories are in that?" he asked.

"Seven hundred and fifty," I replied.

"Jesus," he spat.

"Sometimes I have them add an extra banana. Then it cracks eight hundred."

"You're a weird guy, Ounstead."

"A weird guy who wants to hear who might have had reason to want Lawrence dead."

Dillon took a deep breath and exhaled slowly. "Look, what I'm about to tell you, it's kind of confidential. And if it got out, it could cause a lot of problems."

"Got out where?"

"Derby. I'll tell you what I know, but please don't share it with Daze or any of the Sallies."

"I'll tell my clients whatever the hell I want."

Dillon crossed his arms and slumped in his seat. "Fine. But just so you know, this news could really upset the girls and cause a lot of chaos. I'm just looking out for them."

"Duly noted," I said, nodding.

Dillon continued. "There have been rumours floating around for awhile now that there's a very wealthy group of investors seriously considering launching a national roller derby league that will all but put the WFTDA out of business."

"WFTDA?"

"Women's Flat Track Derby Association. It's the international governing body for the sport and a membership organization for leagues to collaborate and network. You see, even though the WFTDA helps link together teams from all over North America, it's also pretty hands off. They allow independent leagues to do things their way. It's unity without conformity. Our Pacific Northwest League is much more hardcore and extreme than most of the other leagues out there because that's the way we like it. But this group I mentioned, they want to straight up commercialize derby. They want to try and take it mainstream."

I took another sip of my shake. "What, like the WNBA?"

"Pretty much."

"I don't understand. Wouldn't bringing women's roller derby into the mainstream be a good thing?"

"It would be the worst thing."

"Why?"

"Derby isn't like other sports. It's renegade. It's radical. It's punk rock. At its core, it's about empowering women, rebelling against the status quo, and telling the corporate establishment to fuck right off."

I took a moment to consider Dillon's words. Stormy had alluded to the importance of female empowerment in roller derby when she first hired me to find Lawrence. And I had wrestled in some indie promotions myself back in the day that prided themselves on being fiercely anti-WWE and mainstream pro wrestling, so this wasn't a concept I was unfamiliar with.

"So what does this group have to do with Lawrence?" I asked.

"About six months ago, the rumours started to grow. Whispers became a few words here and there. Then those words became conversations. Apparently this group was taking their plan to the next level. Feelers were going out to derby management and coaches all over North America. Then three months ago, someone from this group made contact with a derby coach from Seattle whom Lawrence and I happen to know well. He responded enthusiastically to this person who contacted him, plans were made for them to start coordinating efforts in order to poach WFTDA talent and further explore making a big budget national roller derby league a reality, all while considering what the Pacific Northwest's role could be within it. Except, this Seattle coach, he was playing along. He was pretending to be excited about this blasphemous idea even though it turned his stomach. But he did it anyway so we could have someone on the inside."

"Like a spy."

"Exactly. So now that we had a pipeline into what this rich group of pricks was planning, we were able to start to organize and mobilize a resistance. And I'll give you one guess who spearheaded our efforts to keep roller derby pure."

"Lawrence."

Dillon nodded. "He was like fucking *Braveheart*, man. Rounding up people left and right, convincing coaches and management that this was a legitimate threat to the sport we love, and that if these corporate assholes got their way, the derby as we knew it would wither and die."

"Did it work?"

"It was starting to. But for these people, money is no issue. They pushed back. They're very determined to see the formation of a national roller derby league. Although Lawrence had made some headway, suddenly people in our resistance movement were either dropping out or going radio silent. Lawrence figured they were taking payoffs, so he decided to get a bigger soapbox and microphone and accelerate his plans. Last time I talked to him, he had just finished talks with the head of broadcast of the WFTDA about releasing an official, joint, and very public rejection of any proposed national roller derby leagues. Lawrence was going to get team after team to sign a pledge to resist, and then blast the idea of a mainstream roller derby league across all platforms on social media. He was going to do a goddamn blitzkrieg so every last coach, player, referee, NSO, or derby fan would be aware of the threat to the sport."

"NSO?"

"Non-skating official."

"So what happened?"

"A couple of days after we last spoke, Lawrence disappeared. I didn't know what had happened to him until you walked into my gym."

"So there was no blitzkrieg?"

Dillon shook his head. "I even emailed the WFTDA head of broadcast myself to follow up, but never heard back. Without Lawrence, it all fell apart."

"Why didn't you just take over?"

"Because I didn't want to be the public face of a movement that was about to go up against millionaire investors and send shock waves throughout the sport," he scoffed. "I love derby,

I really do, but I have a family and a business to worry about. Lawrence, he didn't have anything else. He didn't even really have me, despite how much I cared for him. He knew what we had would never be more than it was."

I leaned back in my chair and slurped more shake. "You keep talking about this group of wealthy investors who want a national roller derby league. Who are they, exactly?"

Dillon shrugged. "Again, it's mostly rumours. I'm fairly sure some owners of NLL and Major League Soccer teams are involved, and there's been chatter that there's some significant interest from a NHL team owner back east."

"That's who you think wanted Lawrence dead? Some rich sports team owners?"

"I don't know, man. I just know Lawrence was starting to really piss them off."

"Enough to murder him? So what if they couldn't get a national roller derby league going? They're loaded and can buy any sports team they want. Why take the risk of bumping a guy off for the already risky chance of commercializing a fringe sport?"

"Hey, you're the detective, okay? All I know is that some seriously wealthy dudes are pushing hard to make this new league a reality. Maybe someone involved has more of a reason to see it happen than the other rich old farts and didn't take kindly to the fact that Lawrence was on the brink of blowing it all up."

"It's pretty thin," I said. Dillon shrugged his shoulders. "That's seriously all that you have for me? A half-baked theory that someone would care enough about women's roller derby going mainstream they'd be willing to take a life?"

"There is something else. That Seattle coach I mentioned, he not only got the name of a multimillionaire potential backer who apparently is one of the driving forces behind a potential national roller derby league, but he also had a brief telephone conversation with the guy. And apparently he's quite eccentric. In one five-minute call he went from enthusiastically ranting about how successful mainstream derby could be, to rambling about how he would bring in celebrity endorsements and strike all kinds of television and broadcasting deals, to threatening the coach by telling him that everything they had just talked about was strictly confidential, and that if he repeated a word of it to anyone there would be dire consequences."

I leaned forward in my chair. "Okay, now we're getting somewhere."

"It gets better. This guy, he lives right here in Vancouver."

"What's his name?"

Dillon leaned forward and lowered his voice. "Hector Specter," he said slowly, in a hushed and ominous tone.

I hesitated before responding. "Did he murder Colonel Mustard in the study with the candlestick?"

"What? Fuck you. That's his real name."

"I've never heard of him."

"Well, you should have. The guy is everywhere. He's a multi-hyphenate whirlwind and beverage baron."

"The only baron I know is the red one Snoopy fights in the *Peanuts* comic strip."

"Ever heard of Horned Viper Vodka? Gryphon Gin? Pegasus Pilsner, or Cyclops Stout?"

"You're telling me he's the guy behind all of those tacky Greek mythological booze products that have flooded the market in the last few years?"

"Yeah. And that's not all. He also has a line of energy drinks and owns Cerastes Brands, which has Greek-fusion frozen foods in supermarkets all across Canada."

I took another sip of my shake as I considered Dillon's words. "How could this Specter character even have an interest in taking roller derby national if he's so busy with so many other business ventures?"

"I don't know. But he does. And he also owns a flashy restaurant in town. The Poseidon Supper Club."

"Now I have a place to start," I said, getting up from the table.

"You'll never get an audience with him," cautioned Dillon. "Lawrence tried like hell when he was organizing the resistance. This guy has a security detail wherever he goes. You won't get within ten feet."

If what Dillon said was right, then it might take a lot more than just rolling into a restaurant looking for some souvlaki and a sit-down. But I had my resources. "I'll figure something out," I said, before sliding my chair back under the table.

"Aren't you forgetting something?" snapped Dillon.

"Let's just see how this plays out. Then I'll give you back your camcorder."

"I played ball, Ounstead. I told you everything that I know."

"I hope for your sake that's true."

Dillon's famous temper returned, and he slammed his hands down on the metal table and sprung to his feet, seething. "Give me back that fucking camera," he growled.

I waited for people walking by's gawks and glares to fade away before responding. "When I'm good and ready."

I turned and walked back toward my truck, feeling Yosef Dillon's blazing eyes burning holes into my back as if he had heat-ray vision.

TWENTY-TWO

It took me the rest of the day to procure the two special items, but the moment I strolled through the door of the Emerald Shillelagh and saw my cousin staring at me while drying a pint glass with a dishtowel I knew it was worth it. I took a seat at the end of the bar and placed both items I was carrying on its polished surface. Declan looked between the two items, then back at me. He wordlessly retrieved a couple of tumbler glasses off the wall, then opened the bottle of Glenfiddich IPA I brought for him. The single malt whisky had been aged in a cask already seasoned with India Pale Ale. Declan poured us each three fingers' worth and we enjoyed a sip. I nodded toward the second item, and Declan picked up the wrapped package before tearing into it like a kid on Christmas morning. When opened, he cradled the medium-size canvas in his hands. In the painting a rudimentary but recognizable Clint Eastwood, as the Man with No Name, chomped on a cigar and squinted, just as he did so many times in *The Good, the Bad and the Ugly*. The shades of muted tan and yellowish-brown gave the grim gunslinger's portrait an additional

Wild West vibe. It was signed with the initials BRF, and directly above them was an imprint in black paint of the artist's genitalia.

Declan sniffled and wiped away a tear that was forming in the corner of his eye. "It's bloody deadly, Jed. I love it."

"It's the least I could do."

"I can't take me eyes off o'it."

"For what it's worth, I'm sorry about before. What you said about me being careless in meeting with Lawrence was true."

"Aye, but I didn't need to be such a gouger about it."

"No, I needed to hear it."

"Fair enough, Mate," said Declan, before extending his hand. I gave it a firm squeeze as I shook it. "I love you, brother," I said.

"Aye, I love ya too, ya stubborn sack o'shite."

Declan walked to the middle of the bar and took down the brightly coloured testicle painting, replacing it with the Clint Eastwood portrait.

"Where are you going to hang the other one?" I asked.

"Above me mantle."

"You're taking it home?"

"Jed, by the time I'm done collecting this genius fella's work, I may need an extra flat."

Declan tucked the painting under the bar before jolting upright in a panic. "Bollocks!"

"What?"

"David Hasselhop is loose again."

"Who?"

Declan smacked his palm down on the bar top a couple of times. "All you eejits listen up! First lad or lass to find the rabbit gets a round on the house!"

Although the pub wasn't at capacity, the handful of regulars quickly leapt out of their seats and started bunny hunting. I leaned over the bar and saw that beside the painting stood an open empty cage containing wood chips, a leaf of lettuce, some sliced raw carrots, and quite a bit of rabbit poop.

"Got him!" hollered a skinny film student in a *Star Wars* T-shirt, and before I knew what was happening, Declan had brought the kid a pint of beer and returned with a fluffy, white bunny in his arms.

"What the hell is this?" I asked, bewildered.

"Remember me furry lady friend from the kink club? She's out o'town on business so I'm bunny-sittin' for her 'til she gets back."

An image of the short, busty blonde shaking her fluffy cottontail and twitching her nose while Declan hand-fed her baby carrots flashed in my mind. "You've got to be kidding me."

"Careful, Boyo. This gal might be the one." Declan made a clucking sound while he nuzzled David Hasselhop and scratched the rabbit between his ears.

"What about Trixie Titties?"

Declan flashed a million-dollar smile and winked at me. "Oh, she's still in the picture. The bunny babe is a swinger."

"Does she have a name? Or do you just call her 'Bunny Babe?'"

"Her name's Candy."

"If you don't mind me asking, what does Candy do when not engaging in group sex or indulging her furry fetish?"

"She's a student recruitment and support officer for Douglas College," replied Declan, matter-of-factly.

"Of course she is."

Declan retrieved the leaf of lettuce from the cage and started humming the pop song "Hips Don't Lie" while feeding the bunny. After a moment, Declan noticed me gawking. "Quit looking at me like that, ya tosser."

"You're singing to a rabbit."

"David Hasselhop only eats while listening to Shakira songs. I'm under strict instructions."

I shook my head in disbelief. "Is the old man upstairs?"

"Aye."

"I'll leave you to it then," I said, before heading toward the staircase at the back of the pub while Declan resumed his humming of the catchy song.

I found my old man behind the desk in our office. He was hunched over his computer with his glasses down the bridge of his nose while he hunted and pecked on his keyboard with his two sausage-like index fingers. I took a seat in the chair across from him and placed my right ankle on my left knee, although I regretted it when I felt tightness in my hip. I suddenly remembered taking a hard blow from Spudboy's sack of potatoes during our match a few days earlier, and decided that if I was going to continue wrestling, my thirty-five-year-old body was going to need to invest in some regular yoga and massages in order to keep up with the up-and-coming spry whipper-snappers I would be facing off against in the squared circle.

My father grunted and shoved his keyboard away from him like a man unsatisfied with his dinner. He took off his glasses and rubbed his eyes.

"You really should let me type up your reports for you, Pop."

He waved me away with one of the giant paws he called hands. "It's an email. And what's that say right there?" he asked, pointing at the sign on the door.

"Ounstead and Son Investigations."

"Exactly."

"I don't understand."

"Ounstead *and* Son. Not Ounstead *with* Son. *And* Son. As in partners. Which means I'm sure as hell not dumping off any of my caseload on you just because I crap faster than I type. I can pull my own weight, boy."

"All right, take it easy."

"Sorry," he replied, taking a sip of water from a glass on his desk. "Been catching up on correspondence for hours and it's left me a bit cranky. What's up?"

"I might have a lead on Lawrence Kunstlinger's killer." I summarized my recent encounters with Yosef Dillon, including following him from his gym to Lawrence's apartment and swiping the box of items he had retrieved before returning to lay a pounding on Troy Whitlock. My father chuckled.

"What?"

"That was a pretty slick move—albeit a tad unethical—snagging the box out of his trunk. What was in it that was so valuable?"

"This is where it gets interesting." I told my old man about the sex tape and how I had used it to leverage Dillon into sharing any insight he had into who may have wanted Lawrence dead. I started explaining about the wealthy investors and the plan to create a national roller derby league, but my father interrupted me.

"Wait—you mean those two fellas were really...." My pop trailed off, instead pinching his thumb and index finger together and shaking them in the air.

"You know, Pop, just saying the word gay doesn't magically turn you into a homosexual."

"Didn't you say this Dillon guy was married with kids?"

"Closet case."

"But if he's gay, then why does he stay married?"

"Personal choice, I guess."

My father shook his head and sighed. "I don't understand the world anymore."

"Well you'll understand this." I filled him in on all I had learned about the proposed national roller derby league and Lawrence's efforts to stop it.

"So the head cheese behind this proposed roller skating league is right here in town?" he asked.

"Yes. And he's the person I need you to start compiling a detailed background check on. Apparently he's quite the character."

"How so?"

"Dillon described him as a 'multi-hyphenate beverage baron.' He has lines of energy drinks, liquor, frozen foods, and even owns a restaurant in town."

"What's his name?"

"Hector Specter."

"Hector Specter?"

"Hector Specter."

"You sure he didn't stab Professor Plum with a dagger in the billiards room?"

I chuckled at his Clue board game wisecrack and was reminded that, despite our many differences, in some ways my old man and I were a lot alike. My father opened a drawer and dug out a yellow legal pad and a pen. I shared everything Dillon had told me about Specter while my pop jotted down notes. When I was done he leaned back in his chair.

"I just this morning finished up that fraud case I've been working on the last few weeks so as of now I've got a clean slate. I'll get on this right away."

"Thanks, Pop," I said, getting up out of the chair.

"Where are you off to?"

"Figure I'd head over to the Poseidon Supper Club. See if I can rattle a few cages."

"I like your spirit, son. But I thought this Specter had a security detail that won't let you get close?"

I shrugged. "Maybe he's a wrestling fan."

My old man chortled as he fired up the PI software on his computer. I stopped at the bar on my way out, grabbed a bottled water to go, and, at Declan's insistence, agreed to hold David Hasselhop. I watched the fluffy little guy's nose twitch while I fed him a few slices of carrots as Shakira's "Whenever, Wherever" played over the sound system. I had to admit, stroking the bunny's head was quite soothing, and I was going to need all the calmness I could muster.

TWENTY-THREE

The Poseidon Supper Club was located on Granville Island. The thirty-eight-acre peninsula was a favourite destination of mine because I always enjoyed the architecture, and the island itself immediately brought back countless fond memories of my mother. In the late seventies, after manufacturers had left the area formerly known as "Industrial Island," almost all of the manufacturing sheds were repurposed, and give the abundance of restaurants and shops their unique and distinctive character. By the early eighties, provincial and federal governments had converted a fifty-thousand-square-foot building into the now famous Granville Island Public Market. I spent many Sunday afternoons in my childhood strolling up and down its aisles with my mother while she shopped for groceries. I would sample meats, seafood, and artisanal cheeses before always being treated to banana milkshakes as a reward for my good behaviour. As I grew older I struggled to accept that over time I was remembering my mother less and less, but visiting places we used to frequent together always served to bring vivid recollections of her back to mind.

I parked my truck by Granville Island Brewing and, as I walked by, saw a group of people inside at the bar sampling flights of beer. The bartender was holding up a bottle and speaking about their seasonal Sunshine Coast Hefeweizen. I made a mental note to pick up a six-pack after my visit to Hector Specter's restaurant. I crossed the street and discovered that the Poseidon Supper Club was in the same spot as a hole-in-the-wall fish and oyster café I used to frequent back when I was working on my acting skills by taking part in the nearby Vancouver TheatreSports. My experience in the improv comedy league had been instrumental in developing my professional wrestling persona—it was there that I first conceived the character Hammerhead Jed and his penchant for busting two-by-fours over his head and drinking beer as part of his in-ring celebration after winning matches. I was sad to see that the oyster shack was gone, but my dismay was replaced by curiosity once I entered the restaurant.

The former café had been completely gutted. Instead of a dozen tables and multiple crab and lobster tanks, there was now a long marble bar, dark tile floors, tacky wallpaper, and faux-mosaic murals of Greek temples and mythological characters. The restaurant was empty save for two goateed, heavy-set men in matching black suits and ties and a waifish blonde bartender leaning on the bar top scribbling into her notebook. The beefy boys were both hunched over a table in the back of the restaurant wolfing down giant gyros as though they were in a food eating competition. When one of them noticed me, he sat up and spoke with a thick Greek accent.

"Restaurant not open for forty-five minutes," he snapped, as spittle of lettuce and Kalamata olives flew from his lips.

"Just looking to have a quick drink," I replied, easing my way toward the bar.

The big guy wasn't having it. His chair screeched loudly on the tile floor as he got to his feet, plucked the cloth napkin tucked in the front of his collar, and threw it down on the table. "There fucking brewery across street. We closed."

I was struggling to come up with a way to defuse the situation when the blonde bartender looked up from her notebook and did it for me.

"Holy smokes," she said. "Holy smokes!" she repeated, excitedly.

The big guy on his feet was confused. "What?"

"Do you know who that is?" she said, pointing at me. The big guy shrugged his lumpy shoulders while his partner, who still hadn't moved, continued to devour his gyro. "That's 'Hammerhead' Jed Ounstead."

"Who?" asked the big guy.

The blonde bartender waved him away with one hand and motioned me over to the bar with the other. "Just never mind, Vlassis, I know him," scolded the bartender. Apparently relieved to be done with me, Vlassis sat back down and resumed eating.

I pulled up a stool at the bar and the peppy, blonde bartender extended a hand, which I shook. "What the frick are you doing here?" she asked.

"Just in the neighbourhood," I replied. "Figured I'd wet my whistle."

"Whatever you want, it's on the house."

"That's not necessary."

"No, I insist. You're 'Hammerhead' Jed for Pete's sake!" The bartender put a palm up in the air. Not wanting to leave her hanging, I gave her a high-five. "What can I get you?"

"A beer is fine, thank you," I replied.

She turned around and grabbed a pint glass before filling it up with a blackish brew. I glanced at the tap handle, which featured a cartoonish one-eyed monster and read "Cyclops Stout." The girl served me the beer. I thanked her and took a sip, and it was all I could do not to wince and scrape the acrid taste off of my tongue with my fingernails.

"Sorry," she said. "I know it's not very good. But the owner only allows us to serve his own brand of alcohol here."

"It's like someone blended a Guinness with a rotten egg," I muttered, wiping my lips on my forearm. She giggled and leaned forward on the bar, gawking at me like I was a movie star. I slid the rancid ale away from me. "What's your name?" I asked.

"Jenny."

"I take it you're a wrestling fan, Jenny?"

Her face lit up even more. "Dude, you have no idea. My brothers and I are obsessed. We watch everything. WWE, Impact!, ROH, New Japan. We were even ringside at your show last week in Burnaby!" Jenny's eyes popped wide open as she had an epiphany. She ducked behind the bar, found what she was looking for, and jumped back to her feet holding a backpack. She pulled out one of my new T-shirts and held it up proudly. "See?"

"That is a solid fashion statement."

"Would you autograph it for me?" she asked.

"Of course," I replied, before she handed me a Sharpie. I signed the shirt and Jenny clutched it to her chest like her most prized possession. She then folded the shirt carefully and placed it beside her notebook, which sat next to a college textbook on environmental studies. Jenny put her elbows on the bar and leaned forward.

"You're here for the show, eh? I can't believe Hector landed you as a guest."

"What show?"

"Hector's."

"Hector Specter has a TV show?"

Jenny smirked. "Well, yeah, but it's not really a show," she said in a hushed voice while glancing at Vlassis and his buddy to ensure they were out of earshot. "It's more of a joke."

"I don't understand."

"Hector tried to pitch a talk show starring him to all the local stations but nobody was interested. So instead he buys late night infomercial time every Friday on CHEK TV, then puts on a talk show that he films right here in the basement."

"The basement?"

"Yeah, he converted it into a little talk show set. He brings in an audience, does a monologue, has a band, interviews guests—everything you see on late night TV, just super lame and not funny at all. Hector likes to think he has the charisma of Conan O'Brien, but it's more like Conan the Barbarian. It's kind of pathetic."

"Sounds like it."

"That's not even the worst part."

"There's more?"

"He also does commercials of him doing skits and advertising his energy drinks, booze, and frozen foods in order to break up the show and make it seem legit."

"Are you kidding me? How have I not heard of this? It sounds like a train wreck."

"Oh, it totally is. But Hector keeps on doing shows week after week and none of the sycophants he keeps around him have the guts to tell him how awful it really is. They just keep doing whatever Hector wants and collecting their paycheques."

This Hector Specter character was shaping up to be a real piece of work. "Do you know anything about Hector and women's roller derby?" I asked.

"What is that, like roller skating?"

"Kind of."

"Nah, never heard anything about that."

"How well do you know Hector?"

"I don't know him at all, Hammerhead."

"But you bartend at his restaurant and you seem to know everything about him," I said, confused.

"That's just from gossiping with the other staff. I see Hector, like, once maybe twice a week, if that. And even then it's just a glimpse as he walks by with his security detail on his way to do the show downstairs or to dine in the VIP room in the back with special guests. He's barely ever looked at me."

"What's the deal with the security, anyway? It's not like he's the prime minister."

Jenny shrugged. "He's had them around ever since I started working here a few months ago. I think it makes him feel like a big shot. Hector's ego is off the charts."

"I'm getting the impression you don't like the guy."

Jenny winked at me. "You're pretty sharp for a guy who breaks two-by-fours over his head, Hammerhead."

"You really like calling me Hammerhead, don't you?

Jenny giggled and blushed. "Sorry."

"I don't mind. But I guess you wouldn't be able to put me in touch with him then."

"I wish I could. I'd do anything for you, man."

"Thanks, kiddo."

"Do you know what my favourite match of yours is?" she asked.

I sighed and wondered if Jenny would finally be the first person to pick my all-time favourite match as her own. "Let me guess. Steel cage match for the Intercontinental title against Bubba Hickok, Jr.?"

"Last Man Standing versus Napalm Nixon at SummerSlam."

I nodded and smiled. It may not have been my personal favourite, but it was a hell of a match. Jenny clearly knew her stuff. "Good choice," I said.

"Do you have a card or something? I could at least give it to Vlassis and ask him to try and run it upstairs to Hector."

I retrieved my wallet out of the front pocket of my jeans, slid out a business card, and handed it to Jenny. A big grin crept across her face as she read the card. "You're a frickin' private investigator?" she asked, incredulously.

"Gotta do something between matches," I replied. "What's your last name, Jenny?"

"Matthews," she said.

"And how many brothers do you have?"

"Two."

"I'm headlining a show at the Commodore the last Saturday in June. There will be three tickets at will call with your name on them.

"Are you serious?"

"Absolutely. Just be sure to wear the T-shirt."

Jenny beamed before darting from behind the bar and giving me a big hug. After I agreed to take a selfie with her on her phone I decided to try and play matchmaker. "Are you single?" I asked, out of the blue.

"Oh my God, yes!"

I almost smacked my hand against my forehead for being so hardheaded. Maybe breaking all those two-by-fours over my skull was taking its toll after all. "I have a new friend, his name is Troy. He's kind, nice-looking, about your age, and not a beat-up, broken-down, old chunk of coal like me. He's a good kid. And he's going to be at the show too, sitting right beside you and your brothers. Maybe you two will hit it off."

Jenny flicked my business card against her thumb a few times as she considered my words. "Yeah, maybe!" she said excitedly. She hugged me again and I headed for the door. I stopped after a few strides and turned back around.

"Sorry, Jenny, I just have one more question."

"Shoot," she said.

"You don't ever happen to see a guy in a nice suit and a bowler hat around here, do you?"

"Are you kidding? There's a guy like that in here all the time."

TWENTY-FOUR

I was back at the bar in an instant. "What did you just say?"

"I said there's a guy like that in here all the time."

"In a bowler hat."

"Yeah."

"Slim build, about five-foot-ten?"

"I'm not sure about his height. That could be right. But yeah, he's a slender guy."

My mind was racing. Had I just cracked the case wide open and located the creepy bastard who'd been spying on me? Did Hector Specter hire Chauncey Gardiner to follow me and kill Lawrence?

"There's a picture of him over there," said Jenny, pointing at a wall at the end of the bar.

"May I see it?"

"Sure," she said, retrieving it for me. She handed me the photo. My heart was pounding as I turned it over. However, instead of seeing the well-manicured and murderous voyeur, the metal frame held a snapshot of a middle-aged man in a black suit and matching fedora with a red feather in the band, singing and playing a piano. On the piano was a tip jar, a bottle of ouzo, and a half-full glass.

"His name's Joey. Not sure about his last name. He's here pretty much every weekend. Plays a lot of classics, like Sinatra songs and stuff."

"Jenny, that's a fedora," I said, pointing at the piano player's hat.

"What?"

"A bowler hat is rounded. Like the kind you'd see on Charlie Chaplin in an old movie or on a leprechaun."

"Oops. Sorry, Hammerhead. I thought that's what it was."

I sighed and placed the photo flat on the bar. "It's all right." With my hopes dashed, I decided that I had wasted enough time at Hector Specter's restaurant. "I'll see you at the wrestling show," I said, heading toward the door.

"You know it!" squealed Jenny excitedly.

I was two steps from the exit when I felt Vlassis' hot feta-cheese breath on the back of my neck. Before I could react, he grabbed me by the shoulder and aggressively spun me around, no small feat considering my size.

I wanted to play nice. I really did. But sometimes I just can't help myself. "Sorry, Vlassis, but if you're looking for a Tic Tac I'm fresh out."

"What?" he grunted.

"You should give Listerine Cool Mint Breath Strips a try. Very potent."

I could see the gears in Vlassis' head turning slowly, and he stared at me dumbly for a few moments before catching on. Then he cupped one of his hands and blew into it, before sniffing his wafting, rebounding breath like a dog.

"Perhaps some Binaca?"

Vlassis had had enough. He shoved me hard and I stumbled back into the door. "You *Malaka!* What you doing hugging girl and looking at pictures on wall? Who are you?"

"Vlassis!" yelled Jenny, running to my defence.

I held up a hand and encouraged her to stay back. "It's okay, kiddo. I got this."

"You no got shit, you *Poustis*," he snarled. Vlassis' black-suited buddy, who had finally finished his gyro, lumbered over beside his partner, trying to intimidate me by flexing his chubby bulk while licking tzatziki sauce off his thick fingers.

"You guys ever eat at Swiss Chalet?" I asked. Vlassis and his buddy looked at each other, puzzled. "It's really great. And because their chicken and ribs are so saucy, they give you a little bowl of warm lemon water afterward so you can rinse off your sticky fingers, rather than licking them like a goddamn gorilla."

That was the last straw for Vlassis. He cocked a big fist behind his ear, and while it certainly looked like it could do some damage, his windup was slow. Before he could swing, I fired off a quick, hard right-hand punch and drilled Vlassis square in the solar plexus. Although my hand made a fist, I had kept my index and middle finger knuckles slightly elevated, which gave the strike a sharper impact. It worked like a charm because Vlassis immediately barfed up a little bit of gyro, which dribbled down his chin, before crumpling forward and falling onto the ground.

"Vlassis!" exclaimed his partner, and Jenny and I watched as he waddled side-to-side like an elderly person getting into a bathtub as he slowly lowered himself to the ground to check on his friend.

"Sit him up and hold his arms above his head," I said, and Vlassis' partner, whose eyes were wide open and face displayed utter shock, obediently followed my instructions. I had a feeling Vlassis, and especially his partner, were all brawn with no bite. I had known quite a few big guys who, despite their intimidating size, were useless in a fight back when I worked as a bouncer. Vlassis' breathing improved. I pointed at his partner. "You tell your people I'm a private investigator and that I need to have a word with Hector. Jenny has my contact information." Vlassis' partner nodded vigorously.

I looked back at Jenny. "Is there anywhere Hector goes or hangs out other than here and his businesses? Anywhere public where I could try and run him down for a chat?"

Jenny thought for a moment, and then snapped her fingers. "He loves the ponies. I know he goes there quite a bit."

"You mean Hastings Racecourse?"

"Yeah. Hector owns several champion horses that race there."

"Please tell me he doesn't also own a wiener dog."

Jenny's face scrunched up in confusion. "What?"

"Never mind," I replied, before shooting Jenny a wink and exiting the Poseidon Supper Club. Five minutes later I had a chilled six-pack of Granville Island Hefeweizen sitting on my front passenger seat while sunshine shimmered across False Creek as I drove over the Cambie Street Bridge. I dug my phone out of my pocket and made a call that I had hoped never to make again.

TWENTY-FIVE

"Mr. Ounstead. What a lovely surprise."

"Hello, Sykes."

"To what do I owe the pleasure of this call?"

"I'm thinking about placing a bet on Napoleon's race."

"That would be a wise wager."

"I also wanted to ask you a question."

"Pray tell."

"Do you know of a guy named Hector Specter? Apparently he's down at the racecourse a fair amount where you often conduct your, uh—business."

"Ugh, Hector," spat Sykes. "Yes, I know him, but not for a lack of trying not to."

"Does he place bets with you?"

"No, but a couple of men in his entourage regularly do."

"I need to speak with him about an investigation of mine but he's proving quite difficult to meet.

"That's because of his ridiculously over-inflated ego and the barrage of bumbling bodyguards he surrounds himself with.

The only thing Hector needs protection from is his malignant narcissism."

"I was just down at his restaurant in Granville Island."

"I have heard it is garish beyond belief."

"Yeah. And I didn't even see the TV studio."

"I had forgotten about his insipid little show. That man does not have a shred of class."

"No, but he may have some answers for me, which is why I need to chat with him ASAP. Can you help?"

"I suppose I could broker a meeting between the two of you."

"Just like I suppose that by doing so you would like something in return?"

"Funny how that works, is it not, Mr. Ounstead?" he said. Sykes was a crafty son of a bitch, but he was nothing if not consistent. Despite my frustration, I respected that.

"Another collection?" I asked.

"I am afraid so."

"Please tell me it's not at another kink club."

Sykes chuckled. "No, not this time. I have a very special client who works in the film industry. He makes millions of dollars a year, but enjoys gambling most of that money away, quite often with me. He owes me a substantial sum, and although I have never had a problem with him before, he is delinquent on his payment."

"Where can I find him?"

"At the Hard Rock almost every night. High-stakes poker or roulette tables."

"Name?"

"Alan Kressberg."

"And how much does he owe?"

"Seventy-five thousand dollars."

"What the hell, Sykes?"

"As I said, he gambles a lot away."

"Can you reach out to Hector Specter and get the ball rolling now in good faith?"

Sykes went silent on the other end of the phone. After a moment, he spoke. "Very well. But until I have what's owed to me you will not be meeting with Hector."

"Understood."

"And Mr. Ounstead?"

"Yes?"

"Let us keep your 'collecting' quite cordial this time, shall we?"

"Heard about the spanking I doled out, eh?"

"Indeed. But unlike Forrester, Kressberg is a whale of a client, and I know that he is good for it. It could simply have been a scheduling conflict as he often travels all over the world for his film and television projects. He is also very discreet about making his wagers. Although he has several personal assistants, he has always dealt with me directly. It is clear he does not want those he works with to know of his expensive hobby."

"It sounds to me like the man is an addict, Sykes. And you're asking me not to ruffle any feathers so you can keep profiting from his illness."

I heard Sykes sigh on the other end of the line. "If he did not come to me, Mr. Kressberg would surely be placing bets somewhere else. He is an adult, regardless if what you say is true. At least with me he is treated with respect, professionalism, and courtesy. Trust me when I say most of my colleagues are a lot more unsavoury."

I considered Sykes' point of view and remembered what my old man often told me since I became a private investigator—"You can't save them all."

"I'll call you when I have the money," I said, before clicking my phone off and taking a sip of Hefeweizen. I leaned back against the hood of my truck, looking out on the water from where I had parked in Coopers' Park. Bordering False Creek and tucked under the Cambie Street Bridge, the park was an urban oasis that featured a playground, skate park, vibrantly green open lawns, and some of the best and most expansive views in the city. I took another sip of the wheat ale and watched a fit, young mother jog by pushing a souped-up, sporty stroller with tires and tread nearly as big as my Ford F-150's. I lost track of the lady as she rounded a corner and disappeared behind a large shrub and a planting of magenta blooms. I returned my gaze to the water as a rainbow-coloured Aquabus chugged by, and found myself desperately hoping that all of the hoops I was having to jump through just to meet with Hector Specter were worth it. But if what Yosef Dillon said was true, and Lawrence Kunstlinger had indeed been murdered because of his efforts to stop the formation of a national roller derby league with Specter the driving force behind it, then I had a feeling at the very least a chat with this wannabe talk-show host, restaurateur, frozen-foods-selling beverage baron was going to be worth the wait.

TWENTY-SIX

"Hit you again?"

"You know it, Bub." An ace dropped on the felt.

"Blackjack," announced the dealer.

I took a sip of my Guinness, but it wasn't the same. To this day I still didn't know what magic my cousin worked when swapping out the kegs at the Emerald Shillelagh, but whatever it was spoiled me and our customers rotten and prevented me from truly enjoying Sir Arthur's stout pretty much anywhere else, save for Ireland.

I glanced around the Hard Rock Casino Vancouver, so named despite the fact it was located in the industrial strip of the suburb of Coquitlam. There was no sign of Kressberg. I had done a web search on my phone after talking to Sykes and dozens of images immediately came up, in addition to his numerous credits. Kressberg was a writer, executive producer, and co-creator of several popular superhero TV shows that were filmed in Vancouver, and he had recently added writing and producing a soon-to-be-released, big-budget, action-adventure feature film to his credits.

I tapped the table for the dealer to hit me again and smirked when a jack landed in front of me. I had never been much of a gambler, but for whatever reason tonight Lady Luck was with me as I was up three hundred bucks while I killed time waiting for Kressberg to make an appearance. It was nearly 10:00 PM and the late night crowd was filing in, along with an influx of patrons who had just left a stand-up comedy show in the adjoining Molson Canadian Theatre. A few hands later, I was closing in on four hundred dollars when I spotted Kressberg at a roulette table. He sported thick, black, Clark Kent-style glasses and was wearing a rumpled button-down shirt and jeans. He looked dishevelled and tired. Nevertheless, he dutifully placed big stacks of chips across the table and watched intently as the dealer spun the wheel one way and the little white ball shot off in the other direction. I collected my chips, tipped the dealer five bucks, and then headed toward Kressberg.

Stale, over-oxygenated air lingered while an endless cacophony of poker chips clacking and slot machine chiming echoed throughout the gaudy casino's main floor as I made my way toward Sykes' prized client. I took a spot at the roulette table next to Kressberg, who looked even rougher up close and smelled like a pack of menthols. I put a hundred bucks' worth of chips on an outside bet on black while Kressberg expertly placed a snake bet across the table. The dealer spun the wheel and when the ball landed on black thirty-three, Kressberg glanced at me and gave me a nod of approval.

"Always bet on black," I said.

"That your policy?" he asked.

I shook my head. "Wesley Snipes, *Passenger 57*."

Kressberg chuckled. "*Die Hard* on a plane."

"Almost as good as *Die Hard* on a bus."

"*Speed*."

"*Die Hard* on a train?"

"*Under Siege 2: Dark Territory*."

"*Die Hard* on a mountain?"

"*Cliffhanger*."

"*Die Hard* at an ice rink?"

That one gave Kressberg pause. He scratched his head as he racked his brain. "Steven Seagal?" he asked.

"Jean-Claude Van Damme, *Sudden Death*."

Kressberg snapped his fingers together like he had just missed the answer to the final round on *Jeopardy*! "Damn it, I knew that. Powers Boothe was the villain."

"Action goes into overtime," I said, quoting the film's cheesy tag line.

Kressberg laughed despite himself. He placed a double street inside bet then extended his hand. "I'm Alan," he said.

"Jed," I replied, shaking his hand.

Kressberg stared at me for a moment. "You look familiar."

"You a professional wrestling fan?"

"Not at all. Have you ever done any acting?"

"Actually, yeah. I did a guest spot on a sci-fi show a few years back just as my pro-wrestling career was blowing up. I was the villain of the week."

"*Time Paradox!*" said Kressberg, excitedly, as he slammed his hand down on the roulette table. "You were the cyborg assassin from a parallel universe."

I smiled, impressed that Kressberg had recalled one of my few non-wrestling appearances on cable TV. "How do you know that?" I asked.

"I was one of the writers on the show. I didn't script your episode, but I was in the writers' room when we broke the story. I was the one who suggested the assassin be a cyborg."

"Then I guess I should thank my maker. That guest spot helped boost my profile in the WWE and as a result, I went on to win the Intercontinental Championship."

"*Time Paradox*," said Kressberg, shaking his head. "I think that may have been the last time I actually enjoyed writing. It was original and edgy. Now all I do is adapt goddamn comic books into TV shows."

"They're pretty popular though, aren't they?"

"Insanely popular," conceded Kressberg. "But if I could, I'd go back to low-rated original sci-fi. At least there my imagination knew no bounds. With these goddamn superhero shows you're constantly being pressured by the network and fans into incorporating the latest heroes or villains from the source material."

"Still, I'd assume that you're doing quite well for yourself."

"Money's not the issue," muttered Kressberg, before we placed another round of bets.

I held my tongue and watched the roulette wheel spin. Kressberg's dejection with his work made me wonder if he was perhaps self-medicating with gambling. It certainly made sense given his apparent frustration. I felt bad for the guy and even worse for deceiving him. Here he was making hit TV shows and earning more money than he could spend, yet he was such a sad sack he was pouring his heart out to a stranger he had just met in a casino. I decided to come clean.

"Listen, Alan, I should probably tell you why I'm here. It's not an accident that I sat down at your table."

"You work for Sykes," he said, nonchalantly, before taking a sip from the bottle of Heineken he had in front of him.

"No, I don't—but … let's just say I'm here on his behalf. How did you know?"

"Because I'm well aware I'm owing, and people here don't ever talk to me. Especially big, muscle-bound dudes who know their nineties action movies."

"Fair enough," I said.

"I have the money in my car. I would have had it to Sykes on time but I was delayed a few weeks in Hong Kong for reshoots on this big summer tent-pole movie I'm working on."

I nodded. "Sykes figured as much."

Kressberg collected his chips and placed them in his tray. I just stuffed mine into my pockets. We walked silently across the casino floor. Kressberg left his tray of chips with a cashier before I followed him out the front doors. After being so chummy at the roulette table, it was starting to feel a bit uncomfortable as neither of us spoke as we made our way toward the multilevel, concrete monstrosity that served as the casino's parking lot.

"You been in the industry long?" I asked, awkwardly.

"My whole life," replied Kressberg. "Sound mixer, cameraman, script supervisor, line producer, editor, cinematographer, writer, director—you name it, I've done it."

"How about stuntman?" I asked.

Kressberg chuckled. "Okay, you got me there." He beeped his car remote and I saw the tail lights on a sleek, black Mercedes-AMG GT roadster flash red and the trunk open automatically.

"Nice ride," I said, admiring the two-hundred-thousand-dollar vehicle.

"Thanks. My parents sent me to boarding school in Germany as a kid and once I got a taste for driving on the Autobahn I was hooked for life."

"Makes sense to me, Bub."

"I just don't want you to think I'm one of those douchebags overcompensating for a micro-penis."

"Nah, not with a beauty like this. A red Ferrari on the other hand…." I trailed off as the hair on the back of my neck stood up. I felt a presence behind us and as Kressberg reached into the trunk to retrieve a navy-blue canvas duffel bag I turned around to find two heavies confronting us.

They stood diagonally on opposite sides of the Mercedes' rear bumper, essentially pinning us in between the giant slab of concrete wall behind us and a minivan and a SUV that were parked on opposite sides of Kressberg's car. The guy on my left was big—six-foot-six and maybe two hundred and sixty pounds of beef restrained under a tight black leather jacket. His hair was slicked back gangster-style and he stared at me with angry brown eyes.

"Alan," said the other man, spreading his hands wide. "We've been waiting for you."

Kressberg turned around and his face drained of colour. He stood there paralyzed, still clutching the handle of the duffel bag.

Between my Spidey-Sense tingling and Kressberg's reaction, I knew we were in a bad situation—I just didn't know how bad. I was angry that I had let them get the drop on us, but now was not the time to chastise myself. The man who spoke was dressed in black slacks with a tucked-in black button-down shirt, and both his thumbs were looped into his belt on opposite sides of a large silver and black buckle of a fleur-de-lys. His red hair was clipped and styled into a lengthy flat-top haircut, making his head resemble a paint brush.

"Aren't you going to introduce me to your friends?" I asked.

My question snapped Kressberg out of his trance. "I, uh, have placed bets with their employer in the past."

"And you're still owing," said Paint Brush.

"No, I'm not," snapped Kressberg. "I paid you the full amount."

"But not the vig."

"There was no vig! I paid the next day!" Kressberg insisted.

Paint Brush didn't like that one bit. "Keep your voice down," he spat venomously, his faux-friendly demeanour having vanished.

Kressberg looked at me in desperation. "I gave these guys every cent I owed and I did it right away, I swear. But they keep coming after me for more."

"How much debt do you say he has?" I asked Paint Brush.

Paint Brush and Beefy Leather Jacket exchanged a glance before the smaller man responded. "How much is in that bag?" he asked, pointing at the duffel in Kressberg's hand.

"You know, I've been around long enough to recognize a shakedown when I see one. You guys probably aren't even here on behalf of your employer, you just think you've found a golden goose. Just because Kressberg here farts out more money in a year than any of us will see in a lifetime doesn't give you the right to come sniffing around for handouts, especially if he's all squared up."

I had a feeling I wasn't too far off in my read of the situation as Paint Brush's face turned redder than his hair. "Who the fuck are you, his lawyer?" asked Paint Brush angrily.

"Think of me as a third-party transporter. And that money there has already been earmarked for someone else."

Paint Brush's brow furrowed. "I think you better take a walk," he growled, before nodding at his partner. On cue, the big man opened his leather jacket, showing off a shiny pistol with black grips tucked into his waistband. Kressberg cowered and meekly took a step forward. Before he could take another, I snatched the duffel bag out of his hand, tossed it back into the Mercedes' trunk, and slammed it shut. All three men stared at me in disbelief.

"Let's try this again," I said, turning back around. "We're going to be on our way, and you numbnuts aren't going to bother Kressberg anymore."

Paint Brush wasn't having it. "And why the hell would we do that? Seems to me, Big Leo and I have you two by the short-and-curlies." Both Big Leo and Paint Brush took a step forward, closing in on us like a couple of lions creeping up on their prey.

"No, no, no. You're doing it all wrong," I replied. "You don't call a guy that size Big Leo. You're supposed to be smugly ironic, which is why you should call him Li'l Leo or Tiny or something. Get it? The fact that he's an overgrown ass with caveman DNA is what makes it funny."

Leo must not have been fond of the new nicknames I had suggested as he pulled his gun. Kressberg stumbled backward until he hit the bumper of his Mercedes.

"You're going to want to put that away," I cautioned.

"I don't think so," snarled Paint Brush.

"It's really not a wise move to pull a gun on a cop."

That stopped them dead in their tracks. They exchanged a confused look before Paint Brush put his hands on his hips. "Bullshit," he said.

"I'm going to slowly reach for my badge, okay?"

Paint Brush hesitated, and then nodded slowly. I slid my hand into my back pocket and found my pop's old VPD badge. I had started carrying it around when I worked my first case un-officially, as it occasionally came in handy when trying to coerce someone into talking or granting me access to certain places where I was otherwise denied access. I pulled the badge out slowly and flipped it open for Paint Brush and Big Leo to see. They both squinted and leaned forward, trying to make out the photo on the badge and confirm it was mine.

Except it wasn't. It was my old man's mug, complete with a mustache, so bristly Tom Selleck and Sam Elliott themselves would have been impressed. Big Leo lowered the gun to his side as he kept leaning forward. I held out until the last second possible—trying to shorten the gap between us as much as I could—but the moment I saw a spark of confusion in both Big Leo and Paint Brush's eyes, I took an explosive step forward with my left leg before swinging my right as hard as I could. My foot connected with the revolver and sent it flying out of Big Leo's grip and across the parking lot. The top of my foot screamed out in pain from where my metacarpals had connected with the hard metal, but I didn't have a moment to spare. Not forgetting about Paint Brush in my blind spot, I snapped my pop's badge shut, pivoted, and flung it at his head like a ninja star. My aim was spot on and the hard corner of the badge's unforgiving leather case hit Paint Brush right in the eye.

"*Fuck!*" he wailed, before clutching his face. I turned back around just in time to see Leo reaching for my throat with the two giant mitts that passed for his hands. The big man latched both meathooks onto my neck, squeezing and violently shaking my head back and forth. Stars and bright spots danced in the corner of my eyes and I knew I didn't have long if I wanted to stay conscious. Fortunately, Big Leo was still leaning forward at an awkward angle, with both his feet spread wide and firmly planted on the ground. I wound up my throbbing right foot and kicked Big Leo as hard as I could in his crotch. The big man howled, released his death grip on my throat, and threw his arms up in the air. Wasting no time, I stomped just above the inside of his left ankle, and he hunched forward, reaching for the injured joint. I slipped around behind Big Leo, swept my foot, and kicked him in the back of the knees. He dropped to the ground kneeling, and I snaked my arm around his neck and put him in a rear naked chokehold. Seven seconds later Big Leo went limp. I let go of the hold and he dropped to the ground. Paint Brush held a hand over his injured eye and blinked furiously with the other, struggling with his lack of depth perception as he gawked at his partner passed out on the concrete.

"Back the car up and wait for me," I said hoarsely to Kressberg, who was wide-eyed and frozen as he leaned on the bumper of his Mercedes roadster. He nodded obediently before scurrying around to the driver's side of the vehicle.

I rubbed my aching throat and walked cautiously over to Paint Brush. It was clear he wasn't packing a pistol, but he could still have had a knife or some other weapon on him. He trained his good eye on me as I approached, before putting up both of his hands in surrender.

"Don't hurt me, man, please," he begged.

I picked up my old man's badge off of the ground and tucked it in my back pocket. "Are you and Leo going to leave Kressberg alone from now on?"

"Yes. I swear. We just—he was an easy mark, you know? We weren't ever gonna hurt him or anything," he said, his face contorted as he looked at me with one eye and kept the other one squinted shut.

Kressberg drove past us ten feet then stopped, the Mercedes' magnificent engine idling smoothly. "I'll be checking in with him. If I hear of anything, I'll be a lot less nice next time. Do you understand?"

"Totally," said Paint Brush. "Won't happen again. Just—just don't tell anyone about this, okay? Bygones."

I nodded my approval before glancing at Big Leo, who had regained consciousness and was groaning and writhing on the ground. I walked to the passenger side of the Mercedes, and then turned back around. Paint Brush's other eye was half-open now but watery. "I'm telling you, Li'l Leo is the way to go."

Paint Brush nodded dumbly. I got in the car and told Kressberg to drive.

"Where?"

"Do you like milkshakes, Alan?"

TWENTY-SEVEN

Because of the late hour, all of the Dairy Queens were closed, so I had to settle for a vanilla milkshake from a McDonald's drive thru. It was okay, but drinking a shake without banana in it made me feel like I was cheating on my wife with a mistress in our marital bed. Kressberg had barely said two words since the two goons had tried to shake him down and was nervous about driving me back to the casino so I could pick up my truck and he could cash in his chips.

"Trust me, those guys are long gone. And I'm pretty sure they won't be coming back. If they do, give me call," I said, placing a business card on his console directly beneath the Mercedes' radio.

"Take one of mine from the glove compartment," said Kressberg. I did and slipped his business card into my wallet. "I don't know how to thank you for this."

"Springing for a milkshake was a good start," I replied, before sipping more bland vanilla.

"If I can ever do anything for you—VIP set tours, meet-and-greets with the stars of any of my shows—hell, I can even get you another guest-star role if you'd like."

"Thanks, but I think my acting days are behind me. I'm pretty happy just sleuthing and laying the smackdown in the squared circle."

"Are you sure? There's nothing I can do?"

I thought for a moment. "Actually, there is one thing."

"Name it."

I took a slurp of my shake. "Take one of the big chunks of money you usually gamble away and instead make a donation to a charity."

"Which one?" asked Kressberg.

"Spinal Cord Injury BC."

Kressberg looked at me funny for a moment before giving a curt nod. "How's fifty thousand dollars sound?"

"Pretty damn good, Bub," I replied.

Kressberg steered his Mercedes into the parking lot of the casino and pulled up to the curb behind an idling suv limo. I got out of the sports car, and stood beneath the glowing, purple-and-red, thirty-foot electric guitar featuring the Hard Rock logo mounted on the exterior wall. He rolled down the passenger-side window and leaned over toward me.

"Kind of an odd combo, you know. Wrestler-detective."

"Beats being a fencing-proctologist."

Kressberg chuckled. "Thanks again, Jed."

I nodded. "If I were you, I'd stick with Sykes and forget placing bets with any other bookies. He's a bit cagey, but for the most part seems like a decent guy."

"I will."

"And Alan?"

"Yeah?"

"Pop the trunk."

Kressberg extended his hand and I shook it. I grabbed the duffel bag containing the seventy-five thousand dollars in cash from the Mercedes' trunk and headed toward my truck before stopping in my tracks. I turned around, marched back into the casino, cashed in the chips I had in my pocket for a cool three hundred and eighty dollars, and then made my way to my Ford F-150. I checked my phone as I buckled up behind the wheel, saw that I had one missed call from Stormy, and felt bad. I had been so caught up the last twenty-four hours trying to secure an audience with Hector Specter I had forgotten all about the intimacy we had shared the night before. I rang Stormy's number, put the call on speakerphone, then drove my truck up an on ramp and merged with westbound traffic on the Trans-Canada Highway.

"Jed," said Stormy softly.

"Hey," I replied dumbly.

"Are you okay?"

"Yeah, I uh—I saw you called and just wanted to check in."

"Check in?"

"Yeah. I didn't want you to think ... I mean, I thought I should ... uh, well, you know, after last night...."

"Jed?" she said, mercifully interrupting me.

"Yes?"

"I'm glad you called."

I exhaled a breath I didn't even know I had been holding. "Me too. It's been a long day."

"Did you want to stop by?"

I scratched the stubble on my face and sniffed the armpit of the army-green, long-sleeved American Eagle shirt that I had been wearing all day and winced. "I would love to, but I really need a hot shower, a shave, and some clean clothes."

"I understand," she said, sounding disappointed.

"I don't suppose you'd want to come over to my place tonight?"

"Of course I would."

I glanced at the clock on my dashboard. It was nearly 11:00 PM. "You sure it's not too late?"

"I'm sure."

"Okay, great. I'll text you my address."

"See you soon," she replied.

Fifty minutes later I was freshly showered, into a pair of sweat pants and a comfy, worn out wrestling T-shirt from my

WWE days and snuggling with Stormy Daze under a throw blanket on my couch while watching SportsCentre. Stormy nuzzled her head under my neck as the highlights of that night's Stanley Cup Playoffs flickered across the wall-mounted big-screen TV.

"This is nice," she said softly.

I had my arm around her shoulder, gave her a squeeze, then kissed the top of her head. It had been awhile since I had been with anyone and I'd forgotten how comforting the companionship could be. I thought of Rya and how she had held my hand at the scene of Lawrence's murder and my heart skipped a beat. There had always been chemistry between us, but the timing never seemed to work out. I had opened up to her as I never had to anyone before and ever since our relationship had felt deeply intimate to me. I thought I had blown it for good when I failed to fully trust her while working my first case, but our interaction at the Lamplighter, however brief, had given me hope. But Stormy's sudden arrival appeared to snuff out that flickering flame, and now here I was with a beautiful, supportive, and kind woman on my arm. Our connection was easy, playful, and drama-free, whereas despite my feelings for Rya, our dynamics had always suffered from a certain degree of complexity.

My thoughts shifted from Rya to Lawrence's murder and how it could be directly related to his efforts to stop the formation of a national roller derby league. From the sound of it, Hector Specter had business-venture ADHD, so it didn't track that he would take the risk of bumping off a lowly coach merely for gumming up the works of only one of his many deals. But if Specter really was a driving force behind taking the sport mainstream, odds are he would know best if there was anyone who had the most to lose by the aborting of such a league. I thought about the man in the grey suit with the bowler hat and how with his stealthy surveillance skills he must be a professional hit man. Leaving behind the bowler hat was a sloppy move, but I assumed the van was stolen and that there would be no prints inside because one would most certainly wear gloves if planning to ditch a vehicle after using it to commit vehicular homicide. The only chance Rya and the VPD had to nail him was with DNA from his hat, but without a comparison sample, it would be useless. I still didn't know how the man in the suit first got onto my tail, unless one of the Split-Lip Sallies was in on it and leaked the info about me being hired by the team. Or perhaps he had simply been staking out Lawrence's apartment and took notice of me sniffing around. Either way, despite the fact I had only glimpsed him twice, he had proven himself to be a rather formidable foe.

Stormy sighed softly and nuzzled me some more, snapping my mind out of its wandering and into the moment. I didn't really know what to make of things with Rya or what the future might hold for Stormy and me. I just knew that I liked her a lot.

I excused myself and went to the washroom. I splashed some cold water on my face to fight off the fatigue setting in, and then called out to Stormy from behind the bathroom door. "I'm gonna grab a beer. Did you want anything?"

There was no response. I dried my hands and opened the sliding door only to see Stormy on her knees in the kitchen, holding stacks of hundreds in both of her hands, as the navy-blue duffel bag on the floor in front of her hemorrhaged wads of cash from its open zipper. Stormy looked up from the money she was holding and stared at me, looking stunned and frightened.

I flashed my best million-dollar smile. "You would not believe the luck I had at blackjack tonight."

TWENTY-EIGHT

"What the hell is this?" Stormy demanded.

"That would be seventy-five thousand dollars."

"Are you … are you involved in illegal activities?"

I hesitated before answering. I really didn't want to lie to her, but the truth was that I did have a habit of occasionally skirting the law in order to get ahead while working a case. Like the time I impersonated a police officer so I could gain access to the Vancouver morgue in order to perform an illegal necropsy on a dead snake, only to cut it open and find out that the reptile had died by ingesting a large quantity of rare methamphetamines from Thailand. You know, that same old story.

"I'm no criminal," I said, defensively. "It's just sometimes in order to do my job I have to do things a little … out of bounds."

"So that's why you have tens of thousands in cash in a bag in your kitchen?"

"Pretty much. You see," I said, pointing at the bag, "I only have that money because I had to run an errand."

"An errand?" she asked, exasperated.

"A gambling debt collection errand. For a particularly slick and well-connected bookmaker with a prize-winning racing wiener dog, who would only agree to arrange an audience for me with a beverage baron—and person of interest in Lawrence's murder—if I retrieved the money he was owed."

"What?"

"I'm sorry, I shouldn't have said wiener dog. Napoleon is a thoroughbred dachshund."

Stormy shook her head and tossed the wads of cash she was holding onto the floor in disgust. "I think I should go."

"Stormy, wait," I pleaded.

"I'm sorry, Jed. I can't be around sketchy stuff like this. I've worked too hard to get my life back on track."

"Fair enough. But to be honest, I don't really know what's happening here. I mean, between us. Whether it's something real, or if we're just enjoying each other's company—I'm not sure. But what I do know is that I feel a connection to you. I don't know what that means, and I certainly don't have it figured out, but I would hate for things to end before they even really had a chance to start."

Stormy climbed to her feet and crossed her arms.

"I'm not perfect," I said. "Hell, I'm far from it. But I like to think that I'm a good enough man that I would always treat you right and never intentionally let you down. I'll admit that I get pulled into some arguably shady stuff from time to time due to my investigations, there's no doubt about that. But it's not by design. It's because I'm a horse chasing a carrot and I'll be damned if I don't give my clients the absolute best service I can."

"I'm your client," she said forcefully.

I sighed. "You're right. But you know why I can't let this one go. Which is why returning that bag of money to a bookmaker allows me to make headway into finding Lawrence's murderer."

Stormy considered my words before speaking. "How?"

I explained to her how Lawrence was leading efforts to block the development of a women's national roller derby and how I thought that may have been what got him killed.

"And you think this Vancouver investor guy could be involved?" she asked.

"I think he could potentially lead me to the person who may have the most to lose if this proposed league falls through."

"You know, I hate to say it, but such a league might not be that bad an idea. I think lot of girls would go for it if derby could actually provide a part-time salary."

"Yosef Dillon said that Lawrence found the idea blasphemous. That it would betray everything that made women's roller derby special. That the sport was punk rock and renegade and helping form a league like this would be akin to selling out."

"Damn it," said Stormy, shaking her head.

"What?"

"He's right. Larry was always right. But I still think a lot of girls might be on board if there was money involved, dishonour to derby be damned. Not everyone shares his unshakeable moral high ground."

I started picking up the wads of bills and putting them back into the duffel bag with Stormy's help.

"Well, regardless, Lawrence's mind was made up and he was making strong moves to stop the development of this league. Dillon said he was close to getting the majority of people affiliated with the WFTDA to go public and reject the idea right before he was murdered."

"So who benefits the most from the formation of a national roller derby league?" asked Stormy.

"That's what I'm trying to find out. You ever heard of a guy named Hector Specter?"

Stormy shook her head. "That's the investor guy?"

"Yes."

"And that's his real name?"

I shrugged, zipping up the duffel and placing it back on the kitchen counter. "Not sure. But douchebag name or not, if he can point me in the right direction, I might be one step closer to finding out who had a reason to want Lawrence dead."

Stormy leaned back against the kitchen counter. "I can't believe that crazy son of a bitch got himself killed because he was trying to defend the integrity of derby. That's, like, the most Larry-way possible for him to have died."

I cracked the lid of the can of beer I had retrieved from my fridge and took a big swig. My mind drifted off momentarily, swirling with a medley of thoughts of all I had learned so far, wondering where it could be leading. "All I know is that Lawrence deserved better," I said finally.

Stormy smiled, pushed herself off of the counter, and slipped her arms around my waist. She stood up on her toes and kissed me on the lips. "So what happens next?" she asked, staring deeply into my eyes.

"I was going to drink this beer and take you to bed," I replied.

"I meant with your case."

"Right. Sorry. I guess we'll find out tomorrow."

Stormy cupped a hand on my cheek. "Just promise me you'll be careful. I've already lost Johnny and now Larry … I couldn't bear to lose you too."

"Are you kidding? I can't afford to get bumped off right now. I've got like half-a-dozen people who've recently done me favours coming to my next wrestling show and they're expecting me to put on a barnburner of a match."

"It's nice to know that's what's motivating you to stay alive," Stormy said sarcastically.

I killed the rest of my beer, stifled a burp, and slammed the empty can down on the counter. "Alllllllllllll righty, then!" I bellowed, in my best Ace Ventura voice.

Stormy didn't stop laughing until we were in my bed and under the sheets.

TWENTY-NINE

I had never heard an animal moan orgasmically before, but I imagined the low, guttural noise being emitted by Napoleon came awfully close. The little dachshund lay on his side on a padded table while his masseuse worked her thumbs up and down his ribcage before starting in on the taut, sinewy, canine muscle that made up the majority of his hind legs.

Sykes sat in a nearby chair inside the private room at Precious Paws Massage in North Vancouver, casually perusing the latest issue of *Cigar Aficionado* magazine, featuring Arnold Schwarzenegger on the cover, grinning from ear to ear and holding up a stogie so long at first glance it looked like it could rival the length of the prized wiener dog itself.

"Mr. Ounstead," said Sykes, before patting the empty chair next to him. "Please, have a seat."

The doggy masseuse ignored me as I walked past her and her client in the dimly lit room and sat down next to Sykes. I placed the duffel bag at my feet and sat through thirty seconds of rainforest sounds before I couldn't take anymore.

"You know, this dog has a better quality of life than most people."

"All elite athletes receive similar treatment, Mr. Ounstead," said Sykes, flipping a page of his magazine.

As if on cue, Napoleon moaned loudly again, and I noticed that his masseuse had moved on from his hind legs to his lower back.

"You really think doggy massages will make a difference in his racing ability?"

The bookmaker closed his magazine and turned to look at me. "I think they will make all the difference." Sykes glanced at the duffel bag at my feet. "I hope no paddles were necessary this time?"

"No. However, there was an incident."

I told Sykes about the two goons who had been moonlighting and tried to squeeze some extra cabbage out of Kressberg. Sykes nodded and listened calmly before crossing his legs and stroking his chin.

"I appreciate you encouraging Mr. Kressberg to keep his wagers solely with me."

"I didn't do it for you, Sykes. I did it for his well-being."

"Regardless, it is still to my benefit."

I slid the bag across the floor with my foot until it was in front of Sykes. "And my meeting with Hector?"

"Taken care of. He is expecting you this Saturday afternoon at the Best Buy location on Cambie Street."

"He wants to meet at an electronics store?"

"He is going to be there doing an in-store promotional appearance with his band. But his security people are aware you are coming and will grant you access."

"That son of a bitch has a band too?"

"Apparently. I am afraid I do not enjoy discussing Hector Specter's extracurricular activities, Mr. Ounstead. So unless there is something else, I believe our business here today has been concluded."

Sykes cracked open his magazine and resumed reading. I headed for the door, but not before stopping to give Napoleon a scratch on the head. The little wiener dog cracked an eyelid open and licked my hand before the masseuse had him flip to his other side. I exited the doggy spa and got in my truck. As I drove away I started a mental checklist of all of the questions I wanted to ask the no-longer-elusive Hector Specter.

My thoughts were interrupted when I realized I was driving over the Lions Gate Bridge, and my mind was flooded with vivid memories of what had gone down the last time I had driven this particular route. The song "Welcome to the Black Parade" by My Chemical Romance snapped me out of my trance once the tune's chorus started rocking. I slid my phone out of my jeans pocket and answered the incoming call from a very familiar number.

"Hey."

"How's she cuttin'?" asked my cousin.

"Not bad. I finally made some headway on the case."

"Well done, Boyo. But your Da just finished up that background check and asked me to give your arse a ring. He wants ya to swing by the pub *tits-sweet*."

"*Tits-sweet?*"

"Aye. 'Tis French. Means right away. Me bunny babe is originally from Montreal so I'm trying to pick up some o'her native tongue so I can impress her when she gets back in town."

"Declan, I think you're trying to say *tout de suite*."

"Pretty sure it's *tits-sweet*, Mate."

I shook my head and gave up. "Did the old man dig up anything interesting?"

"Don't know. Been too busy to ask."

I glanced at the clock on the dashboard. 1:17 PM. Happy hour was still a ways off and it was rare the Emerald Shillelagh got busy before then. "Busy doing what?"

"Tending to David Hasselhop. The poor wee bugger has diarrhea."

"Rabbits get diarrhea?"

"Like you wouldn't believe. I think he may o'gobbled up some bad lettuce or some shite when he got out o'his cage the last time. Little bastard's like a fluffy Houdini."

"I thought he only ate if he listened to Shakira songs?"

"What do ya think I've been playin' over the pub's speaker system non-stop?"

Ten minutes later I walked into my old man's pub to find my cousin cradling David Hasselhop in one arm and trying to pour a little plastic cup of Pepto-Bismol into the rabbit's mouth with the other.

"What the hell? D, you're going to kill the thing!" I exclaimed.

"I bloody well am not. And if you've seen the size o'the sloppy shites I've been mopping up all morning you'd be doing the same thing."

"Is that even safe?"

"O'course it is. I did a Google search and everything. Give me a hand, will ya?"

I shrugged and took the little cup of antacid medicine and proceeded to pour it down the rabbit's throat while Declan used his other hand to prop the bunny's mouth open. The little guy lapped it up before Declan gave him a few strokes on the head and put him back in his cage behind the bar.

"And people say raisin' kids is hard," lamented my cousin.

"We just gave Pepto-Bismol to a rabbit with the runs. It's not exactly the same thing."

"Piss off it ain't. And if me bunny babe and Trixie Titties let me have me way ya might be seein' Declan Jr. runnin' around these parts sometime soon."

"You're planning on impregnating and entering into a poly-amorous relationship with your girlfriend with the bunny fetish and the biggest-breasted bald woman I've ever seen?"

"Bollocks! Of course not. Don't be such a stook."

I let out a sigh in relief.

"I would never knock up me bunny babe. She's way too tiny. Trixie Titties is the one with the perfect birthing hips. Can you imagine the size o'the rugrats she could pump out?"

My father mercifully interrupted us as he made his way down the stairs and lumbered toward me with a large folder. "Sit," he commanded. I did as I was told and pulled up a stool at the bar. My old man slid his seat to the left to make space for his massive girth before sitting beside me. He slapped the blue folder down on the bar top and grunted at my cousin. "Some black stuff, son."

"Aye, Frank, don't get your bloody knickers in a twist," Declan replied. "I started on it the moment I heard ya comin' down the stairs like King Kong." Declan proceeded to pour several pints of Guinness. We left my cousin to work his magic and my father opened the folder and slapped a ham-sized palm down on top of it.

"This goddamn Hector Specter is something else," my father announced.

"How so?" I asked.

"For starters his name ain't Hector Specter. Legal name is Hector Spanopolous."

"That sounds a bit more Greek."

"Yeah, well the name's not the only thing. His father died when he was in his early twenties and he inherited about ten million dollars and his family's frozen food empire, Cerastes Brands. He has one sister, but she moved back to Greece not long after they lost their father. Hector dropped out of college to run the company and spent the next twenty years expanding and growing the business. He's taken it from a relatively modest frozen-food company to a top-tier brand by incorporating Greek-fusion meals, energy drinks, and most recently liquor. It's now one of the biggest frozen-food companies in all of Canada, right up there nipping at the heels of McCain. And Spanopolous has nearly doubled his net worth in the process."

"Is his booze any good?" asked Declan, who had slung a bar towel over his shoulder and crossed his arms while he waited for the two-thirds-full pints of Guinness in front of him to settle.

"As far as I can tell, it's mediocre at best," said my old man. "But he's done an effective job at marketing his liquor line."

"He's behind all of that Greek mythological stuff that's come out the last couple of years," I added.

Declan scoffed and started topping up one of the pints. "I tried some o'that Pegasus Pilsner a few months back. They should call it Pegasus Piss instead," he sniped, before etching a shamrock into the head of the Guinness and placing it in front of my father. The old man flipped a few pages and continued.

"Read through this entire thing. There's more in here about his previous business ventures, mostly failures, but a few successes. Cerastes Brands remains his bread and butter and gives him the capital to try and break into other markets. Spanopolous is nothing if not bold, I'll give him that. But his ambition often gets the best of him. Anyway, here's what really caught my eye. The shady bastard has been sued over two dozen times."

"For what?"

"Fraud, defamation, stiffing contractors, sexual harassment, sexual assault—the guy is a real piece of shit."

"Contractors?" I asked.

"Spanopolous got into the construction business in the mid-aughts. Went in with some partners and built a bunch of condos around Greater Vancouver. A lot of them turned out to be leaky. Settled a few cases out of court, but for the most part he got away with building some shitty properties. He has a pattern of behaviour when it comes to his legal affairs—he bullies anyone who challenges him and can afford to tie things up in court for years until the plaintiff either settles or throws in the towel."

Declan placed pints of Guinness with perfect shamrocks etched into their creamy heads in front of us. The three of us wordlessly held up our pints and clinked our glasses, before taking long sips of the delicious beverage.

My old man licked the froth from his lips and nodded approvingly at Declan. "Damn good, Boy."

"'Tis like suckin' nectar from the teet o'Aphrodite herself."

"Tell me about the sexual assault," I said to my father.

He nodded and wet his whistle again before continuing. "This is where it gets icky. Spanopolous is currently in a legal dust-up and headed for court soon. He had a partner a few years ago in a failed role-playing adventure dinner-cruise business. Kind of like those pirate adventures they have for kids on Granville Island, except Spanopolous' was focused on Greek mythology. Customers would take boat rides around False Creek and use water guns to fight off sea monsters and sirens and stuff. Anyway, it was too high-budget and unlike the pirate adventures, Spanopolous' business model wasn't sustainable."

"This guy really does have a taste for the theatrical," I said.

"And then some," replied my father. "But his partner in the dinner-cruise business? Spanopolous had sex with his sixteen-year-old daughter just as their company was going belly up."

"Janey Mack!" exclaimed Declan. "Even I know to bloody well steer clear o'jailbait. Goddamn it, Jed, ya sure know how to pick them."

"Girl claims he got her inebriated and pressured her to have sex. They're headed to court in the next couple of months."

My father closed the Duo-Tang folder and polished off the rest of his Guinness. "You have any idea where you're going to start with this character?"

"Eye on the ball, Pop. Just like you taught me. This stuff is interesting," I said, tapping a finger on the Duo-Tang folder. "And it definitely gives me a better idea of whom I'm dealing with, but I'm going to meet him for one reason and one reason only—to find Specter's connection to this proposed national women's roller derby league, and to learn who may have had the most to lose by Lawrence trying to kibosh the deal."

My father patted me on the back and smiled. The force was so strong I spilled a bit of Guinness on the bar top.

"That's my boy," he said, proudly.

Declan whipped the towel off of his shoulder and wiped up the spilled Guinness. "There's just one thing I don't understand, fellas," said my cousin, before leaning forward on the bar and looking at us both with a solemn expression.

"When are we gonna get our shite together and leg it over to the nearest sports arena so we can watch some o'these brilliant, big-boobed babes on roller skates knock the ever-lovin' hell out o'one another?"

THIRTY

I spent the days leading up to my meeting with Hector Specter hitting the gym, running errands, and lying low at my townhouse while I studied my old man's background report. I reviewed the material and played tunes from the album *Sabbatical* by Vancouver's very own version of Moby, James Landau, whose calming beats helped me both relax yet stay razor-sharp mentally.

When I got into the background report, I realized that it was more of the same that we went over at the pub, with an endnote about Specter's recent dalliances in the entertainment industry, including his weekly talk show, which was given the cringe-worthy moniker of *Late Night Nectar with Hector Specter*. In addition to a traditional talk show interview, Hector and all of his guests were featured enjoying cocktails, beer, and wine from his liquor line during the interviews. I made the mistake of checking out some YouTube clips of the show and holy hell was it bad. Painfully, brutally bad.

Specter's monologue was particularly awful, as he tried way too hard to sell unfunny jokes. It took me about thirty seconds to realize how insufferably smug he was on camera, and perpetually pleased with himself, often laughing at his own "zingers." Specter spent more time looking at his house band for forced laughter than the camera or the audience after delivering a punchline, and there was no doubt the monologue was beefed up with a laugh track. He wore a gaudy three-piece suit with a sparkling, over-sized pinky ring, and had slicked-back, dark hair grown wispy to balding around his widow's peak. Nevertheless, it was clear that Specter thought of himself as quite handsome. After about four minutes, the monologue mercifully ended and, before YouTube could queue up a sketch featuring Specter embarrassingly dressed in drag with a giant blonde bouffant, I clicked my web browser shut, not wanting to prematurely prejudice my in-person impression of the man any more than I already had.

I hadn't seen Stormy Daze since she had slept over earlier in the week. She had headed to Whistler for a girlfriend's stagette, but since she had also been texting me daily, and included an excessive amount of kissy-face emojis in each message, I figured we were okay. We had made plans to get together at some point on the weekend upon her return, but for now I wasn't thinking past my meeting with Hector on Saturday afternoon.

On the day of his appearance at the Cambie Street Best Buy I headed over to the nearby Olympic Village a bit early and treated myself to lunch at Craft Beer Market. A buddy of mine from my bouncing days had moved on to a very lucrative career as a carpenter, and had been hired by the casual restaurant and eatery to build their elongated bar. I arrived alone, walked by the patio into a building that looked like the offspring of a giant warehouse and a rustic red barn, before taking a seat at the giant oval bar. I eyeballed the more than one hundred beers they had on tap, and, despite the fact I was flying solo, realized I was going to have all of the friends I needed to enjoy a delicious meal. I ordered the Phillips Beer Can Chicken with no mashed potatoes but double seasonal vegetables, and chased down with a matching pint of Blue Buck Ale.

I was working my teeth with a toothpick when I noticed a man in a grey suit about thirty feet away walking toward the men's room. We were indoors so naturally he wasn't wearing a hat, but given the man's slight stature and similar height, from behind he looked similar to the murderous voyeur who had been stalking me. I bolted off my stool, chased after him, and charged into the restroom, only to find myself alone. I crept forward cautiously, my arms halfway up and ready in case of an impending attack. I knew that the man in the grey suit had to be in one of the stalls, but he had clearly sensed me coming after him because as I dipped my head and leaned down I saw that there were no feet on the floor in any of the bathroom's three toilet stalls. I moved cautiously and quietly before catching a glimpse of some grey suit in the thin crack of the middle stall where the door met the lock. I squared up toward the stall, dropped into a fighting stance, then kicked open the door as hard as I could.

"Jesus Christ!" yelped the man on the toilet. His heels were on the edge of the seat, his pants were around his ankles, and he was sitting in a squat position. The slim, grey-suited man had soft features and an elongated nose, but unlike the creepy bastard who killed Lawrence, he had brown eyes instead of the pair of icy blue daggers that had pierced holes into me.

"Why the hell are you sitting like that?" I asked.

"Why the hell are you watching me shit, pervert?!"

"I'm not, I'm just—why are you hiding your feet in the stall?"

"I'm not hiding my feet, I have a sensitive colon!"

"What?"

"Haven't you heard of the Squatty Potty?"

"Squatty Potty?"

"It's a stool that elevates your knees when you—wait, why the hell am I explaining this? Fuck off! Let me crap in peace!"

I apologized and closed the door to his stall. He let fly a string of obscenities while I hightailed it out of the bathroom. Thankfully, my bill was waiting for me when I got back to my spot at the bar. I whipped out my wallet, left a generous tip, and got the hell out of the restaurant.

I rounded a corner at Ash and West 7th Street and by the time I hit Cambie I had my game face on. My heartbeat spiked and I found myself a bit nervous realizing I had only one shot to make my meeting with Hector Specter count. I used an old pre-match wrestling trick, took a few deep breaths, and exhaled forcefully while clenching and unclenching my fists. By the time I walked through the entrance to the Best Buy I was calm and focused, although the moment I saw Hector on a makeshift stage singing into a microphone was disconcerting.

"*Yeaaaaaaaaaaaaahhhhhhhhhh, yeaaaaaaahhhhh, yeaaaaaahhhhh!*" Hector bellowed, while a long-haired, hippie-looking trombone player worked the instrument's slide back and forth beside him. Half-a-dozen other musicians surrounded Hector on stage, all vigorously playing their brass instruments, keyboards, and drums in a manner so mediocre I had to fight off the instinct to plug my ears with my fingertips. Hector's rhythm-and-blues song was annoying, and from the way his sweat-stained silk shirt stuck to his gelatinous torso, I could tell that he was at least several songs into his set.

"*I … will … dooooooo … anything that I can! To bring out the cheer in you! No more sad, just smiles for you!*" crooned Hector, whose garbled voice was coarser than a sheet of sandpaper. Despite being taken aback by his terrible performance, Hector and his band were actually not the most painfully awkward thing in the store. Two dozen middle-aged women—some frumpy, some with big hair and faces caked in makeup—crowded around the stage, bopping their heads along to the music. As this collection of aging ladies jived to the song, a man in a *Late Night Nectar with Hector Specter* T-shirt worked a large video camera, prowled around the women, and recorded close-ups of their adoring faces and ungainly dance moves.

"Cut!" yelled out a skinny director, also wearing one of Specter's TV show shirts as well as a black baseball cap. "No, no, no. This is no good. Ladies, we need bigger smiles! We need more enthusiasm! Let's get some clapping going as well. We want the kind of reaction The Beatles or Elvis got, not a Nickelback tribute band!"

The ladies nodded their heads and collectively grumbled.

"Take five, everyone!" ordered the director.

Hector hopped off the stage and grabbed a bottle of water and a towel off a chair. I cut a path through the crowd toward him when one of his security guards intercepted me. He put up a hand, nearly making contact with my chest. Luckily for him he didn't.

"Hold up, big boy," said the guard.

"I have an appointment with Hector. He's expecting me." Before the guard could respond Hector scurried over toward us. He was shorter than I expected, and with the seven or eight-inch height difference, I towered over him.

"He's cool, Jimmy! This is the guy I was telling you about." Hector extended a sweaty palm and I tried not to wince while I shook it. "You're the wrestler," he said, still short of breath from his caterwauling. "Mr. Hammerhead."

"You can just call me Jed."

"Okay, Jed," replied Hector cheerily. "What do you think?" he asked, waving toward the stage and ladies behind him.

"Pretty cool," I said, lying through my teeth. "Those ladies are, uh … die-hard fans, eh?"

"Believe it or not, they're mostly paid extras. I'm having one of my camera guys shoot some footage so we can make a music video for my show. You hungry? We got some great craft service set up over by the Home Theatre section."

"Sure."

Hector gave Jimmy a pat on his shoulder. "We're good, Jimbo." Jimmy nodded obediently and stepped aside. Hector started toweling himself down as we walked through the store. "So I hear you've had a real hard-on to meet with me."

"You have to admit—you're not exactly an easy guy to track down for a chat."

"Is that why you tuned up my guy at my restaurant? You were frustrated?"

"Not at all. Your guy moved on me."

Hector nodded. "Vlassis can be a bit overzealous."

We reached the craft service table, full of more pastries and sweets than a bakery run by Willy Wonka. I looked for a veggie tray or a fruit plate, but there was nothing save for a couple of badly bruised bananas by a bowl of red punch, which immediately made me crave a banana milkshake. Hector helped himself to a glazed donut and took a big bite. He looked me over up and down as he licked some frosting off of his lips and continued to dab the sweat from his brow and the back of his neck with a towel.

"I looked you up online, you know."

"Then there's a pretty good chance you've seen me break a two-by-four piece of Western red cedar over my head," I replied.

Hector smiled. "How the hell do you do that by the way?"

"It's weakened beforehand. They're not terribly difficult to snap in half, but when you do it, it still stings every time. Trade secret."

"You were kind of a big deal in professional wrestling, weren't you?"

"I had my moments."

"'Hammerhead' Jed. That's some great goddamn branding right there. Did you come up with that yourself?"

I nodded. "You're not too shabby yourself. Your Greek mythological liquor line seems to be working out well for you."

Hector finished his donut and started licking his fingertips. I tried not to cringe at the loud slurping sounds he was making.

"Fucking genius, right? I'm making a killing off of that shit. Horned Viper Vodka, Gryphon Gin, Pegasus Pilsner, Winged Horse Whisky—plus I got a new one we're getting ready to launch."

"Let me guess. Titan Tequila?"

"No, Apollo Absinthe. But damn, that's fucking golden! Do you mind if I use it?"

"Have at it, Bub."

Hector smiled. "People are stupid. They love alliterations and stuff that rhymes. They eat it up."

I kept my mouth shut while Hector continued to insult the masses, not wanting to reveal that I disagreed with his cynical perspective. He kept talking.

"I had a feeling I'd like you, Jed. You know what you've got?"

"You mean besides a thick skull?"

Hector laughed heartily and gave me a pat on the back. He was either warming up to me or playing me, but I still couldn't tell which.

"You've got gumption. And a sterling silver set of balls as well. I'd really like to help you out if I can. Sykes said something about you being a private investigator?"

"Yes. And you happen to be a person of interest in a case that I'm currently working."

"Fair enough," said Hector, chuckling. "Sykes hinted as much. He's such a snobby prick. He acts like he's better than me even though he's still hustling on the street while I'm worth a hundred times what he is."

"I won't deny that he's into some questionable stuff, but the guy has always been above board with me," I replied earnestly.

Hector shrugged and continued. "Did you know my last name isn't actually 'Specter?' he asked.

"You're kidding," I said, feigning surprise.

"It's Spanopolous."

"That's not so bad. You wouldn't believe how many times I've been called 'Hammerhead' Jed *'Oooon-sted.'*"

"That's not how you say it?"

"Phonetically it's pronounced *'OW-n-sted.'* But it's spelled *'O-U-N-S-T-E-A-D.'*"

"Well, screw it, I say. Change it if you don't like it. I did. I became Hector fucking Specter. You know how I came up with that? I stole it from that lawyer show, *Suits*. That guy on the show Harvey Specter, he's baller as hell. And now, so am I."

I nodded politely, despite thinking that this was quite possibly the stupidest reason ever for a man to change his name.

"Plus it allows me to call my show *Late Night Nectar with Hector Specter* and promote my booze by having everyone drink it on the show. People love rhymes, remember? Fucking idiots."

It was getting more and more challenging to accept Hector's tangent thoughts. He grabbed a can of Sprite from the craft services table, popped the top, and took a big slurp.

"I'm inclined to help you out, Jed. Provided you do the same for me."

"I'm listening."

"Here's my proposition—you come on my show as the headliner guest and I'll do everything in my power to assist you. Trust me, I have a lot of resources."

I shook my head despite myself. Between Sykes and Hector, I was cutting deals left and right. Just once it would be nice getting some help without having to engage in some quid pro quo.

"I'm kind of looking to avoid the spotlight."

"I was told that you're wrestling again and drawing big crowds."

I sighed and thought about the recent matches I had been having with XCCW. Then I thought about the large cash donations I was regularly making to Spinal Cord Injury BC and the reason for why I was doing it.

"You're a local celebrity, Jed," continued Hector. "Don't fight it. Own it. And if you come on my show I guarantee you'll increase the turnout for your wrestling matches."

Since Hector's television program was late night, pre-paid, infomercial time, I highly doubted it could help increase attendance at all. That being said, if making an appearance on his crappy show would make him keen to assist in my investigation, I didn't really have a choice.

"All right, I'll do it."

Hector smacked a hand on his thigh victoriously. "Fantastic!" he exclaimed. "I've actually been playing with the format of the show—next week we're going to go live for the first time ever. And screw it—I'm bumping my first scheduled guest for Mr. Hammerhead!"

"It's just 'Hammerhead' Jed."

"Fuck yeah, it is!" A few of the middle-aged lady extras, who were still being coached by the music video director, lost focus and gawked at us after taking note of Hector's exuberance. "At the end of the interview, can I pull out a two-by-four from behind the desk as a surprise and have you crack it over your head?"

I sighed and wondered if my former wrestling gimmick would haunt me for the rest of my days. "I'd hate to disappoint."

Hector clapped his hands. "That's great TV! Okay, so do you have like a card or something? My assistant will be in touch and conduct a pre-interview so you'll be properly prepped."

I handed Hector my business card and he tucked it in the breast pocket of his sweaty silk shirt. He slapped both of his hands onto my shoulders and a big, shit-eating grin spread across his face.

"Jesus, your deltoids are like boulders! What kind of weights are you lifting? Cast iron cannonballs?"

"Something like that," I replied, somewhat pleased that the addition of kettlebells to my workouts seemed to be having the desired effect.

"Awesome. All right, big fella. You'll hear from me soon." Hector grabbed a chocolate donut hole from a Tim Hortons box, popped it into his mouth, and started to walk away.

"Uh, Hector?"

"Yeah?"

"The deal was that I would go on your show in exchange for you helping me with my investigation."

"Shit, right!" he said, snapping his fingers together. "Sorry, Champ. Hey, were you actually a champ?"

"Tag Team and Intercontinental."

"Nice. I fucking love gold," he said, running his fingertips along the thick gold chain he was wearing around his neck.

Just then the music video director scurried over. "We're all set, boss."

"Gonna need a few minutes." The director nodded obediently and hurried off. "Sorry," said Hector. "Got a lot of irons in the fire."

"No worries and this won't take long. But I do have a few important questions."

Hector nodded and crossed his arms over his silk shirt. I could see the sweat sparkling on his hairy forearms. I diverted my gaze and tried to stay on point.

"Do you know of a guy named Lawrence Kunstlinger?"

"Ha!" Hector kept laughing until he realized that I wasn't. "Wait, seriously?"

"Yes, that's his name."

"Who is he? Some cowboy porn star or something?"

"He's the coach of a local women's roller derby team. At least he was, until he was recently murdered."

Hector's eyes widened as he clued into where I was going. "You know about the league, don't you?"

I nodded. "I also know that Lawrence was the person mobilizing a resistance to halt the formation of your league. He had gathered a tremendous amount of support and almost had the WFTDA on board when he died."

"WFTDA?"

"Women's Flat Track Derby Association. And don't play dumb. You know who they are."

"I knew there was an association. I just didn't know what it was called."

"Word is you're the driving force behind the whole effort to create a professional league and monetize women's roller derby."

"You're goddamn right I am," crowed Hector proudly. "Think about what you just said. Can't you smell the money? You're a wrestler, for Christ's sake. You of all people should get it. Roller derby is just as colourful as what you do—except with hot chicks on roller skates. It's an untapped gold mine."

"A gold mine that someone who had a vested interest might not have appreciated Lawrence getting in the way."

Hector uncrossed his arms and put his hands on his hips. "You think that's why he was killed? Because he was trying to stop the league from happening?"

"Who has the most to lose by it not taking off? You? Some of your fellow investors?"

"I could take it or leave it. I just love new business opportunities and think this is a money idea. Do you know how much I'm worth? Trust me, babes on roller skates would be a blast, but if the league doesn't come together I'll be just fine. I have plenty of other ventures to keep me busy. I mean, look at those hotties over there," he said, waving to the decidedly non-hottie-like, middle-aged ladies. "They've been here for two hours already because they all want a piece of Hector Specter."

"I thought they were paid extras for your music video."

"Whatever, they're still here. And between my upcoming EP dropping, a concert tour across Western Canada, my talk show, restaurant, food, energy drink, and liquor lines, I barely have enough time to take a crap."

"And your partners who want to start a national roller derby league?"

"Are all a bunch of rich assholes like me who think trying to make bank off of some tits and trim on wheels is a fun idea. I mean, come on, man! How many times do I need to keep saying it? Hot chicks on roller skates knocking the hell out of one another! It's unreal. But this roller derby league is just something we want to use our play money for. If you honestly think any of us would take it so seriously that we'd actually try and have a guy bumped off then you're nuts. It's not like any of us involved have anything to lose if the league doesn't … *oh, shit*."

"What?"

"Nothing."

I took a step closer to Hector, who, despite continuing to wipe himself down, still managed to be glistening with sweat. "That didn't sound like nothing."

"It's just, me, the other guys—you have to understand. We're all multi-millionaires. Collectively we're worth, like, over seventy mil, easy. And while the prospect of this league has mostly just been talk and a handful of meetings up until now, we did make one deal."

"With whom?"

"An athletic wear company. We recently signed a contract to give them exclusive merchandising rights for the National Roller Derby League."

That caught my attention. And it suddenly gave someone a clear motive.

"What's the name of this company and what can you tell me about it?"

"Ninja Mouse Apparel. They're relatively new. Started by a former lululemon exec who wanted to go into business for himself."

"Does this executive have a name?"

"Todd McTavish."

"Do you know him?"

"I know of him. Look, we wanted to get the ball rolling on the NRDL but were looking to keep the start-up costs down. This guy had interest in what we were doing and undercut all of the competition."

"But he would still make a significant profit if the league were formed."

Hector took another long slurp of his Sprite. "Tits. Ass. And chicks on wheels fighting. What the fuck do you think?"

"Okay. Thank you for your time, Hector. I appreciate it."

Hector snapped his fingers at me and flashed a smile. "If you really want to thank me then share some funny wrestling anecdotes on my show next week. Do you have any midget stories? Midgets are hilarious."

I immediately thought of my friend Pocket, the loquacious dwarf wrestler for XCCW who, despite his short stature, has one of the biggest hearts of anyone I've ever known. "Can't say that I do," I replied.

"Too bad," said Hector, before pounding the rest of his soda, slamming the can down on the craft service table, and belching. He shook my hand before marching back toward the stage on the other side of the electronics store.

"Hector," I said, calling after him.

He spun around so fast his gold chain whipped around his neck like a hula hoop.

"Yo!"

"Last question. You ever see a thin, well-dressed guy around? Wears a nice suit and a bowler hat?"

Hector stared me dead in the eyes. "What, like that rap singer Pharrell Williams?"

"Sort of. But smaller, more rounded, and a little less Smokey Bear."

Hector stroked his chin for a moment before shaking his head. "Don't think so. Only guy with a suit and a hat I know wears a fedora and sings at my supper club."

I nodded accordingly and Hector jaunted off back toward the stage. I glanced at the craft service table before I left and noticed the empty can of Sprite. While it wasn't crushed, there were indentations on the sides of the aluminum from when Hector had squeezed it tight. I couldn't help but wonder if it was merely from habit, or perhaps something more.

THIRTY-ONE

It had been a couple of years since I had driven over the Port Mann Bridge. The cable-stayed roadway hosted ten lanes of Trans-Canada traffic and connected the suburb of Coquitlam with Surrey, the second largest city by population in Metro Vancouver. From a distance, the bridge's long cables shot down from two concrete towers. They looked like giant spiderwebs, and it was hard not to admire those thick and powerful cables of coiled steel wrapped in white sheathing.

I found myself waxing nostalgic as my Ford F-150's engine purred while escorting me over the Fraser River, and despite the impressiveness of the replacement, my mind was flooded with memories of driving over the rusty old orange bridge that had been torn down. I recalled sitting in the back of my old man's Cadillac Coupe de Ville as we drove under the bridge's arch while my father drummed his fingers on the steering wheel and my mother sat in the front seat humming Irish hymns. Once a year we made the hour-and-a-half trek from Vancouver to Bridal Falls. Sometimes a rascally, young Declan—in town visiting from Ireland—would accompany us, and during those years the long drive usually involved a lot of snickering on our part and a lot of scolding by my parents.

I was still reminiscing when the exit sign for 200th Street caught my eye and I scrambled to cross three lanes in order to get off the freeway. I turned left and drove north through Walnut Grove, a quaint commuter town that resides within the Township of Langley. I looked out my window at the monstrosity that was Cineplex Cinemas Langley, complete with a gigantic, silver UFO on the top of the building that was part of the movie theatre's extraterrestrial theme offering viewers an "other-worldly entertainment experience." I shook my head at the colossal corporate construction and yearned for the days when the biggest novelty of going to the movies was getting extra butter on your popcorn.

I followed Siri's directions as my iPhone's Maps app guided me through Walnut Grove's commercial area until I pulled into a large industrial park. I rolled my truck to a stop in front of a small, warehouse-like building. A large sign above the entrance read Ninja Mouse Apparel and featured a caricature of a muscular mouse sporting a long Rambo-like headband and wearing a martial arts gi while performing an aerial karate kick.

The door chimed as I entered the store. No one was around, so I spent the next couple of minutes perusing the showroom. Sweat-wicking T-shirts, running shorts, yoga pants, hoodies, and tracksuits were all on display. I was examining some slim-fitting elbow pads, thinking about how I had banged mine recently after Spudboy's bag of potatoes had knocked me down hard to the mat, when a colourful item immediately grabbed my attention. I approached a female mannequin outfitted in a low-cropped red top and a pair of white leggings, that were covered with zombies. Undead heads chomped on severed arms and legs while necrotic flesh and eyeballs drooped from their rotting faces and drops of blood were splattered everywhere across the pants. The colourful zombie attack was very eye-catching and I had a feeling I knew someone who would absolutely love this particular piece of clothing.

"May I help you?" asked a young man with glasses and a shaved head. Despite working around an abundance of athletic wear, he was dressed casually in a polo shirt and blue jeans.

"Just admiring these zombie pants," I replied.

"Pretty badass, eh?"

"I'll say."

"How much are they?"

"Ninety-nine dollars."

"I'll take them." The young man looked at me funny. "I have a lady friend who's really into zombies."

"I'm sorry, you must be confused. This isn't a retail store. This is just a showroom."

I glanced around and realized he was right, as while lots of sportswear was on display, there wasn't a checkout or cash register in sight.

"We make all of our merchandise in the back of the warehouse. This showroom is just for store reps who want to check out our product line in person."

"Why Ninja Mouse?"

"You mean the name?" I nodded. "Take a look at that picture over there," he said, pointing toward the wall behind a rack of windbreakers.

I walked over to a large framed photo on a wall. In the picture a short, skinny, long-nosed, man with a thin beard and wearing a red martial arts gi posed with a giant golden trophy that was nearly his own size.

"That's the owner of the company. Ninja Mouse was his nickname back when he used to compete in martial arts tournaments."

"That's Todd McTavish, then," I said, walking back toward the young man.

"Yes, Sir."

"May I speak with him?"

"I'm sorry, he's not in today."

"Do you know when he will be?"

"Mr. McTavish is actually on a business trip at the moment."

"When does he return?"

"I'm not exactly sure. A week or two? I can ask some of the other staff if you'd like?"

I waved off the offer. "You guys are a relatively new company, right?"

"Yes, Sir."

"How's business been so far?"

"Great!" he exclaimed a bit too forcefully, while plastering a trying-too-hard smile across his face. "Ninja Mouse Apparel is really starting to take off. Customer reviews for our athletic wear are through the roof!"

"Impressive."

"We're also in the midst of launching our online store and our products are now available in a few select sports stores across the Lower Mainland."

"Just a few?"

The young man's smile faded fast and he gave up the ruse. "Yes, unfortunately," he said, before letting out a big sigh. "Things have been … tough. It's a really hard market to break into, especially when you're going up against a juggernaut like lululemon."

"Probably doesn't help that their corporate headquarters are in Vancouver either."

"No kidding," said the young man dejectedly. "I'm Mark by the way," he said, offering his hand.

"Jed," I replied, before shaking it.

"Why are you looking for Mr. McTavish?"

"Just want to ask him a few questions about a case that I'm working."

"You're a cop?"

"PI."

Mark's face lit up again, although this time it was definitely more genuine. "You mean like Jessica Jones?"

I didn't know who that was and wasn't inclined to ask. "More like *Magnum, P.I.* Except without the Ferrari and sweet 'stache."

"Jay Hernandez doesn't have a mustache."

"Who?"

"The guy who plays Magnum, P.I., Jay Hernandez." I stared at Mark, utterly baffled.

I clenched my teeth and suddenly related to Declan's fury over the film student not knowing about the movie *Cocktail*.

"They remade *Magnum, P.I.*?"

"I don't think it's a remake."

It took all the restraint I could muster to keep from smacking Mark on the back of the head and dragging him to the nearest computer so I could show him some YouTube clips and set him straight. "Let's get back on track here, Mark. I'm going to leave you my card. Can you text me and let me know when McTavish is back in town?"

"Absolutely," he said, before taking the card out of my hand and carefully tucking it into his wallet.

"Last thing. I heard a rumour that you guys recently signed an exclusive merchandising deal with a start-up national women's roller derby league."

"How did you hear about that? It's supposed to be confidential."

"PI, remember? What can you tell me about the deal?"

Mark shrugged. "Just that it was a pretty big get for Ninja Mouse. We're barely staying afloat as it is and I don't know how much longer we'll be able to. But if they launch that league then holy hell we'd be in the money."

I nodded curtly. Hector had been spot on with his info and Yosef Dillon's instincts had been right—someone involved in the launch of a National Women's Roller Derby League did have something to lose more than any of the other people involved. And his name was Todd McTavish.

"I appreciate your time, Mark. And I really want to buy a pair of those women's zombie pants. Size large."

"We're really not supposed to make any sales.…"

I plucked two hundred dollars from my wallet and handed it to him. "Keep the change."

Twenty minutes later I was driving back over the Port Mann Bridge while the face of the most gruesome, blood-thirsty, living-dead woman chomped on a human femur bone on the rear of the spandex pants folded neatly on my truck's passenger-side seat.

THIRTY-TWO

I called Rya. If Detective Constable Shepard was surprised to hear from me, she certainly didn't show it in her voice. I told her I had dug up some info on Lawrence's murder. After a long silence, and an even longer sigh, she agreed to meet at the Emerald Shillelagh later that evening.

I arrived early and took a seat at a booth my cousin had reserved for me in the back of the pub. Declan had his hands full at the bar, and I noticed that there was an extra waitress whom I didn't know working the evening shift. The pub was busier than usual, because the lone Canadian team left in the Stanley Cup Playoffs, the Winnipeg Jets, were taking on the Vegas Golden Knights and the series had been tight. While the three big-screen LCD televisions in the pub displayed the game, I perused the background check my father had compiled on Hector Specter while I waited for Rya to arrive. Declan managed to spring himself free from behind the bar and sauntered over to my booth with two pints of Guinness and plate of delicious-looking food that I didn't recognize from the Shillelagh's menu.

"Cheers, Boyo," said my cousin, sliding into the booth and placing the pint and plate in front of me. We clinked glasses and took long sips.

"What's this?" I asked, examining the bone-in meat and generous medley of steamed vegetables.

"Special o'the day. And I brought you extra veggies and no potato cuz I know what a little bitch ya are about your carbs these days, unless it's a beer or a banana milkshake."

"Thanks, D," I said, laying a cloth napkin across my lap.

"So? Any closer to findin' Kuntpounder's killer?"

"Kunstlinger."

"Close enough."

"I'm making progress. Sussed out a guy who has a clear motive earlier today, but he's currently out of town."

"Who in the bloody hell would have reason to off a roller derby coach who looks like Mr. Kotter if the bloke were a registered sex offender?"

"I'll catch you up later. Rya is meeting me here soon."

"Deadly. You two love birds finally gettin' together then, yeah?"

"Not even close. She's the homicide detective assigned to Lawrence's murder and I've come across some info that I'm pretty sure she doesn't know about."

"Aye, that's brilliant. Use your sleuthin' skills to get her all hot and bothered. Frank's gone for the night, by the way, so feel free to use the office upstairs if you two need some privacy."

"That's not going to happen. Besides, she's actually a bit miffed with me at the moment because I've been working her case and seeing Stormy."

"Who?"

I reminded Declan about Stormy and how we had reconnected because of Lawrence's disappearance and subsequent death.

"I remember that lassie. The Amazon babe ya thought may have iced yer mate last year. And now you're in a bloody love triangle? You bollocks! Between the derby dame and the hot cop, you got flange fallin' into your lap!"

"It's not like that."

"All I know is that if beautiful birds keep comin' your way I may have to borrow a pair o'your tights and some baby oil so I can whip your arse in the ring and get in on some o'this action."

I chuckled heartily. "Declan, I would never wrestle you."

"Why the hell not?"

"Because you'd take one bad bump, completely snap, and then kill your opponent with your bare hands."

"Aye, that's probably not far from the truth."

"Stormy's roller derby team has a big game coming up. I promise I'll bring you along, okay?"

"You sure as shite better. And ya can treat me to a nice dinner before. Rodney's Oyster House by me flat so I can knock back a dozen o'those slippery suckers before we watch them big-knockered gals go at it. Oysters are natural aphrodisiacs, ya know."

I shook my head, already regretting the offer. I cut into the seasoned meat and took a bite. It was tender, juicy, and delicious. "This is fantastic. What is it?"

"That, Mate, is the late, great David Hasselhop."

I dropped my knife and fork loudly on my plate and stopped chewing. "I'm eating your girlfriend's rabbit?"

Declan shrugged. "Wee bastard got loose again and made a beeline out o'the front door as a customer was walking in. Got smoked by a Prius."

"But why on earth would you skin and cook him?"

"Do you know how much money I've spent downloading Shakira songs and fattening up that plump little bastard this past week? I wasn't about to let that investment go to waste."

"Does your bunny babe know?"

"Aye, she came by earlier today to pick up his ashes."

"Ashes?"

"I told her I had him cremated. Instead, I dumped me ashtray into an empty Folgers coffee tin and gave it to her."

"How'd that go over?"

Declan frowned. "Let's just say any prospect o' future three-somes is over. But at least I still got Trixie Titties."

"I never knew you had a thing for full-figured women."

"Are you kidding? Between Trixie's fleshy bagpipes and her bingo wings, I'm in chubby-chasin' heaven."

"You have such a way with words," I said. "Like a perverted Cyrano de Bergerac."

Declan smirked and waved a hand across his face. "Stop, yer gonna make me blush."

Just then the front door swung open and Rya stepped inside. She was wearing a billowy black floral blouse, a pair of navy skinny jeans, and Birkenstocks, which showcased her well-manicured toenails, all painted crème white. She looked lovely and I never got used to seeing her in casual clothes. As a result, her effortless beauty always took me aback when I saw her in outfits other than her work pantsuits. She scanned the pub until she spotted me in the booth, then slid a hair elastic off of her wrist and pulled her wavy mane back into a ponytail as she approached. Declan hopped out of the booth and started back toward the bar.

"Detective," said my cousin, nodding politely.

"Hi, Declan," she replied, as she passed him and took a seat across from me.

"It's good to see you, Rya," I said cautiously, before taking a sip of Guinness.

She gave me a dubious look as one of her eyebrows raised slightly. "Mmm-hmmm," she murmured, almost sarcastically. "What are you having?" she asked, before reaching out with her fingers and tearing a piece of meat off of what I now assumed was one of David Hasselhop's hind legs. Before I could reply she popped the meat in her mouth.

"This is really good," she said, chewing on the bunny I had cuddled not too long ago. "What is it? Pheasant?"

"Rabbit."

"Isn't gamey at all."

I was going to try and explain that was because David Hasselhop was a domestic rabbit rather than a wild one, but decided to let it go. "Go ahead," I said, sliding the plate across the table. "I only had one bite."

"You sure?"

"Yes, I, uh … sort of have a conflict of interest with that dish, anyway."

Rya shrugged and unwrapped cutlery out of a cloth napkin and dug in. I tried my best to keep visuals of David Hasselhop's adorably twitchy nose out of my head.

"So? Why am I here? This is your meeting, Ounstead."

Rya was being friendlier than expected, but her calling me by my surname threw me a bit. I much preferred it when she called me Jed.

"Right. Well, as you're aware, I've continued looking into Lawrence's murder."

"Despite an officer of the law directly instructing you not to do so."

"I had to do something, Rya. Otherwise the guilt over my role in the guy's death would eat away at me until there's nothing left."

Rya looked at me for a moment, before I saw the sympathy slowly materialize in her eyes. "I've realized that, Jed. Despite all your strength and combat ability, you've got a giant marshmallow for a heart."

"I don't know if I'd say *marshmallow*.…"

"Bullshit. You're a two-hundred-and-fifty-pound teddy bear and you know it."

"Two-thirty-five."

"Whatever. You've got to stop beating yourself up over things like this. You did it with Johnny Mamba and now you're doing it again. When I work homicides, I keep emotion out of it. If you don't, then you'll get shredded by the terrible things that happen. Kunstlinger was marked for death. If they didn't get him that day with the van, they would have gotten him another way."

"You're probably right."

"I know I'm right," she said confidently.

I stared at her for a moment while things clicked into place. "You have the forensics back on the van and bowler hat, don't you?"

Rya nodded and speared another piece of David Hasselhop with her fork.

"And?"

"Zip."

"No fingerprints in the vehicle? Not even partials?"

"Every last square inch of that van had been wiped down with an industrial-strength cleaner. Even the car keys left in the ignition were spotless. The lab boys have never seen anything like it."

"DNA?"

"A couple of hairs inside the hat. But nothing to match them to."

"What about the hat's make?"

"Mass-produced and thoroughly generic."

"Nothing to go on?"

"It's probably why the killer didn't care if he left it behind."

I leaned back in the booth and considered this development. I knew Chauncey Gardiner was a smooth operator from the way he had stealthily spied on me and twice given me the slip, not to mention tailing me to the Lamplighter despite a cursory check on my part. "What about the van?"

"No reports of anything matching stolen. Serial number had been pried off. Completely untraceable."

"Damn it."

"We've got no leads, Jed. This guy knew exactly what he was doing. It may have been staged like a haphazard vehicular homicide, but everything was by design. That's why I'm saying you can't let the possibly of you leading the killer to Kunstlinger get to you. He was dead no matter what. I don't know who this guy is, or if it was a hired hit, but it was done by a professional."

"But ... if he was a hit man, why wouldn't he have just sniped Lawrence from a rooftop? That would have been more precise, easier to execute, and involved significantly less risk. Not to mention a more humane way to bump a guy off. Why go to the trouble of crushing him to death against a wall with a van and taking the chance of being IDed as you're fleeing the scene?"

"That I don't know. The only thing I can think of is that it must have been personal. Maybe he wanted him to suffer."

I slumped in my seat as I considered this development. I thought about McTavish and his athletic apparel line. Sure, he would have been pissed that Lawrence was jeopardizing his business by rallying the roller derby community to reject a corporate league, but even if he were behind the hit, I didn't see why the way in which Lawrence was murdered would matter to him. All he would have cared about was taking him out. Something didn't track and it was gnawing at the back of my brain.

I snapped out of my swirling thoughts when the waitress I didn't know stopped by our table. "Can I get you guys something to drink?"

"I'll have a Grey Goose martini, straight-up, with three olives, ice-cold," said Rya. I glanced at her and smirked. "What? I'm off-duty."

I tapped the rim of my half-full Guinness glass. "I'm good, thanks."

The waitress nodded and headed straight for the bar. I saw Declan behind the beer taps with his eyebrows raised and holding up a tentative thumbs up. I caught his eye and gave the slightest of nods. He snapped his fingers, clapped his hands, and smiled, before returning to pouring pints.

"You know," said Rya, "the last time we had a drink together you ended up getting pretty drunk."

"I did. And I seem to remember waking up in your condo the next morning."

"In the guest room, Casanova."

"Still counts as our first official sleepover."

Rya smiled despite herself. She ate more of David Hasselhop and some veggies while we waited for her martini.

"All right, big guy. What do you have for me?"

I recounted everything that had happened since I saw her at the crime scene at the Lamplighter. I knew she had already learned of Yosef Dillon's attack on Troy Whitlock from the NWPS incident report, so I jumped ahead and told her about how I had intercepted Dillon the next day at the Anna's Towing impound lot. Although Rya was aware of the assault, she didn't know that my spooking Dillon at his BossFit gym triggered him to race across town to Lawrence's apartment. Rya listened carefully as I told her about the box I had lifted from Dillon's trunk and the contents within it. Ever the consummate professional, Rya showed no surprise when I explained how Dillon and Lawrence had been secret lovers. I followed up by filling her in on Lawrence's efforts to halt the formation of a national women's roller derby league, and finally how that discovery led me to Hector Specter, who then pointed me in the direction of Todd McTavish and Ninja Mouse Apparel.

Rya's drink arrived. She bit an olive off the plastic skewer and took a generous sip of her martini. "What's your read on this Specter guy?"

"He's a piece of work. And a piece of shit."

I slid my old man's background check across the table. Rya flipped it open and skimmed the pages while I had a sip of Guinness.

After a couple of minutes Rya spoke. "You think he could be involved?"

"I don't know. I mean, I can't really see a good reason why he would be. I got the feeling that a women's roller derby league is just a novelty pet project to him, but Dillon mentioned that he was more intense and threatening when he took a phone call with the Seattle coach who was pretending to be supportive of the league only to gain access to the latest news. Hector has a real ADHD frenetic quality to him. You can see it with his business ventures and it's definitely on display when you have a conversation with him."

"So you're liking McTavish."

"I'm liking that he's the only person so far with a clear motive. And I don't see how Lawrence brings this much heat down on himself unless it's related to the campaign he was organizing. He was literally days away from using the Women's Flat Track Derby Association's publicity department to issue a mass press release signed by dozens of teams, players, and coaches denouncing the formation of any type of professional roller derby league. If that statement came out, it could have very well killed any chance of an NRDL altogether, and McTavish's athletic apparel company needs their exclusive merchandising deal in order to stay in business."

Rya took another sip of her martini and stared at me. After a moment, she spoke. "Damn you, Jed."

"What?"

"Nothing. It's just … this is some solid investigative work. Frank must be proud."

"Not enough to finally come to one my wrestling matches."

"I think you've a better chance of getting him to slap on some makeup and roller skates than you do getting him out to watch you wrestle."

We both chuckled heartily. Our laughter faded, followed by an awkward silence. Eventually, Rya chomped on another olive and asked me a question I was hoping she wouldn't.

"So … how's everything else?"

I bought myself time by taking a big swig of Guinness while I tried to figure out the best way to respond. Going over Lawrence's murder case had instantly defibrillated our chemistry. I was thrilled to be on good terms with Rya again and was enjoying her company so much I had forgotten that I was currently seeing someone else.

"All right, I guess. Had a few unique adventures recently."

I proceeded to regale Rya with tales of bookies with prize-winning wiener dogs, kink clubs, and my cousin's newfound obsession with penis paintings. Rya laughed so hard when I told her about the dog collar with big metal spikes I had to wear in order to gain entrance to the Graf Zeppelin, she snorted a few times and had to wipe tears from her eyes.

"Please, please, *please* tell me you took a selfie."

"I'm afraid you'll have to make do with your imagination."

Rya rubbed a hand over her midsection and downed the rest of her martini. "Oh my God, my stomach is killing me. I feel like I just did an ab workout."

"Then it's probably best if I save the Jabba the Slut story for another time."

"I am so happy that I am not a PI," she replied, shaking her head.

Neither of us spoke as the smiles slowly faded from our faces. Rya opened her mouth to speak, but stopped when she heard raucous laughter coming the bar. We both turned our heads to seek the source of the commotion and I wasn't the least bit surprised to see Declan glad-handing and toasting with a customer. Rya, on the other hand, seemed perturbed.

"Son of a bitch," she muttered.

"What?"

"I told him not to come here."

"Told who?"

Rya looked at me as her lips formed into a thin line. "My boyfriend."

Before I could ask a follow-up question she was out of the booth and making her way to the bar.

THIRTY-
THREE

I caught up to Rya near the bar, where Declan was listening
intently to the man who was apparently her boyfriend. He was in
the middle of telling a joke, and Rya stood behind him and to the
left with her arms crossed. Neither Declan nor Rya's boyfriend
noticed her, and she had made the decision to wait until they did.
Her brow was slightly furrowed and she appeared to be clenching
her jaw. Rya's boyfriend put his hands down on the bar top and
leaned forward as he delivered the punchline.

"So he says, 'I don't know who the wingers are, but the centre
is Lanny McDonald!'"

Both Declan and Rya's boyfriend erupted and cackled riotously. Declan topped up both their glasses with Crown Royal
and finally noticed Rya and me when he went to knock back his
shot of whisky.

"Jed! You've got to meet this fella! He's off his nut!"

Rya's boyfriend spun around on his stool with a mile-wide
smile on his face. He was handsome and fit, and with his perfectly
mussed short dark hair and beard stubble, he could have been
mistaken for Jake Gyllenhaal.

"Hey, honey," he said to Rya, before leaning forward and giving her a kiss on the cheek. "How come you never told me what a character Declan is? I love this guy!"

"I thought I told you to wait for me at Steamworks."

"I did. For over half-an-hour."

Rya checked her watch and looked surprised. I knew immediately what had happened. She had lost track of time while we were sharing case notes and enjoying each other's company.

"I'm sorry," she muttered. "Work."

"No worries, babe. I just figured I'd head over and hang out until you were finished. Although if I'd known this crazy son of a gun would be here," he said, jabbing a thumb toward my cousin, "I would have come straight away."

Declan extended a hand and he and Rya's boyfriend slapped their palms together twice before fist-bumping one another. "You're welcome anytime, ya grand bastard." I was still trying to figure out how Declan and Rya's boyfriend had already established their own handshake when my cousin ambled off down the bar to refill some drinks.

"Shoot, where are my manners?" said Rya's boyfriend, before turning to look at me. "'Hammerhead' Jed Ounstead. It's *so* cool to finally meet you. Rya talks about you all the time."

"Is that right?" I said, glancing at Rya with a slight smirk on my face.

Rya rolled her eyes.

"Oh, yeah. But she never talks about your wrestling career. I, on the other hand, happen to be a big fan."

Rya uncrossed her arms and put her hands on her hips. "Jed, this is my boyfriend, Darren Stein."

"Everyone just calls me Rocket," he said, extending a hand.

I shook his hand. "Nice to meet another guy who goes by a nickname. How'd you get yours? You an astronaut?"

"Ha! No, I'm afraid not. But that's a story for another time because I've been dying to ask you something ever since Rya mentioned that she knew you."

"Darren, stop," pleaded Rya.

"No, it's okay, I don't mind," I replied. "I'm always happy to chat with fans."

"See?" said Rocket giddily. "He wants me to ask him."

Rya sighed and resigned herself to the situation.

"Fire away," I said.

Rocket downed his shot of whisky before rubbing his hands together excitedly. "Okay, now I'm sure you've probably been asked this a thousand times—so my apologies if you find the question annoying—but I just have to know. What is your all-time favourite professional wrestling match?"

Rocket wasn't wrong that I found the topic annoying, however, people rarely asked me what *my* personal favourite was. Instead, they usually just blurted out their own and waited for me to start doling out anecdotes. Despite his affable nature, I still hadn't made up my mind about Rocket and was looking for a reason to dislike the guy, so I decided to play things a bit cagey.

"I'll tell you what—you tell me your favourite match of mine first and then I'll do the same."

Rocket clapped his hands together and smiled. "Aw, heck, that's a no-brainer right there, 'Hammerhead' Jed!' Without question, my absolute favourite—and I think your best match ever—was on an episode of Raw when you and Artemis Artifice ended your epic feud in the most dramatic way possible. I can't remember where it took place … Memphis? Lexington, Kentucky?"

"Greensboro, North Carolina," I said quietly, not believing what I was hearing.

"That's it!" said Rocket, enthusiastically. Anyway, there were no gimmicks or stipulations or anything. It was just a good old-fashioned match that had been brilliantly built up to for months. I remember it vividly. Before you guys came out, the crowd was as dead as a doornail, but by the time you and Artemis were finished beating the hell out of one another and the ref raised your hand in victory literally everybody in the arena was on their feet giving you both a standing ovation! Never seen anything like that before."

I couldn't believe it. Finally, after years of desperately wishing a fan would pick my personal all-time favourite match as their own, the person who finally did it was the boyfriend of the woman who had always made my heart skip a beat. I *wanted* to dislike Rocket. But try as I might, I couldn't *not* like the charming son of a bitch.

"Let's go, Darren," said Rya, clearly having heard enough.

"Okay, babe," said Rocket, before pulling out his wallet and cracking it open.

I waved a hand and shook my head. "It's on me."

"No way. The Rocket ain't no deadbeat."

"I insist."

Rocket sighed and tucked his wallet back into his jeans pocket. He clasped one hand down on my collarbone and shook my hand with the other. "You're a good man, Jed. It was great to meet you."

"Right back at you, Bub."

"I'll be outside in a minute," said Rya.

Rocket started toward the door, but stopped in his tracks after a few steps and turned around. "You never told me your favourite match."

I smiled. "Same as yours."

Rocket grinned from ear to ear then headed off, but not before stopping to high-five Declan behind the bar on his way out.

I opened my mouth to speak but Rya stuck a hand in my face. "Not a word."

"But—"

"Not. A. Word."

"I like him, Rya. I really do."

She shifted uncomfortably on her feet before blushing ever so slightly. After a moment any insecurities in her expression had vanished, immediately replaced by the confident and professional demeanour I was used to. "You let me know if you hear from McTavish. I'll see what I can dig up on my end. In the meantime, stay in touch."

"Roger that."

Rya walked briskly out of the pub. I sat on a bar stool as Declan appeared with a couple of pints of Guinness for us both.

"I gotta be honest, Mate. If that posh gal can't be with you, then I'm bloody well glad she's with a jolly bloke like Rocket."

I took a sip of my Guinness and tried to sort through my feelings. Reconnecting with Rya had been intoxicating, and our renewed relationship had my heart a flutter. Meanwhile my stomach was suddenly in knots from actually seeing her with her boyfriend. I was happy Rya was with a good guy, but it still stung that she wasn't with me. Then again, I was also conflicted, as I found myself caring more and more for Stormy Daze. I really liked her—and our growing intimacy was both enjoyable and a welcome break from my usual solitude—but part of me wondered if she'd ever be as special to me as Rya already was. I wondered if anyone would. I shook my head, trying to rid it of its soap-opera theatrics. I didn't have time to brood over affairs of the heart. Not while Lawrence's killer was still roaming free.

"You all right, Boyo?" asked my cousin.

"Yeah, I'm fine. But I'm going to need your help."

"Why's that?"

I took a long sip of my Guinness. "Because I'm going to be on TV."

THIRTY-FOUR

The green room for Late Night Nectar with Hector Specter
was green. Literally. The walls were painted emerald and the
couch and armchairs were green as well. However, unlike the
bright walls, the velvet furniture was upholstered in a darker
shade of forest green.

A production assistant had brought me to the green room
when I arrived ninety minutes prior to the show as requested. She
met me at the hostess podium of the Poseidon Supper Club and
escorted me through the restaurant, past the kitchen, and then
down a flight of stairs into a very large, windowless basement. The
storage space had been crudely retrofitted into a makeshift studio
with metal folding chairs for the audience, cramped music stands
for the band to the side of the stage, and a talk-show set featuring
a cheap backdrop of the city of Vancouver at night underneath
the program's logo. It looked even worse than it did on TV. The
only thing that was impressive was the array of professional television cameras that surrounded the set. Hector certainly didn't
skimp there. Then again, he was such an unabashed narcissist I

was hardly surprised those would be the items where money was no object as he would want himself to look as good as possible.

After a quick tour of the set and showing me the hallway that led to Hector's private dressing room, the PA led me into a small space, that I was sure was either a converted storage room or janitor's closet. She congratulated me on being selected as the debut guest for the first-ever live episode of *Late Night Nectar with Hector Specter*. I feigned as much excitement as I could, which was minimal, before the PA confirmed that I had read over the pre-interview questions they had sent me a few days earlier. She then informed me that Hector was so thrilled to have a celebrity of my stature on his show that they were giving me an extended interview. Once Hector had finished his monologue and comedy skits, I would be the only guest for the remainder of the show.

The PA left me in the room and closed the door behind her. I wandered around the confined space, taking in what was without question the worst green room I had ever been in. A fifty-five-inch, 4K Ultra HD, Smart TV was mounted on a wall across from a paltry craft service table, which had a smattering of Greek-fusion food from Cerastes Brands, including spanakopita, skewers of chicken and lamb, Mediterranean salad, pita bread, tzatziki, and hummus. Next to the craft service table an overstuffed bar and cocktail cart featured all of his liquor brands.

I sifted through cans of Pegasus Pilsner, Cyclops Stout, and bottles of Gryphon Gin and Kraken Cognac. I grabbed the Kraken Cognac and examined the label that featured a giant squid holding snifter glasses in each of its tentacles.

"Moron," I muttered to myself. I knew Hector was out of touch, but this was just egregious. Unlike the mascots for his other brands of liquor, the Kraken was not a creature from Greek mythology. It was a sea monster from Norse mythology, and tales of the massive cephalopod living between the Arctic and Atlantic oceans off the coast of Iceland recounted how the great beast would eat ships that passed by. Hector was such a shallow, ignorant idiot he clearly didn't even research the Kraken before slapping it on his liquor bottles. He was also clueless that a green room, universally known as space for guests to relax when not performing or appearing on air, is not actually supposed to be green. Having experienced firsthand how tawdry and gauche Hector's sense of style actually was, I now understood why Sykes found just the mere thought of Hector so distasteful.

My skin crawled as a sense of embarrassment washed over me. What the hell was I doing going on this farce of a talk show? Sure, I wanted to stay in Hector's good graces until McTavish got back into town, just in case the struggling businessman were to have an alibi for Lawrence's murder and be cleared as a suspect. But potential resource or not, Hector was a buffoon, and I had worked hard to earn a respectable reputation as both a PI and pro wrestler. And I certainly wasn't looking to tarnish either by appearing on television so terrible it would be deemed cruel and unusual punishment to force incarcerated inmates to watch it.

I gave serious thought to bolting. I started running through exit strategies in my head when the screensaver on the TV disappeared and was replaced by clips from previous episodes of Hector's show. I grabbed the remote and muted the TV, put the Kraken Cognac back on the cart, and picked up a bottle of Winged Horse Whisky. I popped the lid, sniffed it, and almost gagged, assaulted with pungent scents of sour oak and a hint of something that smelled like sulfur. I rooted through the cart until I found the Horned Viper Vodka, poured a shot into a glass, then mixed it with ice, club soda, and a generous amount of lime juice. I sat back down on the couch, wincing with each sip of the beverage. While somewhat tolerable, it still felt like drinking diluted gasoline. But if I were actually going to go through with appearing on Hector's phony talk show, I figured I could use a little liquid courage.

I was on my third sip of the subpar spirit when Jimmy Hendrix's opening guitar riff for "Purple Haze" started playing and my phone began vibrating in my pocket. I answered the call and was pleased when I heard the voice on the other end of the line.

"Hey, handsome," purred Stormy Daze.

"Hi."

"What are you doing?"

"Oh, not much, other than being moments away from going on the worst talk show of all time as the headliner guest and potentially ruining both of my careers."

"What?"

I quickly filled Stormy in on Hector Specter and how I believed he was connected to Lawrence's murder.

"You know what? Just have fun with it," suggested Stormy.

"Seriously?"

"Yeah, why not? What's the worst that could happen? Besides, if it's as crappy a show as you say it is, then I don't think a lot of people will be watching."

"Good point. Thanks, Stormy."

"Do you know how cool it's going to be for me to tell the other girls on the stagette that my boyfriend is about to be on live … *oh crap*."

There was silence on her end of the line and I was tongue-tied. While I had been very much enjoying Stormy's company of late, I was definitely taking things one day at a time and hadn't given a lot of thought to where things between us might be going.

"Jed, I, uh … I didn't mean—"

"Stormy?"

"Yes?"

"It's cool."

"Are you sure?"

"Yes. Plus now I can plug my girlfriend's roller derby team on the air if I get the chance." She let slip an excited giggle, and I could almost feel her beaming through the phone. There was a knock on the door.

"Five minutes," the voice said from outside the room.

"I have to go," I said.

"Break a leg, Jed."

I hung up the phone and walked over to a full-length mirror. I slammed back the rest of my drink, tossed the cup in the waste bin, and checked out my reflection. I had taken Declan's advice and dressed smart casual so I would look respectable enough without having to wear a stuffy suit and tie. I smoothed out a couple of slight creases in my black slacks and matching black UNTUCKit French-cuffed dress shirt, then dipped a napkin in some water and shined up my large, silver-and-pink Bret "The Hitman" Hart cufflinks.

By the time I was ready to go, the PA had returned. She quickly fastened a small microphone to my shirt above my sternum and then clipped its battery pack to my belt below the small of my back. She then escorted me to the set. I followed her down a hallway until we were behind a royal-blue velvet curtain. The band was playing jazz and the audience was chatting away as everyone waited for the show to return from a commercial break. I glanced at a television monitor mounted high up on the hallway wall and saw Hector sitting at his desk, scribbling furiously on several note cards.

"Okay, people!" hollered a voice from the other side of the curtain. "We're back in ten! Nine! Eight!…" The countdown continued as I took a deep breath and exhaled forcefully. I watched Hector on the monitor and waited for my cue.

"Welcome back, everyone, to the first-ever *live* episode of *Late Night Nectar with Hector Specter!*"

The crowd applauded more enthusiastically than I expected and I wondered if perhaps there may have been some pro-wrestling fans in attendance.

"My guest tonight is a hometown boy, born and raised right here in Rain City! He went on to find great success as a professional wrestler, having spectacular matches all around the world until he became a star in World Wrestling Entertainment. His distinguished career includes winning both the WWE Tag Team and

Intercontinental championships and, after a hiatus of several years, he is now wrestling professionally again—right here in Vancouver! Please give a warm welcome to 'Hammerhead' Jed Ounstead!"

The crowd popped loudly and the band was silent save for the guitarist who started wailing on his axe as he played the intro to "Hammerhead" by Jeff Beck. I walked through the blue velvet curtain and the applause got even louder. I smiled and waved at the crowd, then stepped up onto the elevated set and was greeted by Hector. I noticed at once he was several inches taller than when we met at Best Buy, and after a quick glance at his shoes, realized he was wearing lifts. Hector extended a hand and I shook it. Hector immediately pretended I was crushing his hand and collapsed to one knee, mugging for the camera. His cheap theatrics elicited a few chuckles before he flashed a winning smile, stood up, and waved his hand at the audience in an I-was-just-messing-with-you kind of way. Hector directed me to my seat. By the time I turned around to sit, I noticed that Hector was already in his chair. Now, I don't watch a lot of talk shows, but even I knew that proper etiquette was for the host to always allow the guest to sit first. I eased myself into the chair and said a silent prayer in my head hoping that the interview would not be a disaster. The applause subsided and I glanced out at the audience and multiple cameramen who all had me in their crosshairs. I gave a slight nod before turning my attention back to Hector.

"Welcome to the show, 'Hammerhead' Jed."

"Thanks for having me."

"Okay, I'm going to ask the question that's on everyone's mind right off the bat."

I tried not to clench my jaw as I braced myself.

"What kind of nectar will you be having with Hector Specter?"

There were a few chuckles from the audience. "How about some Horned Viper Vodka on ice with club soda and lime?" I said.

Hector got a kick out of that answer. "Ha! Look at that! The big, tough guy wrestler wants a 'skinny bitch' to drink!"

Scattered, uncomfortable laughter was peppered throughout the crowd. I was tempted to make a crack about Hector's crappy liquor and how his vodka was the only thing I was able to choke down, but maintained my composure and decided against it. Instead, I patted my stomach and smiled.

"Need to make sure I can fit into my wrestling tights," I said pleasantly.

The audience chuckled, less from my half-assed joke and more from the fact that the crack I had made defused the awkwardness of Hector insulting me. Never one to miss out on a cheap pop, Hector immediately patted his belly as well.

"Smart man! Plus this way we can spend those extra calories on some baklava later!"

After drumming his hands on his tummy, Hector came around his desk to the drink cart in front and whipped up two vodka sodas on ice with lime juice. He talked briefly about the distillation process required to produce Horned Viper Vodka while making the drinks to avoid dead airtime. Once the cocktails were made he took his seat again and we clinked our glasses together in a toast.

"*Yamas!*" exclaimed Hector cheerfully.

Not knowing what he had just said in Greek I simply nodded slightly and took a sip of my skinny bitch.

"So I'm dying to know—how did you get the nickname 'Hammerhead' Jed?"

"Well, long story short, when I was just starting out in the wrestling business I had a run where my opponents kept cracking me over the head with all kinds of foreign objects—"

"You mean two-by-four pieces of wood?"

"Two-by-fours, metal chairs, garbage cans, kendo sticks—you name it, they tried it. But I kept winning matches despite all of the headshots so the nickname sort of stuck."

"And they say that I'm hard-headed!" bemoaned Hector, before hammily jabbing a thumb over his shoulder toward me. Polite chuckles ensued before Hector continued his line of questioning. "So how did you get your start in professional wrestling?"

"I had been a lifelong WWE fan and wrestled competitively in high school and later at Simon Fraser University. After I finished my senior year, a buddy of mine dared me to attend a six-week professional wrestling camp run by one of Bret 'The Hitman' Hart's brothers with him in Calgary. After the first day I was hooked. The rest is history."

"Fascinating," said Hector, stroking his chin, although I thought he was full of shit. "But now that you've started wrestling again, how come you're doing it here with a local independent promotion in Vancouver instead of making the big bucks back in the WWE?"

"I love this city. It's my home and where I want to be. Plus, I only wrestle part-time nowadays as my priority is my other career."

"Which is?"

"I'm a private investigator."

"Wooo-weee! Looks like we got ourselves our very own suplexing Sherlock here, folks!"

There was forced laughter from the crowd. I noticed the applause sign above the audience flashing repeatedly.

"Actually, I work with my father at his detective agency. Ounstead & Son Investigations. He's a retired VPD officer and one of the best cops this city's ever seen. I guess you could say I'm kind of like the Robin to his Batman."

"Ha! Does that mean you wrestle in those gay little green speedos and elf shoes he wears in the comic books?"

I ignored the homophobic remark and tried to answer the obnoxious question as politely as possible. "Actually, I wrestle in black spandex pants with hammers and lightning bolts on them."

"Hammers and lighting, folks!" crowed Hector. "*Sooooo* alpha male!"

I smiled and gritted my teeth so hard I may have ground out a filling. I wondered how much more of this "interview" I had to endure.

"Okay, moving on," said Hector, shuffling his blue index cards. I took a sip of my crappy vodka soda and tried my best to down as much as possible without making it obvious while I remained on camera.

"Is it true the reason you left professional wrestling a few years ago was because you accidently paralyzed your friend and former tag-team partner 'Mad Max' Conkin during a rehearsal for a show?"

There were audible gasps throughout the studio before it became so silent you could hear a pin drop. I felt a tightness in my chest and a wave of light-headedness washed over me. I was frozen in my chair. Everyone was staring at me, including Hector—who I swear had the slightest, most subtle of smirks on his face.

What happened next occurred so fast I can barely remember it. Before I even knew what I was doing my left hand curled into a fist and my arm shot out with a vicious jab that contained every ounce of strength I had in my body. My fist clocked Hector square in the face, my knuckles connecting perfectly between his right cheekbone and his nose, which I felt crumple and shift out of place. My arm snapped back as if it were an elastic band. Suddenly, I was sitting in the chair with both my arms on the armrests again, as if the punch hadn't even happened.

The audience's gaze shifted from me toward Hector, who was sitting upright in his chair and wobbling ever so slightly. The wobbling slowly increased and blood started flowing from Hector's nose down onto his three-piece suit. After a few seconds that felt like minutes, Hector's arms dropped to his sides like wet noodles. His eyes rolled back into his head, his mouth fell open, and then he fell forward, smashing his face down hard on his desk. People in the audience winced and grimaced at the sound of the thud, while Hector remained there unconscious, a pool of blood slowly forming on his desktop.

I looked back out into the audience and saw everyone gawking at me. I stood up, removed the microphone from my shirt and its battery pack from my belt, placed them on the couch beside me, and walked off the set past the band and through the blue curtain.

THIRTY-FIVE

After the incident on Hector's talk show I went straight home and right to bed. I turned off my phone and hoped my father, cousin, Rya, Rocket, Stormy, her girlfriends, and pretty much anyone I had ever met, avoided witnessing the live television debacle.

I slept in the next morning, not checking my phone when I would wake, and tried hard to fall back asleep in order to escape my reality. By 11:30 AM my body refused any more rest and I forced myself to get up. I left my phone charging in my bedroom and made my way to the kitchen where I cooked myself some scrambled eggs with chopped green peppers, diced tomatoes, and feta cheese, then slathered on copious amounts of hot sauce, before enjoying them while watching the previous night's highlights on TSN's SportsCentre. After getting caught up on the latest in sports news, I grudgingly retrieved my iPhone from my bedroom and took a look at what was waiting for me.

I clicked the home button and so much had blown up overnight there wasn't enough room on the screen to report all of the recent activity. I was still scrolling through the texts, emails, and missed calls when my phone lit up with my cousin's name and a photo of him wearing aviator sunglasses and flipping off the camera with a rude gesture.

"Hey," I said, answering the call.

"Shite in a sack! Look who finally decided to answer his mobile."

"I needed some time after last night."

"From what? Being a bloody star on the internet?"

"What are you talking about?"

"Jed, what you did was brilliant! Please don't tell me you're mopin' around yer pad all scundered and sad. You should be celebrating! Do you know how many folks'll be comin' to your wrestling shows and hiring you and Frank now?"

"I don't understand."

"Your live TV interview, Boyo. It went viral online overnight and makes you look like a badass."

I raced to my office, which doubled as my townhouse's second bedroom, fired up my iMac, and directed the web browser to go straight to YouTube.

"You're gonna wanna search for 'Douchebag talk show host gets his due!'"

I heeded Declan's suggestion and performed the search. My stomach lurched when a video clip of me socking Hector in his smug face popped up and I saw that it had already received over six hundred thousand views in under twelve hours.

"Oh please no," I said, shocked by what I was seeing.

"What's got your goat? This is fantastic!"

"Most people have no idea how Max became paralyzed, Declan. The WWE purposefully kept it hush-hush at Max's request before he quietly left the company. And now, because of me, it's on YouTube for everyone to see."

"Do ya even know how that Greek son of a bitch found out about your past?"

"Not a clue. But it didn't stop the prick for going for some gotcha journalism."

"Poor bastard shoulda taken better notice o'the kind o'jab you can throw."

"I didn't even mean to do that. It just happened."

"There's no off position on the genius switch, Mate."

My phone beeped and I saw that I had an incoming call. It was from a number I didn't recognize with a 250 area code, which meant it was from either Vancouver Island or the interior of British Columbia.

"I've got another call coming in," I said to my cousin.

"Aye, well stop by the pub for a pint when you get a chance, ya deadly bastard."

"Will do," I replied, before ending the call and accepting the incoming one. "Hello?" There was nothing but silence on the other end of the line. "Hello?" I said again. I was about to hang up when a voice I never thought I would hear again spoke up and sent chills down my spine.

"Jed."

I knew immediately who it was. Even worse, I knew exactly why he was calling after all of these years.

"Max."

More silence.

"It's good to ... how are you?" I asked.

Seconds ticked by. Then he asked a question that ripped open a wound I had worked so hard and spent so long trying to close.

"Why, Jed?"

I didn't know what to say. How do you tell the person you accidentally paralyzed that you contributed to the outing of a private tragedy because you were trying to stay in the good graces of an asshole who is a person of interest in a murder case you are working? And how would they even understand when all you have done is brought them pain and suffering?

"Max ... I'm a private investigator now. With my father. I ... I help people."

"How does grandstanding on a talk show do that, exactly?"

"Max—"

"No one knew, Jed. Denise and the kids and I, we've all made a new life for ourselves here in Kelowna. I've been making progress in rehab. I even got a great new job."

"Max, that's amazing."

"It was. Except now everyone will know. Your little publicity stunt just sentenced me to an eternity of rehashing how I got hurt and our entire community pitying us. How could you have let this happen?"

I opened my mouth to speak but there were no words. I collapsed onto my couch, my insides twisted and cramping. I felt sick and it was all I could do not to vomit. I sat there for I don't know how long until I realized the line had gone dead. I dropped the phone as the numbness overtook me. All I could think was how for the longest time I believed the worst thing I had ever done in my life was paralyze my friend. In that moment, I realized I had done something worse—I single-handedly dredged up the past and sentenced Max to having to relive the worst day of his life over and over again, just as he and his family had found hope for the first time in years. I don't know how long I sat there, my heart aching while a few tears trickled down my cheeks. At some point my phone rang, and although I had no intention of answering, I looked at the caller ID anyway. It was Rya.

I wiped my face, cleared my throat, then answered the call. "Hey."

"You need to meet me at YVR right now."

"Why?"

"Because Todd McTavish was just found dead in his car in the long-term parking lot."

THIRTY-SIX

A Boeing 767 jet whined loudly overhead as I drove over the Arthur Laing Bridge to Sea Island in Richmond. Once I had crossed the Fraser River, I continued on Grant McConachie Way toward Vancouver International Airport as expressways snaked around me in loops, above and beside the main roadway.

It was a straight shot to the long-term parking. As I pulled in it wasn't hard to find the crime scene. I followed the flashing red and blue lights of several RCMP cruisers and parked as close as I could to the cordoned off area. The RCMP officer serving as a buffer between the crime scene and the public had been expecting my arrival. He was less than pleased however when he saw the large Dairy Queen banana milkshake in my hand.

"You can't have food at a crime scene," said the officer.

"It's a banana milkshake."

"I don't care what it is. Throw it out."

I took one last big sip, respected the officer's wishes, then tossed the empty cup in a nearby garbage can.

"I'm a private investigator and VPD Homicide Detective Constable Shepard specifically requested my presence at this crime."

With that, the RCMP officer let me through the blockade, and pointed me toward Rya, who was standing alone next to a silver Lexus RC and jotting down notes. I walked past several RCMP officers taking statements from a few witnesses and turned my head when I heard a loud clang, and saw that the coroner's assistant had dropped a metal gurney as he was unloading it from the back of the official's van. As I neared the Lexus I saw a dark figure slumped over the steering wheel and a great deal of blood splatter on the inside of the driver's side window and half of the windshield.

"Why can't we ever get together for a nice steak dinner and a bottle of Chianti by a crackling fire? It would be a nice change of pace from all of the dead bodies."

I watched Rya fight off a smirk while refusing to look up from her notebook. "How did your talk show appearance go?" she asked.

"You haven't seen it?"

"No, but I recorded it on my PVR."

"Do yourself a favour and just delete it when you get home."

"That bad, eh?"

"And then some."

Rya finished scribbling in her notes and then snapped the book shut. "Well, at least it looks like we've gotten some closure on McTavish."

"How's that?"

Rya motioned to the body of the athletic apparel mogul inside of the Lexus. "Appears to be a pretty clear case of suicide. He even left a note."

I circled the vehicle until I was beside Rya. She handed me a pair of latex gloves that I snapped on before I opened the passenger-side door and examined McTavish's corpse. With his body sprawled over the steering wheel and a pistol on the floor of the Lexus, at first glance it seemed quite obvious that McTavish had put a SIG Sauer P226 to his right temple and pulled the trigger. There was also a typed message on a piece of paper that rested on the passenger seat. The note read:

"I'm so sorry. I killed the roller derby coach. I thought it would save my business but I can't live with the guilt. Forgive me."

I stood up and peeled the gloves off of my hands. "This is bullshit."

"Excuse me?" said Rya.

"Don't tell me you're buying this."

Rya waved her arms in the air, exasperated. "Is there some great conspiracy theory that I'm missing here? If so, please enlighten me."

"This guy has been out of town for over a week since I started looking for him," I said, jabbing a thumb toward the dead body. "Specter serves him up on a platter with a crystal-clear motive for murdering Lawrence. Then the son of a bitch just offs himself at the airport before either of us gets a chance to question him? No way. It's too neat."

"Jed, I'm working half-a-dozen priority cases and have my supervisor's foot so far up my ass when he wiggles his toes he tickles my tonsils. Neat is good. I like neat."

I crossed my arms across my chest and shook my head, still resolute in my opinion.

Rya sighed. She reached out and tenderly squeezed my forearm. "Look, I get that you're frustrated. But I think that maybe you're trying to jam a square peg through a round hole here."

"McTavish didn't commit suicide, Rya. And Hector Specter is in on it somehow. I'm not saying he took him out, but he's at least covering for whoever did."

"That makes for a nice story, but unfortunately as an officer of the law, I require actual evidence to build my case."

"Then you should start by asking yourself how a typed suicide note left on the passenger seat of a car doesn't have a speck of blood on it, despite the guy who supposedly wrote it blowing his brains out two feet away," I said, before walking away from the crime scene.

THIRTY-
SEVEN

I spent the rest of the weekend hanging around the Emerald Shillelagh. My old man and I had a little meeting in our agency office, and he concurred that McTavish suddenly turning up at the airport as a victim of suicide, after Hector Specter had plopped him in my crosshairs, was definitely suspicious. When I told him about the blood-splatter-free suicide note, in which the alleged author didn't even refer to Lawrence by name, my father was pretty much sold on my theory and encouraged me to trust my gut, but to also cut Rya some slack. He reminded me that as a PI I had the luxury of taking my time with cases, while Rya, who was by far the most talented detective in the VPD's Homicide Unit, was tasked with an unending string of murders. So it was unfair to judge her for wanting to clear as much off her slate as possible. He was right.

Stormy returned from her stagette after I got back from the airport and we spent the rest of the weekend at my townhouse. We talked, watched movies, made love, ordered in food, watched more movies, made more love, and generally just enjoyed each other's company. Our connection was definitely deepening, but we didn't allow ourselves to overthink things, or to look a gift horse in the mouth. We just hung out and made each other laugh. I'll be damned if it wasn't wonderful. Perhaps what I appreciated most was that not once did she bring up my appearance on Hector's talk show, though I knew she was dying to talk about it. She just gave me lots of hugs and kisses, and while I knew I would eventually open up to her, I was still reeling from my phone call with Max. Not to mention guilt over that video going viral. Having Stormy around my place was a welcome distraction and kept me from berating myself, which during difficult times I was prone to do.

On Sunday afternoon, Stormy went back to her place to pick up some clean clothes and I swung by the Shillelagh. Two dozen Vancouver Film School students were having an impromptu wrap party for a short film on which they had just finished principal photography, so I ended up jumping behind the bar to help my cousin keep the drinks flowing. About halfway through the party, the Kangol cap-wearing kid, whom my cousin had fired for not knowing the Tom Cruise movie *Cocktail*, wandered into the pub. I intercepted him to serve as a buffer between him and Declan, who was giving the poor son of a gun the worst case of Irish stink-eye I had ever seen.

"I just wanted to have a couple of beers with my friends," he pleaded, pulling up a stool at the bar.

I served the kid a pint of Red Truck Lager. He accepted the drink gratefully and knocked back nearly half with his first gulp. "First round's on me, Bub," I said.

"Thanks, man. And hey, just so you know, I watched *Cocktail.*" Declan had caught wind of the Kangol Kid's apparent apology, and I heard him grumble grudgingly while drying a glass with a dishtowel.

"Well done," I said, before glancing at Declan who nodded ever so slightly. "Keep up the retro film fest and I think we can consider your ban lifted."

"Really?" he asked excitedly.

"Sure. Go on, join your pals."

"But what should I watch next?"

"You ever heard of Shane Black?"

Kangol Kid shook his head. "Who is he, a rapper-actor like Common or something?"

"Jaysus Christ!" bellowed Declan, having overheard the remark. I ignored my cousin and focused on the kid.

"He's a filmmaker. Start with the original *Lethal Weapon* and then work your way up to *The Last Boy Scout*." Kangol Kid dug his phone out of his pocket and typed down my recommendations into the device's notepad. "And throw in *Kiss Kiss Bang Bang* for good measure," I added.

"Seriously?" replied Kangol Kid. "That sounds like the title of a porno."

"You thick wanker!" barked Declan. "I honestly don't think he is the full shilling, Jed."

I motioned for the kid to take off. "Remember what I said." Kangol Kid scurried over to a booth and was enthusiastically welcomed to the table by his fellow VFS students.

"I'm proud of you, D. That's big of you to lift the kid's ban."

"Aye, well, ya can thank me by taking me to one o'them roller titty shows ASAP."

"It's roller derby. And they're games, not shows. Anyway, I'm one step ahead of you. Stormy gave me a couple of tickets to their playoffs this Thursday."

Declan slapped a palm down on the bar, pumped his fist, and cut loose with a wicked front kick he snapped off so fast I felt air whoosh against my face. "About bloody time!"

Once the VFS wrap party wound down, Declan shooed me away and told me to head home and spend some more time with Stormy. She had texted to say that she would be running late, but would be back in time for us to make our reservation at Cardero's Restaurant across the street from my townhouse. I tried to distract myself by channel surfing, reading a sniper thriller by Stephen Hunter, and catching up on emails. But it was no use. I simply couldn't focus.

With a heavy heart I closed the mail app, opened a web browser, and went to YouTube. I searched for the video clip of me punching Hector Specter and was devastated to see that the number of views had quadrupled since I had first seen it posted online. I skimmed a few comments, and while all painted me in a positive light and enthusiastically supported Hector's come-uppance, I still felt like crap. Max was right. It was on me that the video had gone viral. If I had simply maintained my composure, given a vague response, and changed the topic, hardly anyone would have seen the clip or learned of the tragedy in our past. Thankfully, Stormy arrived just then and snapped me out of my self-induced sorrow. I put my computer to sleep and met her in the living room as she came up the stairs with an overnight bag.

"How you doing, handsome?" she asked, either sensing my melancholy or seeing sadness lingering on my face.

I cleared my throat and nodded. "I'm fine."

She dropped the bag, slipped into my arms, and nuzzled her cheek against my chin. "You know, our reservation isn't for forty-five minutes."

She kissed me gently on the lips and for a little while I escaped the swirling medley of thoughts that had been haunting me ever since I broke Hector's nose, stepped off his stage, and forced my friend to relive so publicly the worst moment of his life.

THIRTY-EIGHT

"Hey, Jed! Over here!"

I glanced up into the crowd looking to put a face to the voice calling my name.

"What are you, blind? I'm right here!"

I finally spotted a small, stocky woman waving her stubby arms over her head. Although she smiled when she saw me, I had no earthly idea who she was.

"Who the hell is that?" asked Declan.

"I don't know."

The woman patted a hand on the two empty seats beside her and motioned for us to sit with her. I looked at my cousin and he shrugged. "Beats standing room only," he said.

I did a quick scan of the nearly century-old sports venue. The majority of the seats inside Queen's Park Arena in New Westminster were filled to capacity for a double-header of women's flat track roller derby playoff action. The arena's iconic green wooden floor shimmered under the overhead lights, although the black, oval roller derby track laid down on top in the centre of the Sportsplex was less reflective. The track also obscured most of the twin logos for the New Westminster Salmonbellies Lacrosse Club painted on the floor at the centre of the arena, although you could still make out the giant red fish swimming through the letter W on both sides.

Stormy and her teammates were on the track sporting all kinds of colourful leggings, socks, and skates, while a few players wore over-the-top makeup.

"Jaysus, them birds look like a Jackson Bollock painting come to life," said my cousin.

"Pollock," I replied.

"Pretty sure it's *Bollock,* Mate."

Their opponents, the Shevil Knevils, were huddled around their bench listening to their coach as he drew plays on a dry-erase board. Although not as colourful as the Sallies, the team sported some impressive gear, and the majority of the women were intimidatingly big, athletic, and physically imposing, especially when compared to Stormy's mostly smaller teammates.

Declan and I shuffled down an aisle until we reached the stout woman and sat in the seats next to her. She gave me a punch on the arm and smiled. "Nice to see you again! Stormy had me save a couple seats for you."

"Thanks, uh … I'm sorry, I seem to have forgotten your name."

"It's me, Pippi." She immediately noticed I was clueless as to who she was. "Pippi Longstomping? We met at practice when Stormy hired you?"

Then I remembered, but barely recognized her without her painted-on freckles and bright red pigtails. "Right. You look a lot different without your derby gear."

Pippi rubbed her spiky, pixie-cut, black hair. "No wig tonight, big guy."

"Why aren't you down there?"

Pippi pointed to her ankle and the big plastic boot she was wearing on her left foot. "Hairline fracture. Jabba the Slut got a bit rough during our last practice."

Just hearing that woman's name caused phantom pain in my buttocks and images of my spilled banana milkshake flashed in my head. "That woman is a menace."

My cousin couldn't stop laughing. "Jabba the Slut? That's a gas! Which one o'these lassies is she?"

As if on cue Jabba roared and beat her chest like a gorilla while leading her teammates around the track for another lap.

"Christ on a bike!" exclaimed Declan. He gave me a nudge and nodded toward Jabba the Slut. "I think Trixie Titties may have some competition."

I rolled my eyes as a horn blared and the punk rock music blasting over the arena's speaker system slowly faded. The Split-Lip Sallies finished their final lap and Stormy glanced up directly at us as she passed by and locked eyes with me. She looked like the sexiest member of the living dead in her Amazombie makeup, and was proudly wearing the zombie-themed spandex pants that I had purchased for her from Ninja Mouse Apparel's warehouse. Stormy smiled and blew me a kiss.

"Something tells me you're dressin' up for Halloween this year," said my cousin.

I winked at Stormy and leaned back in my seat as three referees on roller skates glided toward the track.

Declan clapped his hands and rubbed them together excitedly. "Here we go! All right then, Miss Peepee Dongthumper. How long 'til I see me some bodacious blamps? Five minutes? Ten?"

"It's Pippi Longstomping. And I have no idea what you're talking about."

"You know, a pair o'chapel hats." She stared at my cousin like he was insane. "Some whamdanglers?" continued Declan. "Jalobies? Lung warts? Cupid's kettledrums?"

I sighed, leaned over to Pippi, and lowered my voice. "He's talking about breasts. For some reason he thinks the contact in women's roller derby causes the players' boobs to pop out."

"Yeah, that, uh … never happens," said Pippi, scowling at my cousin.

"Are you bloody kidding me?" he snapped, outraged.

I elbowed Declan and he grumbled and settled down. I was about to ask Pippi a question when I heard the sound of two cans being cracked open. Declan took a swig of Parkside Brewery's Dawn Pilsner with one hand and handed me an open can with the other.

"You're not allowed to have alcohol in here," warned Pippi.

"Listen, love—if I ain't seein' any nip slips tonight then I'm sure as shite gonna enjoy me some pints."

"Enough, D," I said, before placing my can of beer on the floor between my feet. "So what exactly are the rules for roller derby?" I asked Pippi, desperately trying to change the subject.

She gave Declan a funny look as he slurped his beer before leaning forward and pointing at her teammates, who were all huddled up for a group cheer.

"Okay, the rules for derby are actually fairly simple. People just figure since we're not chasing a ball or a puck that it's overly complicated. It's not."

"Aye, but with no ball, puck, or nets how do these gals score points?" asked my cousin.

"I'll get to that," said Pippi. "It breaks down like this. Each team fields five players at a time. They compete in a series of two-minute jams that take place over two thirty-minute periods. Four of the five players per team are blockers. Think football, but if the offensive and defensive lines were combined."

"Pussyball," snapped my cousin.

"I beg your pardon?" asked Pippi.

I shook my head. "He takes offence over the term football being used to refer to any sport other than soccer," I said to Pippi. "Just ignore him."

Pippi glared at my cousin for a moment before continuing. "The fifth player is called the jammer. She's the player who scores the points."

"And so for every bum or boob they smack makin' their way through the pack, the jammer ups the tally then?"

"What? No. Jed, who is this guy and what's his problem?"

"He's my cousin. And unless you have a few hours, it's best just to skip it."

Declan took another big swig of his beer before stifling a burp. "How the bloody hell are we supposed to know who the jammer is?"

"The helmet cover," explained Pippi. "Also known as a jammer panty," she said, pointing at a waifish woman on the track pulling yellow spandex over her protective headgear. Once she was done, her now-yellow helmet had big black stars on either side. "We're starting Infernal Myrtle tonight. She's slim and wiry, can slither through blockers like a snake, and skate like the wind. Once the jammer breaks through the pack, every opponent blocker she passes on any subsequent lap counts as a point until the jam is over."

I sat upright in my chair and gripped my armrests.

Something was stirring. I couldn't put my finger on it, but I could feel a little tickle in the back of my brain, like a thought scratching to get out.

"So them's all the rules, then?" asked Declan.

"Those are the brass tacks and enough for you guys to understand the—"

"Say that again," I said, interrupting.

"Say what again?" asked Pippi.

"The other name for the helmet cover Infernal Myrtle just put on."

"Jammer panty?"

A split-second later the floodgates opened and the memory broke through. I flashed back to the Lamplighter patio and standing next to Lawrence as he died. Pinned against the brick wall at the waist by the van, flopped on its hood, and spitting up blood, he had spoken his final words:

"Jam … J-J … Jim … errr … "
"Jim who, Lawrence?"
"Pan … paaant … "
Jammer panty.

Lawrence was trying to say jammer panty as he died.

But why? What for? A moment later I recalled the high shelf in his apartment, the one thing that went untouched when his home was raided and tossed. On that shelf, in addition to a few roller derby trophies and framed photos of Lawrence with the Split-Lip Sallies, sat a roller derby helmet wrapped in a yellow spandex jammer panty.

THIRTY-NINE

"What do ya mean you're leavin'?" protested my cousin. **"The** game is just startin'."

I hustled past dozens of kneecaps as I shuffled quickly down the aisle, then bounded down the bleachers stairs and made my way toward the exit.

"Jed! Wait up, for shite's sake!"

I didn't slow down or look back. I even forgot to say goodbye to Pippi Longstomping because of my sudden revelation. My mind raced. Why would Lawrence try and tell me about a jammer panty? That he was hoping to direct me to the one in his apartment was the only thing that made sense. What could it mean? I dug my keys out of my pocket and my brisk walk became a run. I was out the door and had just entered the arena parking lot when a strong hand grabbed me firmly on the shoulder and spun me around. Declan stood huffing and wearing a scowl on his face.

"What the bloody hell is going on?"

I explained about Lawrence's last words and how I thought he may have been giving me a message with his dying breath.

"I don't get it. What kind o'help could this jammer panty be to ya?"

"I'm not sure. But I need to check it out ASAP."

My cousin lit a cigarette, took a long drag, and exhaled a cloud of smoke. "Bollocks. Fancy some company?"

"You want to tag along?" I asked, surprised.

"Why not? I booked the entire night off at the pub and me roller titty show turned out to be a bust—no pun intended."

I chuckled and gave my cousin a pat on the arm. "Thanks, D. I really think this could be something."

"Aye, well I think we already got a little something on our hands," said Declan, before taking another drag of his smoke and nodding toward something behind me. I turned around to see Yosef Dillon and five other men of varying height and size fanning out slowly in the parking lot like a pack of wolves circling their prey. The six men did have one thing in common—they were all very muscular and fit. By the time I realized Dillon had recruited a crew of BossFit bros to get the jump on us, we were surrounded. I slipped my keys back into my pocket and clenched my fists as I sized up the men around us.

"Who are these hooligans?" asked my cousin nonchalantly.

"A bunch of BossFit guys here to back up the bald one," I said, nodding toward Dillon, who was glaring at me with fiery eyes while he cracked his knuckles.

"BossFit, eh? Ain't that when yer jumpin' like a jackrabbit and swingin' ropes 'round like Tarzan?"

"Something like that."

"What'd ya do to piss him off? Cuz he's lookin' at you like ya fucked his Ma without a Johnny."

"I have something of his that's sensitive in nature. He wants it back. I've been holding onto it as leverage in case I needed to get more information out of him. He's not exactly the most cooperative person of interest."

"Looks like we're in for a hell o'a craic then, Mate."

Declan took another puff of his cigarette and I felt his shoulders brush up against mine. We were now standing back to back as Dillon drew closer and the noose of BossFit bros grew tighter around us. Only about twelve feet now separated us from the six men with an abundance of grim faces and buff muscle.

"Hand it over, Ounstead," snarled Dillon.

"I don't have it," I replied. "Not on me, anyway."

"Wrong answer," spat Dillon. He opened his mouth to continue, but before he could form the words Declan addressed the group.

"Listen up, Gents, cuz I'm only gonna say this once. You best wind yer necks in and saunter off right bloody now, otherwise by the time I'm through beltin' the lot o'ya you'll be pissin' blood and scoopin' brown trouts out o'yer Underoos."

Dillon nodded toward a tall, muscular guy with close-cropped hair wearing a tank top that showed off his chiselled arms. "Shut that fucking mick up, Spencer," he ordered.

Spencer flexed his arms and took several aggressive strides toward my cousin. I looked back over my shoulder and watched as Declan sprung forward. He moved so quickly it was unnerving, and before Spencer could even raise one of his ham hock fists my cousin unleashed a flurry of Dornálaíocht Irish bare-knuckle boxing strikes. Declan tagged Spencer twice with wicked blows to the stomach and sternum, then finished with an uppercut that snapped the big man's head back so fast I half expected his noggin to fly off of his neck. Dillon and his BossFit bros gawked at Spencer as he wobbled slightly on his feet, big arms hanging limply by his side, and glazed eyes staring straight up at the night sky that was bathing the parking lot in moonlight.

Declan took a long drag of his cigarette. He flicked away the butt, then in a flash spun on the ball of his left foot, whipped his right leg around and up—cracking Spencer on the side of the head with the most vicious roundhouse kick I had ever seen. The big man dropped to the pavement. Because he was out cold, he couldn't get his hands up as he fell, so his head made a cringe-worthy thud when it hit the ground.

The BossFit bros stared at their fallen comrade in shock. Even Dillon looked startled. By the time Declan had taken a few slow steps backward until our shoulder blades were touching again our aggressors had turned their gaze from Spencer back to us. Declan slipped into a Dornálaíocht fighting stance, his fists hovering dangerously out in front of him like the heads of venomous snakes ready to strike.

"Are ya startin' or not you divvy bastards?" taunted my cousin.

With that Dillon and the BossFit bros charged at us like it was Custer's Last Stand at Little Bighorn. Dillon sprinted directly toward me and it was all I could do to dodge the wild haymaker he swung my way. Before he could recover and turn and face me, one of his BossFit bros attacked me from behind and delivered a few kidney punches to the rear of my ribcage that made my sides explode in pain. Anticipating another strike, I caught my attacker's arm, twisted it while rotating my body around until I was standing side-by-side with him, then torqued his elbow joint with my left arm, did a one-eighty, and delivered a vicious clothesline to his throat with my right. I knocked the BossFit bro clean off his feet, and while he hit the pavement hard, he was still conscious. I drove my right fist into his face with as much force as I could muster, and the back of his head bounced off of the concrete like a bouncy ball in a game of jacks.

Two down, I thought to myself. However, before I had a chance to see how Declan was fairing, Dillon tackled me to the ground. We wrestled back and forth until he had the advantage, pinning me on my back while he was on top of me, MMA ground-and-pound style. Dillon rained down blows and I instinctively covered up as best I could until I was able to knee him in the groin, roll on my side, and throw a fierce elbow upward. It connected directly with his upper jaw and nose. Dillon shrieked and threw his head back, spewing a mouthful of blood into the night air. I watched as one of his front teeth arced across the glowing full moon above before I shoved him off me. Dillon hit the ground and curled up into the fetal position, both of his hands covering his gushing nose.

I stole a glance at my cousin as I climbed to my feet, but in retrospect it was foolish of me to think that he might actually need my help. Declan was fighting all three remaining BossFit bros at once, and he moved with such nimbleness and precision you might have thought him the lead dancer in a martial arts-themed ballet. I watched in awe as he kept the trio of attackers at bay. He deftly dodged and blocked their clumsy punches with ease, his hands moving like bolts of lightning. The BossFit bro furthest on the right made an impatient move and tried to grab hold of Declan, only for my cousin to duck under, spin, and chop him in the Adam's apple with his backhand. The BossFit bro wheezed, his hands clutched his throat, and Declan delivered a brutal, steel-toed kick to his testicles. He dropped to his knees and Declan finished him off with a side kick to the face. I watched as the BossFit bro toppled over, unconscious.

I checked on Yosef Dillon, who was still curled up in a ball on the concrete trying to stop the stream of blood from his nose. I started toward Declan to help him with the two remaining BossFit bros, but he incapacitated both of them before I could even get there. With attackers on either side, Declan took a moment to centre himself before calmly exhaling. Both men came at him at the same time. Declan dodged a punch from the one on his left, grabbed his wrist, and yanked it downwards. The man stumbled forward and my cousin drove his right knee up into his face. Declan immediately pivoted and snapped his right leg out and up behind him in a reverse high kick, clocking the BossFit bro on his right square in the jaw. In one fluid motion, Declan retracted his right leg, drilled the teetering BossFit bro he had kneed in the face with a hard right hand punch, then leapt in the air and finished off the one on the left with a fierce spinning front kick. Declan landed on his feet like a cat after executing the devastating blows, and stood still until both men collapsed to the ground on either side of him.

At this point a small crowd had formed around us in the parking lot. Declan lit up a cigarette when a lanky teenage boy spoke up.

"*Holy shit, man!* You just destroyed those guys!"

Declan took a long drag of his smoke and winked at the kid. "That's why you should always mind yer manners, Boyo."

The lanky teen looked at his two buddies and then the group ran over to my cousin. "That was, like, the most badass thing we've ever seen, man. Can we get a selfie?" he asked, holding up his iPhone.

Declan shook his head. "Would you lads settle for a smoke instead?"

"Hell, yeah," said the teen.

I left my cousin to smoke cigarettes with minors and walked past the five unconscious BossFit bros over to where Yosef Dillon was still turtled up and clutching his nose. I ripped off a piece of Spencer's tank top and threw it at Dillon.

"Use that to put pressure on it," I said.

Dillon sat up, grabbed the fabric, and tried to stanch his bleeding nose with the piece of cotton shirt. I crouched down next to him.

"When this is all over, and I've found Lawrence's killer, I will give you back that tape. I haven't made copies and you have my word. But I swear, if you come at me again, this little tussle will seem like a mosquito bite compared to the suffering I will bring your way."

Yosef Dillon coughed and spat a wad of blood on the pavement beside him. I stood back up and stared at him until he made eye contact. "Are we clear?" I asked.

Dillon nodded and looked away. I snapped my fingers at my cousin, who had given in to peer pressure and was about to snap a selfie of himself and three underage teenagers smoking cigarettes he had supplied them.

"Not a good idea, D," I cautioned.

Declan heeded my advice and tossed an iPhone back to the disappointed teens. "Next time, Mates," he said, before jaunting over toward me and following me to my truck.

"That was a bit o' fun, wasn't it?"

I smirked. "You know, with the penis-painting obsession, chubby-chasing, and all round, general perversion, I forget sometimes just how deadly you are in a fight."

"Aye, I am a man o'many talents."

"Perhaps one of those talents could one day include not corrupting youth with illegal vices."

"Ah bugger off with ya, already. I did those wee babies a favour."

"By introducing them to a lifetime of addiction?"

"By makin' sure that if they're gonna have a puff, they'll bloody well do it in style," said Declan, before holding up a pack of Carrolls Number One cigarettes and lighting a fresh dart.

We hopped in my truck and I rolled down the windows so Declan could enjoy his smoke without making my vehicle smell like a casino. We drove in silence to Lawrence's apartment in New Westminster where answers were waiting for us.

FORTY

A haze of marijuana smoke drifted out of Troy Whitlock's apartment and into the hallway as he answered the door. The sight of Declan confused him, but when his eyes made their way over to me he grinned wider than the Cheshire Cat.

"'Hammerhead' Jed. Good to see you, Bro."

Troy hugged me tight. I patted the little stoner on the back a few times before gently pushing him off me.

"Jaysus," bemoaned my cousin. "Ya didn't tell me we were goin' to meet up with Cheech and Chong's bastard love child."

"Wait, wait ... what'd you say, man? Cheechie and choo?" Troy giggled uncontrollably. "Cheechie choo ... cheechie choo choo!"

Declan looked at me and shook his head. "You know I'm gonna do it."

"Easy, D. He's just a harmless kid."

"Cheechie chooooooooooooo ... cheeeeeeeeechie"

Declan hauled off and slapped Troy across the face. I was surprised by how light of a hit it was and appreciated him exercising some restraint.

"Hey! What the—hey, man! What's with the hostility, yo?" asked Troy.

"Look, kid, we're short on time. Can you just give me Lawrence's key?"

Troy rubbed his cheek and glared at Declan. "All right, all right." Troy disappeared into his apartment and returned after a few moments with a silver key on a keychain, as well as a pair of pink metal roller skate charms. He handed me the key and gave Declan a dirty look. "I don't like you, man."

"Aye, well then ya best get in line, Buttercup."

I thanked Troy, turned around and unlocked the door to Lawrence's apartment. Troy stared blankly at Declan and I'm pretty sure my cousin was getting ready to give him another smack when I snapped at him. "Come on, D."

Declan left Troy in his doorway and joined me in Lawrence's apartment. Someone had removed the shattered TV and straightened up the place a bit, but with its ripped couch and other damaged furniture it still looked the worse for wear.

I reached up to the shelf with Lawrence's roller derby memorabilia and grabbed the helmet covered in the jammer panty. I pulled off the yellow spandex and searched the fabric until my fingers came across something peculiar—a thin pouch that had been woven into the underside of the jammer panty itself. I could feel something inside of it. I opened the small, Velcro flap and pulled out its contents—an inch-and-a-half long thumb-drive data stick.

"This is it," I said to Declan.

"What do ya think is on it?"

"Only one way to find out."

I glanced around the apartment but there was no computer to be found.

"So what are you waiting for? Let's take that memory stick back to the pub and check it out over some pints o'the black stuff."

I put the helmet and jammer panty back on the shelf with my left hand and clutched the thumb drive with my right. "I know of a closer computer," I said, heading toward the door.

"Oh, bloody hell no, Jed, not again," pleaded my cousin. "C'mon, I'm beggin' ya, Mate."

I marched back across the hall toward Troy's door and knocked. After a moment, he answered.

"I need to use your computer," I said.

"Sure, bro, whatever you need. But he can stay in the hallway," said Troy, pointing an accusatory finger at my cousin.

"Aw, me heart is broken that I can't come inside your dope den, ya smelly gobshite."

Declan waited in the hall while I followed Troy into his apartment. I waved some of the lingering marijuana smoke out of my face as he directed me toward a laptop on his kitchen table. I pulled up a seat, booted up the computer, and inserted the thumb drive into a USB port. An icon for the data stick appeared on the screen and I clicked it open. Inside was a single, untitled folder. I opened the folder to find twelve JPEG files. I clicked the first JPEG and a large, hi-res photograph of Hector Specter and another man I didn't recognize sitting beside each other on a park bench appeared on screen. Both men wore suits and faced in opposite directions. On the bench next to Hector sat a black attaché case. The men appeared to have no idea that they were being photographed. It also seemed pretty clear that Lawrence had taken the pictures using a long-distance, telephoto lens.

I didn't know what I was expecting, but this certainly wasn't it. I clicked through the rest of the photos one-by-one, and slowly the pictures began to tell a story—Hector and the man sharing a few words, Hector passing the man the attaché case, the man opening it, et cetera. However, the second-to-last photo made it crystal clear what the photos had captured. In the picture, the contents of the attaché case were visible—stacks and stacks of unmistakable brown Canadian one-hundred-dollar bills.

I leaned back in the chair as it hit me. It was a payoff. I didn't know who the other man was, but I did know why he was on that bench next to Hector Specter. Lawrence had managed to capture Hector's transaction on camera and I had a pretty good idea how he used these photos after taking them.

Blackmail.

Any doubts I had about my theory disappeared after seeing the last photo in the set. In the picture, the man who received the briefcase full of money was getting up to leave. Hector Specter, meanwhile, was caught still seated—but staring directly at the camera. Had Hector spotted Lawrence snapping pictures of him paying someone off? Is that why he had Lawrence killed? Or did the roller derby coach attempt to blackmail Hector into dropping his efforts to form a National Roller Derby League? In the end, the details didn't really matter. Lawrence found dirt on Hector Specter, who became aware of it, and then the Split-Lip Sallies coach went on the lam only to be brutally murdered.

I closed the laptop, pulled the thumb drive out of the USB port, and tossed Lawrence's spare key to Troy. As I left, I thanked him for his help.

"Yo, you sure you don't want to stay for like a sandwich or something, bro? I make a mean corned beef."

"Another time, kid. And thanks again."

I met my cousin in the hallway and he struggled to keep up with the speed with which I was walking toward the elevator.

"What was on the thumb drive?"

"Pictures of some kind of payoff between Hector Specter and another guy. I don't know what it means exactly but I'm almost certain Lawrence was trying to use it as blackmail to kibosh the National Roller Derby League. That's what got him killed."

"Which means this Hector Specter prick is the one who had Lawrence of O'Labia taken out?"

"It looks that way, yeah."

"Who's the bloke he was meeting with?"

"I don't know. But I know someone who might."

FORTY-
ONE

Rya leaned forward and squinted at the first photograph on the computer screen. Her shoulder brushed slightly against mine and I felt her breath on my neck. I sat frozen in the Ounstead & Son Investigations desk chair, enjoying how close she was to me, but also a bit nervous to make any sudden moves that might make her pull away.

"Can you make that image any bigger?" she asked.

I clicked on a tab and enlarged the photo so it filled the entire screen. Rya leaned back and stared at the man receiving the briefcase containing stacks of hundred-dollar bills.

"*Holy shit.* Do you know who that is?"

"Some guy Hector Specter was paying off?"

"That's not just some guy. That's Richard J. Wilson, Crown Counsel for British Columbia." Rya spun me around in the chair and jabbed a finger at the monitor. "He's the lawyer prosecuting Specter on his statutory rape charge that's going to trial next month."

"So Lawrence really did have something on Hector. This is what got him killed."

"Jed, *we* have something on Specter!" exclaimed Rya. "This is huge. These photos are going to send shock waves throughout the entire legal system nationwide. I mean, not only is Wilson's legal career toast, but he'll also be facing jail time, and Specter is looking at at least a dime in prison for obstruction of justice."

"But not murder."

"What? I'm sorry, but no."

I shook my head. "That's not good enough, Rya."

"What are you talking about? Specter's going to go away for a long time."

"But he skates on Lawrence's murder."

Rya sighed and turned around. She eased herself back and sat on the edge of the desk. "Trust me, I've done this long enough to know that you get the bad guys on what you can and take that as a victory."

I sat up straight in the chair and slammed my fist down on the desktop. "This piece of shit ordered a hit on Lawrence, then had Todd McTavish killed, staged it as a suicide, and tried to frame him for murder."

Rya waited a few moments, then put a hand on my forearm and squeezed. "I know that, Jed. But we've got zero evidence. Nothing we can use to link Specter to either death. Hell, we can't even find the guy who drove the van into Kunstlinger."

"That's not good enough. Lawrence deserves better. And I owe it to him to make sure it happens."

Rya slid her hand down my forearm, then grabbed my palm and held my hand in hers. I looked up into her sparkling green eyes.

"I have to do something, Rya."

Rya smiled softly and gently brushed her fingertips against my cheek. A moment later we both moved our heads forward and kissed. My arms snaked around her as I stood up and pulled her body close. I felt her heartbeat against mine and all I could think in that moment was that I never wanted to let her go. We enjoyed a few more seconds in our embrace before we both heard footsteps on the spiral staircase leading up to the office.

We immediately detached from one another and while I lowered my head, looked away, and scratched my neck, Rya wiped her lips on the back of her hand and fussed with the lapel on her pantsuit blazer.

The door swung open and Declan entered the office carrying two pints of Guinness but instinctively sensed something was up. "I'm just gonna leave these right here," he said, placing them in the middle of the desktop.

"Thank you, Declan, but I'm afraid duty calls," said Rya. She gave him a peck on the cheek and skedaddled out of the office before I had a chance to call her name. By the time Rya was halfway down the stairs Declan was gulping down one of the pints he had poured.

"If you two have yourselves a little fella, I just want to say that Declan is a hell o'a first name."

"You're an asshole," I replied.

"I am not!" protested my cousin. "I just want to make sure me second cousin isn't named after a vegetable or whatever it is you eejits are passin' off as trendy food these days."

I crossed my arms and leaned forward on the desk. "Where's Pop?"

"Out workin' a case. You want me to give him a call?"

"No, leave him be. I don't need his help with this."

"With what, exactly?"

"I've got an idea."

"Does it involve some exceptionally erotic Japanese manga?"

"No, D, and I'm sorry to disappoint. I'm talking about a way to take down Hector Specter for Lawrence's murder."

"Bloody hell. There's the Jed I know."

"You up for it?"

"I'm all ears, Mate."

FORTY-TWO

The Poseiden Supper Club was empty, save for a single, pri-
vate, ten-person dinner party in the middle of the restaurant.
Their table was littered with nearly empty plates, and they spoke
in Greek and laughed loudly while enjoying coffees and desserts.
Vlassis and his tubby bouncer buddy were hanging out by the bar
and spotted me the second I walked through the door, but their
bulk slowed them down so much I had plenty of time before the
brutes were on me.

Vlassis reached out to grab me, but before he could, I grabbed
his wrist, twisted it, then slammed my other hand down on the
back of his extended elbow. He dropped to one knee and I hit
him hard with a right hook to his cheekbone, which knocked him
unconscious and silenced the restaurant. Metal clanged against
plates as diners dropped their cutlery. Vlassis' partner put his
hands up in the air in surrender and backed away. I kept walking
straight through the restaurant. Two men at the table rose to their
feet, but they didn't move any more than the mural on the wall
behind them, so I continued on, marching past the restrooms
until I was in the doorway that led to the TV studio underneath

the restaurant. I bounded down the stairs, and heard Hector's band playing jazz inside the studio. I glanced at a wall-mounted television and saw the audience for the evening's show filing in and taking their seats. A timer on the bottom right-hand corner of the screen counted down the minutes until showtime.

Nine minutes and thirty-three seconds.

"*Where's Specter?!*" I screamed, reaching the bottom of the stairs.

The same PA who had set me up in the green room during my guest appearance on the show sent out a panicked warning on her walkie-talkie. I stormed past her, turned left, and headed down the hallway toward Hector's personal dressing room. I was halfway there when three men in dark suits from Hector's security team charged out of a doorway and came at me. I had just braced myself for a frontal attack when I was tackled to the ground from behind. I fought hard to get them off of me, but their collective strength was too much, and they managed to pin me down while the guard who had tackled me zip-tied my hands behind me.

"*Get off me! Where's Specter?!*" I yelled again.

"Fuck you, you son of a bitch," snapped one of the security men.

They yanked me to my feet before each of the three men in front of me took turns slugging me in the stomach. I coughed, wheezed, and struggled to catch my breath. The security team escorted me roughly back down the hallway. They led me up the stairs, but turned right at the top, instead of going through the door to the restaurant's dining room. In the kitchen the stuffy air was ripe with scents of oregano, garlic, and cooked meat. The skeleton crew of chefs and servers on hand all gawked at me with wide eyes as we moved toward the back of the room, through another set of doors, then down a short hallway until we reached an industrial-sized, walk-in cooler. They shoved me forward through the wide, dangling, strips of clear plastic that served as the entrance to the large refrigerated space. I stumbled but maintained my balance, only to be pushed again from behind. I fell over a pallet-load of large tubs of yogurt and landed hard, rolling onto the cold, concrete floor.

"Stay down, Asshole!" threatened the man who had zip-tied my hands.

I slid across the floor until I was able to sit with my back against a wall. The security team huddled up and talked in hushed voices. After a few moments, one of them spoke into a walkie-talkie while the others crossed their arms and glared at me.

I bided my time and watched my breath form clouds as I exhaled, propped up against the wall in the cooler, surrounded by produce and meats. The chilly air muted the smells, but whiffs of the contents were still noticeable. A few minutes later Hector Specter stepped inside. He was wearing a navy-blue, three-piece suit, and his face was caked with enough makeup that even a Kardashian would suggest going easy. A thin strip of tape lined the bridge of his broken nose, and despite all of the cosmetic effort, some swelling was still noticeable. Hector stomped over toward me with his security team close behind, shooting daggers with his eyes. His ribcage expanded and shrunk dramatically as he huffed like the Big Bad Wolf standing before a straw house, and I could all but feel his seething rage.

"You meddlesome motherfucker," he hissed.

"It's a good thing your crappy little show airs at midnight, Hector, otherwise you'd be facing a fine for using that kind of language on TV."

I didn't think it was possible for Hector to become any angrier, but I managed to pull it off. His face turned red and he barked at his security team. "Stand him up!"

His men obeyed. Two of them grabbed me under my arms and yanked me to my feet. The guards held me in place as Hector undid the button on his suit jacket, stepped forward, and got in my face. He glared up at me before swinging a wild right hook.

The impact was modest and I rolled with the punch so the blow didn't do much damage. Hector was shaking his stinging hand in the cold air when one of his other bodyguards spoke into his ear from behind him.

"What do you want us to do, Boss?" he asked.

"I already contacted Elliot," replied Hector. "He'll be here shortly."

The bodyguard shifted uncomfortably on his feet before responding. "I meant about the show, Boss. You're supposed to go live in less than five minutes."

Hector started pacing back and forth like a caged feral animal. He never once took his frenzied eyes off of me.

"Call the station and have them air a repeat. We'll still tape a show tonight and air it pre-recorded at a later date. Apologize to the audience for the delay and have the band keep playing and the kitchen serve everyone free drinks and appies until I'm done here. I won't be long. I just want to watch Elliot work this piece of shit over a bit first. Trust me, it will put me in a great mood for the monologue."

The bodyguard nodded and hustled out of the cooler with his orders.

"Sit him back down," said Hector.

The two security goons on either side shoved me roughly onto the floor. Hector nodded for them to back away. The men retreated until they flanked Hector on both sides, still close enough to strike in case I tried anything. I didn't.

"Kristos, bring me some ouzo and a Pegasus Pilsner," said Hector to the third bodyguard behind him. "I want to enjoy this."

Kristos hurried off while the other two security guards started grabbing empty milk crates and stacking them until they had created a makeshift seat for Hector. By the time Hector sat down, Kristos had returned with his boss' beverages. Hector downed the ouzo, chased it with a sip of Pegasus Pilsner, and winced.

"You know, my cousin tried your pilsner awhile ago," I said.

"Is that right?" said Hector.

I nodded. "He suggested you change the name to Pegasus Piss."

Hector maintained his composure and crossed his legs. He nodded at his security men and they all took turns tuning me up again with a slew of blows to the gut. My ribcage was throbbing. The bodyguards finished playing Whac-A-Mole with my midsection and I collapsed to the ground and slumped on my side, gasping for refrigerated air.

"I would suggest you keep your mouth shut until Elliot arrives," said Hector.

I coughed and hacked until I was able to get my wind back. "Who the hell is Elliot? Your accountant? You should ask him if you can write off the pound of makeup you layer on your greasy mug every week, but because your show is a glorified informercial put on by a moron with delusions of grandeur, I think you're shit out of luck."

Hector snapped, sprung off of the milk crates, and booted me in the face with one of his brown leather Canali shoes. The hit hurt but I refused to give the son of a bitch the satisfaction, so as I reeled back on my haunches I hoped my blood would permanently stain his footwear.

"The fucking mouth on you!" exclaimed Hector.

"They did use to say I was the best pro wrestler on the mic since The Rock."

Hector stood over me and put his hands on his hips. "You're digging your own grave."

"Are you going to have me killed like you did Lawrence Kunstlinger?"

"You're goddamn right, I am. That fucking roller derby coach deserved to die for all the trouble he caused me. The only difference between him and you is that by the time I'm finished with your dumb ass, what happened to Lawrence will seem like a spa treatment."

Hector's bodyguards looked at each other uncertainly and I figured they might have been nervous being accessories to Hector's murderous crimes. They still backed their boss, but their body language conveyed a lack of the bravado they displayed when they took me down and brought me to the cooler.

"Why'd you have him killed, Hector? Because he was about to torpedo your plans for a professional roller derby league? Or was it because he was blackmailing you for paying off the Crown Counsel before your upcoming rape trial?"

Hector's eyes widened, he gasped, and took a step back. "How … how the fuck do you know about that?!" I spat blood and climbed to my knees. Hector grabbed me by the shoulders and shook me furiously. "How do you know that?!"

"I've seen the pictures. You really should have had your guys do a better job searching Lawrence's apartment."

Hector punched me again. I rolled with it as best I could, but this time he caught a piece of my nose. It wasn't broken but it started to bleed more heavily. I spat more blood.

"You're going to hand those photos over to me before I have you killed," he snarled.

"What's the matter, Hector? Don't have the stones to do it yourself?"

Hector chuckled a little despite himself. "You know what? I don't usually like to get my hands dirty, but for you I'll make an exception."

"I appreciate the courtesy. Do you mind if I ask you one more question before you snuff me out?"

"Go ahead, you stupid fuck."

I nodded toward the black battery pack clipped on his brown leather belt. "That's for your microphone, right?"

"What?" asked Hector, confused, while checking the mic that was clipped to the lapel of his suit jacket.

"If so, I was just wondering what that little green light means."

Hector opened his suit jacket and slid the battery pack around on his belt. His jaw dropped when he saw the small green light glowing brightly.

"That's right, asshole. Your mic is on. And thirty people and your shitty band just heard you confess to murdering Lawrence Kunstlinger."

Hector's bodyguards were stunned and looked back and forth at each other in hope one of them would know what to do. Hector snapped his mic off of his jacket and battery pack off his belt and smashed them on the ground, shattering them.

"What—how—how—"

"There's a guy I know. I did a favour for him recently. Works in the film and TV business. A veteran jack-of-all-trades. So when he filed into your studio as part of the audience tonight it was a piece of cake for him to turn on your mic five minutes before showtime. You just broadcasted your confession live to dozens of witnesses, you gutless bastard."

Hector was in shock. He stared at the smashed mic and battery pack on the ground, took a step back, and put his hands on his head.

"Now, D!" I yelled, at the top of my lungs.

Before Hector or his bodyguards could even turn around my cousin sliced through the hanging plastic strips and into the freezer like a hundred-and-ninety-five-pound dagger of Irish bare knuckles. He grabbed the two closest bodyguards by the back of their necks and smashed their heads together. As they both teetered on their feet, Declan performed a formidable sweep that took out four legs and had both men flat on their backs in a heartbeat. For insurance he kneeled down and drilled both men in the face with savage right hands, and before Hector and the two remaining security men had processed what had happened, both bodyguards were unconscious. The last two guards looked nervously at one another before going for their guns.

Bad idea, I thought to myself.

Declan sprang forward toward the bodyguard on his right, cracking him in the jaw with his elbow, and snatching his gun away. The bodyguard dropped faster than one of Spudboy's sacks of potatoes. As Declan spun to face the last man standing, he snapped back the gun's slide, and ejected both the bullet from the chamber and the clip of additional cartridges below it. He then spun the weapon around in his hand to grip it by the barrel and used his momentum to crack the last man across the face with the butt of the gun. As I watched the bodyguard topple over, Declan turned to me and winked.

"Show-off," I said, with a smirk.

"I've been called worse," he replied.

I climbed awkwardly to my feet with my hands still zip-tied behind me. I walked past Hector, who stood shell-shocked in the middle of the walk-in fridge, mouth agape and eyes wide as saucers as he stared at his fallen security team. I had to step over and around the four unconscious bodies as I made my way toward my cousin. Declan pulled a six-inch folding hunting knife from his back pocket and flicked it open with his thumb as I turned around and he cut my hands free.

Declan handed me a handkerchief and I used it to wipe the blood from my nose and face. Fortunately, the cold air had already helped the flowing blood slow to a trickle. I cleaned myself up as best as I could while Declan searched Hector's bodyguards. He pulled a small wad of zip-ties from one of their pockets and handed me one. I left him to keep patting down the bodyguards and walked over to Hector, who couldn't take his eyes off his defeated men. I spun him around, roughly pushed him up against the wall, and zip-tied his hands behind him. That seemed to snap him out of his trance.

"What the fuck are you doing?"

"What does it look like, Hector?"

"You have to let me go. You—you can't do this. You're not the police!"

I spun Hector back around and delivered a solid punch to his belly. He dropped to his knees, unable to breathe. I crouched down until I was at his eye level.

"Look at me, Hector." He started wheezing while hunched over and staring at the floor. *"Look. At. Me,"* I said firmly. Hector did as I asked. "Every time you talk, I'm going to hit you. Hard. Do you understand?"

Hector opened his mouth to speak but caught himself before he did. Instead he just nodded vigorously, and wore an expression on his face that was so fraught with fear he looked like a little boy suffering coulrophobia forced to attend Pennywise the Dancing Clown's birthday party.

"Let's go," I said, lifting him to his feet and escorting him out of the fridge.

By the time we made it back to the restaurant the studio audience was working their way upstairs, talking non-stop about the confession they had just heard.

"Rya?" I asked my cousin.

"Aye, she and her boys in blue should be here any minute," replied Declan, before lighting up a cigarette and taking a long and well-deserved drag.

I sat Hector down in a corner booth. "Don't move," I commanded. I rejoined my cousin at the corner of the supper club's long granite bar, a few feet away from where Hector was seated.

The kitchen staff had followed us as we walked through their workspace and the collective chatter in the restaurant kept getting louder as the studio audience kept gabbing about being witness to such a stunning and salacious murder confession. I nodded at Declan, he popped two fingers in his mouth, and let out a screeching whistle. Everyone stopped talking and looked at us.

I put my hands up in the air and spoke in the loudest voice I could muster.

"Everyone listen up! The police will be here any minute and are going to want to take some statements about what you just heard, so in the meantime please take a seat. This will all be over soon."

Everyone in the restaurant sat down, including the kitchen staff. The chatting resumed, although it was much quieter. Just then I spotted Alan Kressberg coming up the stairs. He was dressed casually in a hoodie and jeans, but he looked well rested and much better than he did when I met him at the casino.

I nudged my cousin and nodded at Kressberg. "Give me a minute. And keep an eye on Hector for me, will you?"

"If that bitch-bag moves a bloody muscle I'll piss in a cup and show him firsthand what his pilsner tastes like."

"Gross, D."

"Sorry. Adrenaline's still pumpin', I guess."

I patted my cousin on the shoulder and worked my way through the seated crowd until I reached Kressberg. He saw the blood on my shirt and the bits I wasn't able to fully wipe off my face and winced.

"I guess I had the easy job," he said.

"It looks worse than it is," I replied. I shook his hand. "You really came through for me tonight. Thank you."

Kressberg smiled. "It's the least I could do, Jed. Here," he said, handing me a digital audio recorder. "It's all on there. The entire thing."

"Thank you," I said, pocketing the device.

"I also recorded the entire confession on one of the PMW-300s."

"The what?"

"The HD video cameras they have in the studio."

"Right."

I glanced over at Declan who was watching Hector like a hawk. The disgraced multi-hyphenate, beverage-baron, talk-show host hung his head and sat motionless in the booth.

"May I ask you a question?" asked Kressberg.

"Shoot."

"How'd you know Specter was going to confess to the murders?"

I shrugged. "I guess I didn't. But if there's one thing you can count on bloviating narcissists to do, it's talk about themselves. I figured if I could needle him enough to lose his cool, he'd end up boasting about it."

Just then the chimes above the front door to the restaurant rang. I turned to look expecting to see Rya and VPD officers enter the premises but instead a thin, middle-aged man with angular facial features walked purposefully into the supper club. He carried a black briefcase and was dressed in a slim-fitting dark grey suit with a thin tie—as well as a matching bowler hat.

Chauncey Gardiner.

Or more likely the Elliot person whom Hector said was on his way to work me over, then kill me when I was still tied up in the fridge. Either way, he was the same sneaky son of a bitch who had spied on me, flattened Lawrence Kunstlinger against a brick wall with a van, and left his bowler hat behind at the scene of the crime.

Elliot took three long strides into the restaurant before he looked up and took notice of the scene around him. An expression of concern crept across his face as he stood alone in the middle of the restaurant with dozens of people silently staring at him.

Declan appeared by my side in an instant. "Who the hell is that?" he asked in a hushed tone.

"The man who murdered Lawrence with the van," I replied.

The deafening silence in the room was shattered when Hector Specter looked up from the corner booth and hollered. *"Run, Elliot! Run!"*

Elliot spun on a dime and was almost at the door before I had even moved. I started to sprint when the sound of breaking glass crackled throughout the restaurant, causing people to scream. Elliot collapsed onto the floor, having had an empty pint glass shatter against the back of his head, nearly knocking him unconscious.

I looked beside me to see my cousin, who lowered his throwing arm and shrugged. "What?" he said. "The dodgy arsehole was gonna bolt."

"You deal with Hector," I said. Declan went over to the booth and smacked him across the cheek with a wicked backhand while I walked toward his accomplice.

Elliot kept writhing in pain while clutching the bleeding wound on the back of his head. I kicked away his briefcase and then patted him down to see if he was carrying, but it was challenging since he kept squirming and crying out in pain.

I grabbed a dishrag off of the bar and was about to put pressure on Elliot's gash. I wasn't sure why, but I kept seeing Lawrence's face in my mind's eye. Images of his photo with his stoned smile and Instagram pictures of him laughing and posing with Stormy and her teammates flashed in my head. I saw the pure terror in Lawrence's eyes as the GMC Vandura jumped the curb. The last vision I had was of Lawrence flopped on the hood of the van, blood dribbling out of his mouth, as he exhaled his last breath.

Elliot looked up at me in desperation. "What are you waiting for?" I snapped back to the present. After a moment, I tossed the dishrag aside.

"Come on!" cried Elliot. "Help me!"

Before I knew what I was doing, I had lifted my right foot and stomped down hard on the back of Elliot's head. He let out such a loud, high-pitched shriek I thought the windows might shatter. Dozens of people from the studio audience, who were seated and watching the scene unfold, gasped. I pressed down on his head harder and started twisting the ball of my foot back and forth.

Wailing sirens grew louder and a few moments later flashing red and blue lights from outside were bathing the interior of the restaurant with splashes of colour. Two uniformed VPD officers came through the door first, guns drawn, followed immediately by Rya. All three stopped when they saw the unusual scene before them. The entire place was still and the only movement in the restaurant was Elliot squirming on the floor and my foot grinding into the wound on the back of his head.

"*Jed!*" shouted Rya.

Her voice brought me back and I looked up to see her with her gun lowered but the other two cops still pointing their weapons at me. I had never seen the look that Rya had on her face before. It was a mixture of shock, relief, but most troubling—fear.

I lifted my foot off of Elliot's head and took a few steps back. I caught my reflection in the mirror behind the bar and barely recognized the person I saw. My teeth were gritted, my brow was furrowed, and there was fire in my eyes. I rubbed my face in my hands, trying to wash away the mercilessness that had overtaken me.

"Stand down," she ordered, and the cops holstered their guns.

Rya and I kept staring at one another for a few moments, but after everything that had happened I couldn't take the disappointment I saw in her sparkling green eyes. I turned my back on her and walked toward Declan, who was at the bar smoking another cigarette. He had found a bottle of ouzo and poured himself a shot. I wasn't certain, but I thought I might have spotted the slightest of smirks in the corner of his mouth.

FORTY-THREE

The fallout from Hector Specter's downfall was swift. After
Rya and the VPD had arrived on scene at the Poseidon Supper
Club, the EMTs showed up minutes later. They treated Elliot's
head wound. While they were tending to him, a VPD officer
opened his briefcase and found a veritable torturer's tool kit,
including knives, pliers, nails, needles, a Taser, a blowtorch, a
hammer, cocaine, and a couple unregistered and illegal hand-
guns with the serial numbers filed off. As a result, a VPD officer
handcuffed Elliot to the gurney, he was loaded into an ambulance,
and taken to Vancouver General Hospital.

I shuddered to think what would have happened if my plan
had gone awry and I wound up as Elliot's plaything. The cocaine
and firearms violations had initially allowed Rya to place Elliot
under arrest, however, after the VPD ran a strand of his hair, it
was identified as a direct match to the ones found in the bowler
hat left inside the murder vehicle. As a result, Elliot copped a
plea and turned on Hector Specter, who in turn lawyered up,
and had not said a single word while his top-of-the-line legal

team scrambled to try and keep him from spending the rest of his life in jail.

Nonetheless, with the recorded confession, dozens of witnesses, Todd McTavish's "suicide" now being investigated as a homicide, and Elliot ratting him out, the chances of murder charges sticking were looking really good. Hector was also on the hook for obstruction of justice charges for bribing an officer of the court, and still faced a statutory rape charge. That trial was postponed, however, because, as Rya had predicted, once news went public that the province's senior Crown Counsel had taken a bribe, and Lawrence's photos of the payoff were splashed across newspapers and online, the headlines did indeed send shock waves through the legal system. The story was national news for weeks.

In addition to public knowledge that Hector had bribed the Crown Counsel, it was reported that he had ordered the hit on Lawrence Kunstlinger for trying to blackmail him. While most of the news media left out Lawrence's motive for the blackmail, and some even suggested it was nothing more than a simple shakedown of a multimillionaire, the roller derby community knew better. The WFTDA made a formal statement on Lawrence's passing, and lauded him as a champion of their sport and a role model for future generations. Stormy and the Split-Lip Sallies as well as over a dozen other teams rallied around Lawrence's sacrifice and, as a result, were able to pressure the WFTDA into doing what Lawrence had tried to do, namely release a public condemnation on any potential formation of a national roller derby league because turning it corporate would betray the very spirit of the sport. Hector's removal from the group of wealthy investors doomed efforts to form a league, and the actions of the WFTDA provided the final nail in the coffin.

I kept my promise to my cousin and took him to the next Split-Lip Sallies playoff game. Although they lost a do-or-die bout to progress to the finals, they played their hearts out against a team that greatly outmatched them and they dedicated their season to Lawrence. I was in such good spirits seeing Stormy and her teammates so happy that I even took Declan for a round of drinks and treated him to a couple of private dances at Brandi's Exotic Show Lounge. With his desperate desire to see scantily-clad women finally met, he was happy.

As the days passed after the Poseidon Supper Club show-down and Hector Spector continued to dominate the news for his litany of illegal activities, one dark cloud continued to hang over my head. With all the press Hector was attracting I couldn't help but wonder if the viral video clip of me knocking him out was getting more views. I tried not to think about it, and kept myself distracted by doing paperwork and housekeeping in the office. I even insisted on working a few bartending shifts at the Shillelagh. Inevitably, with the non-stop barrage of Hector Specter in the media, I gave in late one evening, and logged onto YouTube.

The last time I watched the clip it had over six hundred thousand views and was climbing. I held my breath and searched for *"Douchebag talk show host gets his due!"* and a moment later it appeared. I clicked on it and then scrolled down slowly to see the number of views listed on the bottom left under the video.

3,745,982.

I stared at the number in disbelief. I refreshed the page in hopes that the total number of views was some kind of glitch. When the page reloaded the number was *3,745,989.* I sagged back in my desk chair, utterly dejected. Eventually, I sat up and grabbed my cell phone from my desk. I scrolled through my recent calls until I found the 250 area code number that Max had called from. My thumb hovered over the number for an eternity. I finally clicked my phone off, put it back on the desk, ran to my bathroom, dropped to my knees, and vomited in the toilet.

FORTY-FOUR

It was a surprisingly quiet day at the Emerald Shillelagh. My pop had been out of the office for days, off on his annual fishing trip with some retired cop buddies. Most of the Vancouver Film School programs had ended and the summer ones had yet to begin so the usual crowd of budding filmmakers were absent.

It was early in the afternoon and the pub was empty, save for two elderly women in a booth, who were sharing a turkey and brie sandwich with fries and drinking half-pints of Molson Canadian, despite Declan having done all he could to talk them out of "punishing their palates with corporate swill" and not-so-subtlety implying that they might not have that many beers left to drink in their lifetimes.

My cousin and I were sitting at the bar nursing pints of Guinness and eating teriyaki chicken rice bowls when the front door opened and Yosef Dillon walked in. Declan gave me a look and I nodded, having previously arranged the meet. He went to check on how our lone customers were enjoying their lunch while Dillon approached. Although he saw the video camera sitting on the bar in front of me, he kept his hands in his pockets and his head hung low. I spun around on my bar stool and handed him the camcorder, which he accepted without a word before walking toward the exit. Declan reappeared and, only moments after Dillon had left, Rya entered the pub.

"Bollocks."

"What?"

"You haven't seen her since the night we took down Specter, yeah?"

"So?"

"So it means I'm gonna have to finish me lunch in the back so you two eejits can piss and moan and make doe eyes at each other."

Before I could respond, Declan scooped up his rice bowl and pint and got up off the stool. He smiled at Rya as she approached the bar.

"Lovely to see ya, Lassie."

"Good to see you too, Declan."

Declan retreated out of sight and Rya pulled up a stool next to me. I took a sip of Guinness and wiped my mouth with a serviette.

"Can I get you a drink?" I asked.

"Sure," she replied.

"What would you like?"

"Bartender's choice."

I walked around the bar and grabbed a tulip-shaped glass off of the shelf. I poured the Guinness until it was two-thirds of the way full, and then let it sit.

"How are things?" I asked.

"Do you even watch the news?"

"Yeah. It's been intense."

"To say the least."

"Lawrence really shook things up by taking those photos."

"And then some."

I filled up the rest of Rya's pint and attempted to etch a shamrock into the creamy head. Surprisingly, for the first time I managed to do it.

"Would you look at that," I said. "Must be my lucky day."

"Cheers," said Rya, and we clinked our glasses together and both took long sips. "Mmmm," she hummed with pleasure, before taking another sip. "I can't believe I'm enjoying this. I don't really care much for stouts."

"It's a Guinness, Rya. And Declan is magic."

"Apparently."

"So what brings you by? I assume with everything that's going on you're busy as hell."

"You can't even imagine."

"Then why am I so fortunate to get a visit?"

Rya took another sip and licked her lips. "Because I wanted to talk to you about something."

I sighed. "Is this the part where you scold me for going off half-cocked with a hare-brained plan in order to get the bad guys? Because we've done that dance before."

Rya placed her pint on the bar. "No, Jed, it's not. You're a big boy and a PI now so go ahead and keep doing whatever crazy shit keeps popping into that melon you call a head. I didn't come here as a cop. I came here as your friend."

"Okay. Well then, friend, do you want to play a game of Jenga or something?"

Rya dismissed my attempt at playfulness and looked at me sternly. "I want to know what the hell that was back at Specter's restaurant."

"What *what* was?" I asked, despite knowing exactly what she meant.

"What you were doing to Micklevick when I got there."

"His name is Elliot Micklevick? What is he from Slytherin House or something?"

Rya slammed a palm down on the bar. "Damn it, Jed! You were torturing the guy!"

I glanced behind Rya and saw that the two elderly ladies were staring and one had stopped chewing. A piece of turkey fell out of the side of her mouth and hit the floor. I turned my attention back to Rya.

"Um, you did see the stuff he had in his briefcase, right? The guy is a murderer, sadist, and professional torturer."

"You didn't know all that when you started grinding your boot into his wound like Dirty Harry stomping on Scorpio."

I took a big sip of Guinness and ran a hand through my hair. "What do you want me to say, Rya? I didn't plan it."

"But why did you do it?"

I stood there for a few moments trying to come up with an answer. "I don't know. Something just came over me."

"Jed, the expression you had on your face … it was like you were enjoying it."

"So what if I did!" I snapped. "I don't know about you, but I'm goddamn sick of people like Micklevick or Specter or Dennings or Kendricks hurting good and decent people! They all deserved what they got! I get that you're bound by rules and regulations, but I sure as hell am not!"

Rya was clearly startled by my outburst. The elderly ladies slowly stood up, silently left cash to cover their bill on top of their table, and walked out of the pub. As soon as they were gone Rya opened her mouth to say something, but hesitated. Instead she slid off of the bar stool, straightened the collar of her shirt and wiped a droplet of Guinness off her pantsuit blazer. She looked at me for a long time before speaking, her sparkling green eyes tinged with a hint of sadness.

"You're going down a slippery slope, Jed. It's not going to end well if you keep playing judge, jury, and executioner. One day it will catch up to you."

Rya turned and headed toward the exit.

"Rya, wait."

She stopped and turned halfway toward me, her raven hair cascading down over her shoulder. Her beauty always snuck up on me and I was again reminded of how stunning she could appear at the most unexpected of times.

"We, uh … we never talked about it. The kiss in the office."

Rya nodded slightly before smiling softly. "I know, Jed. And for now I don't think we should."

And with that, she was gone.

FORTY-FIVE

Two thoughts popped into my head when the starting pistol
went off, and I watched a group of dachshunds take off down the
track like little Oscar Mayer Wienermobiles come to life. My
first notion was that they really were extraordinary little canines
and the athleticism displayed while racing helped me visualize
them working as hunting dogs and flushing out burrow-dwelling
animals. And second, I realized that I should make a trip to the
concession stand because my stomach was rumbling and a hot
dog topped with mustard, sautéed onions, and cheddar cheese
would really hit the spot and nicely compliment the large banana
milkshake I was enjoying.

It was a beautiful but hot day at Hastings Racecourse. The
sun beat down from the sky above. The air was crisp from an
early morning drizzle and the landscape of majestic mountains
in the distance featured a couple of peaks that still had white
tips of lingering snow.

The wiener dogs all went the distance down the hundred-
metre stretch of track and the announcer proclaimed over the
speaker system that a small, black dachshund named Cornelius

was the winner. The second-to-last heat of Hastings Racecourse's annual Wiener Dog Races was complete.

Sykes' prized pooch Napoleon had already qualified for the finals in a previous race, and based upon how he beat the competition in each heat—by leads of up to five feet—I had a feeling the little guy had a pretty good chance of winning the whole thing and being crowned Wiener Dog Champion.

"Get your arse up, ya big lug," chirped my cousin.

I looked over my shoulder to see Declan and Stormy walking down the stadium's steel steps as they returned to our front row seats with a bounty of goodies. I got up out of the aisle seat so they could squeeze by, and when I got a whiff of Declan's chili dog my stomach rumbled even louder and I instantly regretted my order of a small popcorn. Stormy slipped by me next, purposefully rubbing up against me and giving me a kiss on the lips as she passed by.

"What'd we miss?" she asked.

"Just one heat. Finals are up next."

We all took our seats and dug into our snacks.

"I'm so excited to see if your friend's dog will win," said Stormy, cracking a peanut out of its shell.

"He's not my friend. He's a business associate. And a loose one at that. I've just spent some time with Napoleon lately and wanted to come and cheer the little fella on."

"That wee bastard better pull it off," said Declan. "I bet a thousand bucks on that mutt."

"He's a purebred, D," I replied.

"*A thousand?*" exclaimed Stormy. "Jed and I only bet a hundred. I didn't think they let you place wagers that large here."

"They don't," I said. "Declan placed that bet with Sykes."

"He's taking bets on his own dog? Isn't that a conflict of interest?"

"Yes, and, even worse, paying off wagers on Napoleon to win could wipe out his own gains as the winning dog's owner. Those bets he almost certainly lays off with other bookies. In calculating and sharing risk, I imagine that bookmakers are at least as savvy as insurance underwriters."

The racecourse attendants finished raking the dirt and the wiener dog finalists took to the track with their masters to thunderous applause.

"I don't think I've ever seen this place so jammers," said Declan.

"I've never even been here before," replied Stormy.

I spotted Sykes as he and Napoleon made their way toward the purple starting gates. Sykes had forgone his usual crisp blazer with khakis and instead was sporting a designer Hugo Boss tracksuit with matching sneakers, all blacker than his slicked back hair. Sykes walked briskly and Napoleon trotted beside him with his head held high. Once Sykes and the other owners had locked their dogs in their stalls they walked along the grass inside the oval track down to the finish line where they took their spots corresponding to their dog's starting gate. A man in a referee's jersey walked onto the track, took his position, and held a starting pistol in the air.

BANG!

The shot echoed in the air and the gates slammed open. Eight dachshunds came out flying, and it was clear this was going to be a much closer race than the previous ones. Napoleon was the only reddish dog in the race, the rest of the dachshunds were all varying shades of brown and black. After ten metres Napoleon had started to pull away and Declan sprang to his feet.

"That's it ya grand bastard! Keep on goin' and I'll get ya a box o'Milk-Bones and a wiener bitch to hump!"

Declan's excitement was short-lived. Just before the twenty-metre mark tragedy struck. A bulkier, heavier dachshund running on Napoleon's right suddenly veered left and bumped his head into Napoleon's hind leg. Napoleon let out a yip and tumbled, rolling over a few times.

Declan lost it. "Are you kidding me?! Did you all see that shite?! He hit him! He knocked him over!"

Everyone around us was staring at my cousin. "Sit down, D," I said, but it made no difference.

"You cheatin' chunky pooch! I swear I'm gonna come down there and gut ya meself and then cook yer tubby arse on me barbecue!"

I remembered the hunting knife Declan had pulled from his back pocket when he cut my zip-tie, and suddenly what he was threatening seemed quite plausible. Fortunately, what happened next settled my cousin down, because during his ranting Napoleon had finished rolling and without missing a beat popped back up on all four legs and continued racing.

"C'mon ya wee little shite! *Catch up! Catch up!*" hollered my cousin.

Napoleon was in the middle of the pack and still behind three other dachshunds, but he was moving fast. By the time he hit the fifty-metre mark he had caught up to the third wiener dog.

"*That's it, Boyo! That's it!*" yelled Declan.

At the seventy-metre mark Napoleon pulled ahead of the next dog, overtaking second place. He was still a few feet behind the leader but was closing ground. Caught up in the excitement, both Stormy and I stood up and cheered on Napoleon and his gutsy performance. Having recovered from Declan's obscenities, the crowd was now roaring. Napoleon pulled up next to the leader with twenty metres to go but couldn't pull ahead. He and the other dog remained neck and neck.

Fifteen metres to go.

Ten metres to go.

Five metres to go.

Then, incredibly, with only a few feet to the finish, Napoleon stretched his body, strained his head forward, and managed to win the race by half a body length before leaping into Sykes' waiting arms. The crowd went crazy. My cousin thrust his fists into the air as if Ireland had just won the World Cup.

"*Moladh go deo le Dia!!!*" bellowed my cousin, which was Gaelic for "hallelujah."

Stormy jumped up and down and gave me a big hug and a kiss.

"Jaysus Christ," said Declan, flopping back into his seat. "That was such a thrill I almost bricked meself."

My cousin pulled a tallboy of Kilkenny out of the small, insulated cooler-bag tote he had brought with him, cracked it open, and lit a cigarette. I asked Stormy if she wanted to meet Napoleon.

"Of course!" she said excitedly.

We left Declan with his beer and smoke and headed toward the entrance to the track. We walked over to the grass and then down to the finish line where most of the racing dogs were still milling about. Sykes was on his knees massaging Napoleon behind his ears and feeding him treats. Seeing me, Sykes picked up his champion canine and rose to his feet.

"Mr. Ounstead," he said, extending a hand. "What a pleasant surprise."

I shook Sykes' hand and nodded. "Hell of a race."

"Indeed."

"This is my girlfriend, Stephanie Danielson, also known as Stormy Daze."

"Nice to meet you," she said, shaking Sykes' hand.

"You as well, my dear."

"He is *sooo* adorable," said Stormy, admiring Napoleon.

"Would you like to hold him?" asked Sykes.

"Yes!"

Sykes handed Napoleon to Stormy and the little racing hound nuzzled his head up underneath her chin.

"Oh my God, Jed we have to get one," said Stormy.

"No way." The words shot out of my mouth before I even considered what Stormy had said. Stormy looked at me oddly, taken aback by my brisk response. "I mean, maybe," I said, trying to walk it back. "We can talk about it later."

"Mr. Ounstead, I am pleased that you are here. I actually have a business proposition for you."

I looked at Sykes, but as usual with his silver, reflective aviator sunglasses the only thing I could read was the name 'Uncle Daddy' Tony Baroni on the XCCW wrestling shirt I was wearing.

"I'm done playing courier, Sykes."

"It is nothing of that nature. In fact, I think it might be something you would be quite interested in."

Sykes nodded over toward the grass and started walking.

"I'll be back in a minute," I said, and gave Stormy a kiss on the cheek, but she was so enthralled with holding and petting Napoleon I don't even think she heard me. I joined Sykes on the grass ten feet away from the track.

"What is it, Sykes?"

"I saw your appearance on Hector's talk show recently. Remind me to send a gift basket to your father's pub."

"I don't want to talk about that."

"By all means. But when you were on the show I noticed you were wearing a particularly unique set of cufflinks featuring professional wrestling legend Bret 'The Hitman' Hart."

I nodded. "What's your point?"

"My point is that in addition to the work of mine that you are familiar with, I also have other business ventures and organizations I deal with, and one of my duties with one of them is fundraising."

"Okay. So?"

"How would you feel about taking a trip to Calgary for a one-time-only exhibition wrestling match between you and Bret 'The Hitman' Hart, with all proceeds going to charity, one of which you will be able to select yourself?"

My heart skipped a beat and goosebumps popped up and down my arms. I tried to think of what to say, but couldn't find the right words.

Instead, after a few moments, I simply smiled.

ACKNOWLEDGEMENTS

It was a thrill to continue "Hammerhead" Jed's adventures with this book. Thank you to everyone for reading and to those who have been so supportive of the character since his debut.

I would be remiss if I didn't profusely thank my friend and retired Vancouver Police Department Sergeant 1314 Joel Johnston. His guidance on all things law enforcement has been vital to the accuracy of the police elements that are depicted in both *Cobra Clutch* and *Rolling Thunder*, and since he is also a published writer and a mystery / thriller aficionado, his feedback is invaluable.

A huge thank you to my high school classmate and former Terminal City Rollergirls skater Jenna Hauck aka "Hydro-Jenna Bomb." Although I attended roller derby games and researched the sport to the best of my ability, there is no substitute for first-hand knowledge and experience. Because of Jenna I was better able to capture a realistic peek into this counter-culture sport and hopefully do it justice. Jenna is also a Multimedia Journalist with the *Chilliwack Progress* and the grammatical and logistical errors she caught with her eagle eye were so impressive my editor believes she could have another career as an editor herself if she were so inclined!

Thank you to private investigator Alex Jay of Peak Investigations for consulting on some of the inner workings of BC PIs, especially as Jed continues to work at Ounstead & Son Investigations.

A big thanks to Elite Canadian Championship Wrestling and co-owner Alyssa Sargeant for allowing me to not only promote my books at local ECCW pro-wrestling events, but also for providing me behind-the-scenes access that gives me the opportunity to accurately describe this awesome world of sports entertainment that Jed remains a part of. Thank you to pro wrestlers *"Joshi Slayer"* Cat Power, *"Uncle Daddy"* Tony Baroni, Shreddz, Artemis Spencer, and Nicole Matthews for their ongoing support and generosity with their time as I continue to do research for upcoming novels. Thanks to *the* original G.L.O.W. (Gorgeous Ladies Of Wrestling) girl, model, actress, stuntwoman, and celebrity Jeanne "Hollywood" Basone, and writer / music and recording industry survivor / former 1970s All-Star Wrestling co-promoter and all round public relations extraordinaire Bob Harris, as they have both gone above and beyond in their efforts to spotlight the "Hammerhead" Jed series. I cannot express how truly appreciative and fortunate I am to have them in my corner (pun intended).

My continued gratitude to Crime Writers of Canada and everything the organization does to promote Canadian crime fiction, and to all of my fellow authors and friends. It's an honour to be part of such an amazing and talented community, and I love every minute that I get to spend with you all at readings, book launches, cwc events, and crime conventions.

What else can I say about my amazing publisher NeWest Press that I haven't already, other than a heartfelt thanks for giving me the opportunity to continue to share my work. Thank you to my NeWest brother-from-another-mother and acclaimed author of the stellar crime novel *Only Pretty Damned* Niall Howell. Thanks to Office Administrator Christine Kohler and Production and Marketing Coordinator Claire Kelly, who take such good care of every author who is fortunate enough to be part of the NeWest family. Thank you to my exceptional editor Merrill Distad, who is a pleasure to work with and taught me even more this time around. And of course a massive thank you to NeWest Press General Manager Matt Bowes, whose leadership and vision for NeWest Press is not only admirable but also inspiring.

Thank you to my friends and family for their ongoing support. I must give a special shout-out to my "front line" of readers who take the time to give me excellent notes on early drafts, including Sean O'Brien, Mike Smith, my incredibly supportive mother Dianne, and "Hammerhead" Jed's biggest fan, Darren "The Rocket" Stein, who cameos in the book you just read as a *slightly* fictional version of himself. Thanks to my aunt and uncle Margaret and Jim Gillis, Kathy Findlay, and Coreena Love for all they have done to spread the word about the "Hammerhead" Jed series. And a monster thank you to my man Brad Love, who consistently gives me great constructive criticism on Jed's latest escapades, and helps me promote the "Hammerhead" Jed series at numerous author events, pro-wrestling shows, book clubs, and comic book conventions.

Finally, thank you to my beautiful wife and children Susie, Jack, and Scarlett for everything they do (and all they put up with) as I continue on this exciting journey.

—A.J.D.

A.J. Devlin grew up in Greater Vancouver before moving to Southern California for six years where he earned a Bachelor of Fine Arts in Screenwriting from Chapman University and a Master of Fine Arts in Screenwriting from The American Film Institute. After working as a screenwriter in Hollywood, he moved back home to Port Moody, BC, where he now lives with his wife and two children. *Cobra Clutch*, the first book in the "Hammerhead" Jed mystery series, was released in April 2018 and was nominated for a Lefty Award for Best Debut Mystery and won the 2019 Arthur Ellis Award for Best First Crime Novel. For more information on A.J. and his books, please visit www.ajdevlin.com.